ARIEL TACHNA

INHERIT
THE SKY

Dreamspinner Press

Published by
Dreamspinner Press
382 NE 191st Street #88329
Miami, FL 33179-3899, USA
http://www.dreamspinnerpress.com/

Inherit the Sky

Cover Art by Anne Cain   annecain.art@gmail.com
Cover Design by Mara McKennen

ISBN: 978-1-61372-419-4

Printed in the United States of America
First Edition
February 2012

eBook edition available
eBook ISBN: 978-1-61372-420-0

ARIEL TACHNA
Contemporary M/M Romance at its Finest

Her Two Dads

"…one of the most emotionally rewarding and uplifting love stories that I have read in a long time." —Dark Diva Reviews

"This is one of the best books I have ever read."
—Judging the Book by Its Pages

"…a fast-paced story with a well developed storyline that will leave you begging for more. It's a story about overcoming hatred and bigotry, the joys of parenthood and discovering love when you least expect it."
—Literary Nymphs

"…a sweet and stirring novel about the power of love and family."
—Romance Junkies

Seducing C.C.

"…a great comfort read." —Blackraven Reviews

"…a seductively sexy and romantic story." —Night Owl Reviews

Out of the Fire

"This story tore at my heart." —TwoLips Recommended Read

"…something in it for just about everybody who has a kink…"
—The Romance Studio

Once in a Lifetime

"… a coming-of-age story that introduces heart-pounding firsts and nostalgic lasts." —¡Miraculous!

http://www.dreamspinnerpress.com

To Nicki, who always inspires my muses,
and to Isabelle and Meredith for teaching me about Australia.

ONE

CAINE NEIHEISEL tossed his bag on his childhood bed and flopped down on the mattress next to it. Six years, down the drain. There hadn't been any dramatic fight, any one moment when everything had gone south. It was more a slow, sinking realization that he and John simply weren't going anywhere. They made fine friends, good roommates, but not great lovers. Not even halfway-decent lovers recently. Caine chose to say they'd grown apart rather than to think John didn't desire him anymore. His self-esteem didn't need another blow. It was bad enough being stuck in the mail room at Comcast for nearly ten years. He'd applied for promotions, of course, but he always seemed to get passed over. He didn't think he could deal with losing John's interest that way.

He'd have to start looking for a roommate or another place to live. He couldn't afford the rent on his own. That hadn't been an issue when he'd moved into the condo. John had been more than willing to pay for half in exchange for living in the Gayborhood in Philadelphia. Caine would miss the convenience if he couldn't find another roommate, but that was the way his life had been going recently.

"Caine! Dinner's ready."

Caine sighed and went to join his parents.

"We're having your favorite," his mother Patricia said when he came into the kitchen. "Fried pork chops, Brussels sprouts, and mashed sweet potatoes."

"Thanks, Mom," Caine said, relieved he got the words out without stuttering. He knew why his mother had made his favorite meal from childhood, and it had nothing to do with being glad to have him home for Christmas. She was trying to cheer him up. While he appreciated the sentiment, he didn't want to spend his entire vacation being pitied. He had enough problems with that on his own.

"So what was in that letter from Australia?" his father, Len, asked, joining them in the kitchen.

"I'll tell you over dinner," his mother said. "Let me get the food on the table first."

"Let m-me help," Caine offered, wincing at the stutter. He apparently wasn't as comfortable with being home as he'd thought he was. Chiding himself for dwelling on something he couldn't change, he set the table and carried over the serving bowls as his mother filled them.

When they were all seated and eating, Len turned to Patricia. "So what was in the letter?"

"You remember my mother talking about her younger brother Michael who left England about the same time she married my father and came here?" Patricia asked.

Len and Caine both nodded. Caine had corresponded regularly with Uncle Michael as he was growing up, although their letters had become less frequent once Caine went away to college.

"He had a heart attack last week," Patricia continued.

"Oh, I'm sorry to hear that," Len said immediately. "Had he been ill?"

"I don't know," Patricia admitted. "After Mom died, we lost touch somewhat. We should have taken that trip to Australia we always talked about, but other things always seemed to be more important. That's not all the letter said, though. It's from the executor of his will. It seems he left everything to me."

"To you?" Caine asked. "But why?"

"He never married or had children of his own," Patricia explained. "I'm the only living relative he has. The executor wrote to explain the situation and to ask what I wanted to do with the sheep ranch he owned. Apparently it's a huge chunk of land, several thousand square kilometers. Obviously I'll have to sell it. I don't know anything about sheep, and my life is here. I have no idea what selling it will entail, but hopefully the executor can handle it and transfer the money once it's done and all the taxes are paid."

Len chuckled. "I can just see us arriving on that old ranch. I'm pushing seventy and you're not that much younger. They'd laugh us right back home if we tried to run it."

Caine had to admit the image of his parents on a sheep farm in Australia would be funny to see. "It seems a shame to sell it," he said. "Could you hire someone to run it and have them t-transfer the profits to you? If it's profitable."

"According to the executor, it's quite profitable," Patricia replied, "but I'm not sure how well it would work to have us over here and a foreman over there. We'd have no way of knowing if he was managing the ranch well."

"I could go," Caine said softly, the words out before he realized he had thought them. He'd always wanted to visit his great-uncle, but the trip they'd planned in such detail in all their letters had never come to fruition. Like so much else in his life.

"That's sweet of you," his mother said, patting his hand, "but you have a job, a life in Philadelphia. I couldn't ask you to give that up for this."

There wasn't much to give up as far as Caine was concerned. "Let's think about it for a d-day or two at least," he said, his mind racing with sudden possibility. "Don't rush into a decision."

"Oh, Caine, I know you always wanted to visit the ranch, but there's a difference between a teenager going for the summer and you moving there permanently," Patricia said. "You can't go chasing pipe dreams."

Caine sighed and let the matter drop for now, but after dinner, when he'd returned to his room to sleep, his mother's words echoed in his head. Pipe dreams.

He was thirty-two years old, damn it. He'd tried being responsible and doing all the adult things that were expected of him, and that had gotten him exactly nowhere. In a dead-end job with a lover who didn't love him anymore, and no prospects of anything better anywhere on the horizon. He had a "life" in Philadelphia that was killing all his passion, all his enthusiasm, all his drive. The sheep ranch in Australia could change all that. He'd have a lot to learn, but intelligence had never been his problem. He stuttered. There wasn't a cause for it or a single thing he could do about it. Speech therapy had helped, but when he got nervous, it came back. He'd never get promoted because he'd never manage the interview well enough, and his bosses wouldn't put someone with a speech impediment in a situation of working with customers. He got that, but it left him nowhere to go at Comcast and no real way of going anywhere else either.

In Australia, he'd run the ranch. Technically his mother would own it still, but he'd be the one in charge. He'd have to throw himself on the mercy of his employees and his neighbors until he learned how to manage it, but he wouldn't be passed over for a promotion or a salary increase or anything like that. He'd have a job, a living, and maybe the change of scenery would be good for him. And if it was an absolute disaster, well, so was his life in Philadelphia.

He had no idea what it would take to immigrate to Australia, but he could find out. He might not be the best speaker in the world, but he knew how to research. Pulling out his laptop, he fired it up and started searching.

Two hours later, he had what he needed. Now he just needed to convince his mother not to sell the ranch.

"I'VE b-been thinking, Mom," Caine said when he came down for breakfast the next morning. "I want t-t-to go to Australia."

"Caine," his mother chided. "We talked about this last night."

"No," Caine said, taking a deep breath to calm the stutters. "You talked about it. I looked it up online last night. I can m-m-move there because of the inheritance if you write a letter saying I'll be running the r-r-ranch for you."

"But what about your career?"

"What career?" Caine asked bitterly. "I have a job. I probably won't ever lose it because I do it well, but I'll never advance at Comcast. I've been there for t-ten years without a promotion."

"You could change jobs."

"I could t-try," Caine agreed, "but I probably won't find one, not stuttering the way I do. Certainly not a job where I could advance. It would be trading one dead-end job for another."

"You don't know anything about sheep."

"I can learn," Caine insisted. "I could work outdoors instead of in an office. The sheep wouldn't c-care if I stutter sometimes. Does it make that much of a difference if you sell it now or in a year if I'm wrong and I can't make it work?"

"Not to me, but if you pull up roots here, you won't have even a dead-end job to come back to."

"Then I'll just have to make things work in Australia," Caine declared. He took his mother's hands in his. "P-please, Mom. Give me this chance."

His mother sighed and hugged him. "All right, honey. If this is really what you want to do, I won't sell the ranch. I'll worry about you being so far from home, but you're an adult, even if I still look at you and see my baby. After all, everything that's mine will be yours someday, so I suppose this is your inheritance too."

"Thanks, Mom. I love you."

THREE months later, visa and passport in hand, Caine waited nervously for his big adventure to begin. He wasn't particularly looking forward to the twenty-eight-hour flight. He'd have to change planes in Dallas and then again in Los Angeles before flying on to Sydney, but he could deal with the airports. He'd deal with the long flight, too, because this was what he wanted. He'd been in touch with Macklin Armstrong, the foreman at his uncle's sheep station, as he'd learned it was called in Australia, via e-mail, so the man knew he was coming. He'd decided to stay in Sydney for a few days before heading out to Lang Downs, his uncle's station. As excited as he was about getting there and getting started, he suspected he'd need a day or two to recover, not to mention he didn't exactly have the right clothes for his new life. He wasn't sure he could find them in Sydney either, but he'd look anyway. And if not, he'd throw himself on Macklin's mercy and find the closest town to the station. Boorowa looked like the closest on the map, but he'd gotten lost in Eastern Kentucky in college and learned that maps could be deceiving, and what looked like a straight line wasn't always the fastest route.

First, though, he had to get to Australia.

He'd broken the lease on his condo a month ago, selling most of his furniture and packing up the few things he couldn't live without. Some of them were at his parents' house, to be stored and shipped later. He'd shipped the rest to Australia, hoping they'd get there by the time he did. He had a suitcase with clothes and other necessities, but he wasn't entirely willing to give up his books and CDs.

It was sad to think his entire ten years in Philadelphia could be summed up in a box of books and CDs, but those were the only things he couldn't live without. He'd said goodbye to his friends, and they'd all promised to keep in touch on Facebook or Twitter. Somehow Caine didn't expect that to last terribly long. They were friends, but in the casual acquaintance sort of way. Certainly not a reason to stay in Philadelphia any longer.

The call to board interrupted Caine's musings. He joined the line to show his passport and ticket and take his seat. He'd splurged for the trip, flying business class rather than coach. He'd made enough money selling off his furniture to pay for it, and he wouldn't need a lot of money once he got to Australia. From what he remembered from talking to his uncle as a child and what he understood from his more recent conversations with Macklin, other than his own personal supplies—clothing, toiletries, etc.—the station paid for the rest. He could move into his uncle's house and eat with the men who worked for him, so he wouldn't have rent to pay or groceries to buy.

He could afford to be comfortable on the plane to his new life.

The flight was full, so Caine had a neighbor between him and the window, but the man didn't seem inclined to talk, and Caine wasn't one to strike up conversations with strangers. He had learned to overcome his natural inclinations when it mattered, but his lingering nerves over his stuttering made him timid in unfamiliar situations.

Three hours later, they landed in Dallas, and Caine made his way through the maze of terminals to his next gate, feeling the fatigue of traveling hitting him already. He rolled his neck, trying to stretch the aching muscles, to no real avail. Maybe the hotel in Sydney would have a spa where he could get a massage to ease his stiff muscles before he headed out to the station.

Or maybe he'd better skip that and start to toughen up since he doubted there would be a masseur at Lang Downs.

His stomach churned as he boarded the next flight, nerves assaulting him as he wondered what business a city boy like him had moving to Australia to run a sheep station. He'd grown up in Cincinnati, not a huge city, but the metropolitan area counted over two million people, so it wasn't tiny by any means, and Philadelphia had over five million. He had a feeling he was in for more than a little culture shock out on Lang Downs, but maybe it would be good for him. He wasn't overweight or anything, but he was definitely a little bit on the soft side. The physical lifestyle would harden him up, make him stronger and healthier, and keep him so busy he wouldn't have time to miss the luxuries of town. And if the longing for a museum or a play got to be too much, he'd figure out a way to get to a city for a long weekend. It wasn't like Australia was a complete wasteland. The Sydney Opera House was world-renowned. He could still have bits and pieces of city life if he planned carefully.

By the time they landed in Los Angeles, Caine had talked himself back down from his panic with the help of a couple of shots of vodka. He wasn't falling down drunk or anything, but he was definitely more relaxed than he could remember being since Christmas.

He reminded himself that his e-mails with Macklin had all been cordial, if not quite friendly, and honestly, he could understand the man's concerns. Caine freely admitted he knew nothing about sheep farming. He'd be more ignorant than the rankest beginner on the station because, chances were, even the newest hand there had grown up around the industry. Caine had done some research, trying to learn terms and techniques, but he knew better than to think that was any replacement for experience.

He'd also read up on the table lands in Australia to try to get an idea of what to expect as far as climate. He was arriving in autumn, heading into winter. Crisp, cool, even cold at night, with a cold, dry winter on the way. At least he wouldn't have to worry about snow from what he could tell. That was a relief after the winter he'd had in Philadelphia. He swore it had snowed again every time he'd dug out his car. And it wasn't winter yet. He'd checked the temperatures in Sydney, and it was supposed to be in the upper 70s, warmer than at home.

"Lang Downs is home now," Caine reminded himself softly. If he had any hope of winning the faith of the people who worked for him, he would have to remember that, and not just remember it, but believe it. Truly and deeply believe it, because he was certain they all did.

The stewardess on the flight from Los Angeles to Sydney had an Australian accent, making Caine smile. He loved the way Australians talked. He knew he'd stand out just as much once he got to Lang Downs with his American accent, but he knew it would be a long time before listening to the people around him talk stopped making him smile. He wondered if his accent would be as charming to Australians as theirs was to him. Maybe if it was, that would make up for his stuttering a bit.

Soon after they were airborne, the flight attendants came around with dinner, making Caine glad he had chosen to fly business class. He didn't know if the food was any better, but he had more room to eat it at least. When he had finished, he made himself close his eyes to try and get some sleep.

TWO

CAINE got his first culture shock after the plane landed and the flight attendant gave them all the information about the current weather in Sydney. The airline staff casually announced it was a beautiful twenty-one degrees. It took a good minute as Caine mentally ransacked his suitcase for something warm enough to protect him from freezing temperatures before he remembered Australia used Celsius, not Fahrenheit. Then he had to stop and remember how to estimate the calculation in his head. Multiply by two, add thirty… seventy-two. He could live with that in his short sleeves and khaki pants. Below freezing would have been bad.

He made it through customs and immigration without too much trouble, although the immigration authorities had more than a few questions about his visa and where he intended to work. He produced the letter his mother had provided, giving him authority to run the sheep station, his stuttering growing worse with each minute that passed. Finally, though, they gave him the go-ahead. He made it out to the main area of the terminal, debating whether he wanted to try public transportation with his luggage or if he should break down and take a taxi. He had always prided himself on using public transportation when it was available, but he had two huge suitcases and a hiker's backpack. He wasn't even sure he could make it onto a bus or train that loaded down. Sighing, he trudged out to the cab stand and waited in line. The taxi dispatcher had to ask him three times where he was going before he could get his brain to understand the question and drudge up the answer. "The Medina Grand Sydney," he said finally.

"You're dead on your feet, aren't you, mate?" the dispatcher asked. "No worries, we'll get you sorted."

Caine summoned a wan smile and heaved his bags into the trunk of the taxi when it pulled up without waiting for the driver's help. He kept his backpack with him since it had his wallet. He'd have to find a bank so he could transfer funds to start his new life, but he had enough cash to survive a few days.

He wanted to watch the city go by as they drove to the hotel, but even having flown business class, he was too exhausted, his body on American time still. He closed his eyes and trusted the driver to get him where he was going.

Checking in was another adventure, the range of accents baffling to him as he struggled to find his room and get settled. When he finally got to the room, he dumped everything where he stood, flopped on the bed, and slept for four hours straight.

When he woke up, it was three o'clock in the afternoon and he was starving. First, though, he needed a shower. He unpacked his backpack where he'd put everything he expected to need while he was in Sydney and stood for a long time under the hot water, letting it wash away the remnants of jet lag and the grime from traveling. When he finally felt human again, he got out of the shower and got dressed, slipping his wallet in his pocket before wandering down to street level in search of a place to eat.

He found shop after little shop with food counters in the back, offering a variety of hot dishes. The smells lured him inside finally to find an Indian woman behind the counter, her blue and green sari a bright flash of color. "Can I help you?" she asked.

Caine looked at the menu and at the red sauce on the curries. He liked Asian food, but he had a suspicion this would be too spicy for him. "C-c-could I have a d-doner k-kebab?" he asked, silently cursing the stutter that seemed to have come back in full force.

"You want tabouli and hummus with that?" the woman asked.

"Yes, please," Caine said. "And a cup of tea." He knew better than to ask for iced tea even though that was what he really wanted. At least it wasn't miserably hot outside so the hot tea wouldn't be unpleasant, just not what he wanted. He'd have to see if he could buy some tea bags to keep at the station so he could make a pitcher of iced tea and keep it for himself, even if the other station hands scoffed at him for it.

"Milk?" she asked.

Caine blinked a couple of times, trying to make sense of what was surely an obvious question. "Um, n-no thank you," he said finally, not entirely sure why he would need milk. Then it hit him. Milk for his tea. It was not a flavor he had ever enjoyed so he was glad he had said no. When she handed him a tray a few minutes later, he gaped at the quantity of food on the plate. He had been looking for a snack, something to tide him over to dinner, but this was a meal in itself. Sitting down at one of the small tables near the window, he started to eat, promising himself he'd get on local time starting with breakfast tomorrow.

CAINE had allowed himself two days to take care of the business aspects of his arrival in Australia: a bank account, credit cards, a cell phone that would work in Australia with an international calling plan so he could call his parents occasionally, a new power cord so he could use his laptop without having to juggle converters and adapters. It took him every minute of those two days to take care of his business so that when he boarded the bus for Yass at Sydney's Central station, he kept fighting the feeling of having forgotten something. The drive through Sydney and out toward the airport was not terribly interesting from a scenery point of view, but as they headed southwest toward Mittagong and then on to Goulburn, the cityscape disappeared, replaced by progressively more rugged terrain. By the time they left Canberra and headed to Yass, where Macklin was supposed to meet him, Caine was feeling totally out of his element. Canberra was a decent size city from what he could tell, and it was only an hour away from Yass, but he had no idea how long it would take to get from Yass to Lang Downs. Macklin had said they would drive as far as Boorowa that night and spend the next day getting his gear together before they went out to the station, but that hadn't given Caine any sense of how far it was from there to Lang Downs.

Yass was nowhere near the size of Canberra, but it did seem to be a thriving town. He could see an impressive historic main street from the bus window, making him wonder if Macklin would be willing to give him an hour to wander around before they headed north to Boorowa. Maybe they could even buy some of the things he would need here to justify the delay.

He descended from the bus and reclaimed his bags, looking around for anyone who might be Macklin Armstrong, foreman of Lang Downs. Unfortunately for Caine, half the men at the station looked like they could fit the description he had of Macklin, and none of them seemed to be looking for him.

"Caine Neiheisel?"

Caine turned around and came face to face with the most rugged man he'd ever seen. Not that his life in Philadelphia had given him a lot of opportunity to meet the cowboy type.

"Y-y-yes," he stammered, the jolt of attraction he felt leaving him even more tongue-tied than usual. "I'm Caine."

"Macklin Armstrong," the man said, holding out his hand. "Welcome to the outback."

"Th-thank you," Caine said, taking the offered hand and feeling the calluses as Macklin squeezed, not hard enough to hurt but definitely hard enough to prove the strength of his grip. "I'm g-glad to finally be here."

"Long trip?" Macklin asked sympathetically.

"Not so much today," Caine said, mastering his stutter finally. "Only about five hours on the bus. The flight here was miserable."

"Jet lag is the worst," Macklin agreed, reaching for one of Caine's suitcases. "Are you hungry?"

"Starving," Caine replied gratefully. "I had b-breakfast and I brought along a snack to eat on the bus, but I haven't had lunch."

"There are pubs downtown where we can eat," Macklin said. "We'll toss your suitcases in the boot and walk from here if you're wearing comfortable shoes. You don't want to get blisters now."

"D-definitely not," Caine agreed, hefting his backpack onto his shoulder and picking up the other suitcase. "I'll be the first to admit I don't know much about what I'll be doing once we get out to the station, but being in pain makes the list of bad ideas."

"We've got plenty of station hands with the jackaroos we hired on in the spring," Macklin said, closing the trunk of the Jeep he was driving. "You don't have to worry about doing anything that'll end up with you getting hurt."

Caine recognized the dismissal, but he was determined not to be put off by it. Macklin had no reason to expect otherwise, given Caine's lack of experience. He would just have to change the foreman's mind. "Is it worth doing some shopping here? The main street looked interesting and full of shops when we drove by. If it would save time to do it here rather than having to stop in Boorowa, I don't mind changing our plans."

"The station has accounts with the stores in Boorowa," Macklin explained, his long strides eating up the ground as they walked. Caine had to half run to keep up with him despite being nearly the same height as the foreman.

"Yes, but the station shouldn't pay for my personal gear," Caine said. "You wouldn't buy a new pair of boots for yourself out of the station account, would you?"

"No," Macklin said, "but I don't own the station."

"Neither do I," Caine replied. "M-my mother does. I'm just here to help manage it for her." He chuckled at the ludicrousness of that comment. "Okay, maybe not since I don't know what I'm doing, but b-believe me, I'm not really in charge of anything. I fully intend to rely on your advice for everything. I'm your newest... what was that word you used? Jackaroo?"

"You've got a long way to go before you earn that title, Caine," Macklin said with a shake of his head, "but if you want to learn, there'll be plenty who can teach you. They might play a few tricks in the process, but they're good men at heart."

"I c-can handle it," Caine said, the thought of having to prove himself to a station full of men making him nervous again. He only hoped Macklin didn't realize it.

"We can eat here," Macklin said, gesturing to a building on the corner of the main street. The sign read Yass Hotel. The interior was dark and cool, a welcome respite from the bright sun. The weather wasn't hot, but Caine could feel the effects of the sun. He added a hat to his mental list of things to buy, although he was sure Macklin wouldn't let him forget something that obviously important, given the battered state of his own hat.

Despite the name on the sign, the restaurant was not a hotel at all but rather two distinct bar areas, one that was quiet and nearly deserted while the other one was half-full with people playing pool amid much laughter and noise. Macklin led Caine into the busy room. "You don't mind the company, do you?"

"N-no, of course not," Caine said. "D-do you think they'd m-mind if I j-j-joined them after I order?"

"Probably not," Macklin said. "Unless they have a bet going. If it's just a friendly game, they'll be glad to have one more."

Caine considered the situation again as they found a table and skimmed the menu. In addition to the table crowded with men, there was a second pool table currently unoccupied. They ordered lunch, and Caine leaned toward Macklin. "D-do you p-play? We c-could start our own g-game."

"I'm not really in the mood to play," Macklin said coolly, "but go ahead if you like. The table's empty."

Playing pool by himself struck Caine as scraping the bottom of the barrel, but he'd brought it up. He wasn't going to back down now. Taking a deep breath, he pushed back from the table, wincing as the chair legs dragged along the floor, and went over to the pool area. He took his time picking out a cue. If he was going to play, he refused to make a fool of himself. He wasn't an expert, but he was pretty good. Good enough to impress a casual player if he had a straight cue and a level table.

Racking up the balls, he took a couple of experimental shots with the cue ball, testing the cue and the table before pulling back to break. The balls broke cleanly, one of them shooting off into a pocket right away. Caine smiled. He couldn't pull that trick off often, but it always thrilled him when he did. He checked the ball to see which one had gone in, continuing to play stripes and solids as if he had an opponent. Maybe if his luck held, he would before long. He noticed a couple of the men at the other table glancing his way. He could hope it would lead to someone joining him or an invitation to join them.

Little by little, he worked his way around the table, lining up shots, hitting some and missing others, but pocketing enough of the solid colored balls with enough regularity to draw an audience.

"You know your way around a pool table, mate," one of the men said, finally breaking the silence. "Are you interested in a friendly game?"

"A f-f-friendly game or a friendly w-wager?" Caine asked, smiling to make it clear the question was not intended as an insult.

The other men laughed. "Let's start with a friendly game, eh?" the Australian suggested. "We'll see where things go from there."

"C-caine Neiheisel," Caine said, offering his hand. "N-newly arrived in the area."

"Aidan Johnson," the man said, shaking Caine's hand. "Welcome to Yass."

"Thanks," Caine said. "I always meant to come sooner, but this is the first chance I've had. Shall we p-play?"

Aidan nodded and set the table up, offering to let Caine break. He didn't pocket a ball that time, but it was still a clean break. Aidan took his turn, missing a pocket shot by a matter of millimeters. Aidan's friends jeered at him, but Caine pushed all that out of his head. They didn't have a bet going, so it wouldn't matter to his wallet if he lost, but he felt like he had something to prove. To Macklin, if nothing else. He didn't need a babysitter or a pat on the head. He might not know anything about sheep stations, but he wasn't a child or an imbecile.

They played in silence for a few more minutes, cheers and playful boos echoing after each shot. Caine was pleased to hear his good shots got as many cheers as Aidan's did. When they had cleared the table, Aidan offered his hand again. "You're not half-bad. Let me shout you a beer to welcome you to Australia."

Before Caine could accept, Macklin loomed over them suddenly. "Lunch is on the table."

"I'm g-going to have a b-b-beer with my new friends," Caine said, feeling a bit like a teenager defying his parents for the first time. He reminded himself again that he was thirty-two and that, while he might need Macklin's help and approval once they got to Lang Downs, he didn't need it in the Yass Hotel. "I'll come g-get my p-p-plate."

Macklin looked like he wanted to protest, but he let it go, much to Caine's relief. While he didn't want Macklin viewing him as a child or worse, he also knew he would need the man's help out on the station, so he couldn't afford to alienate him completely. "You c-could join us."

"No thanks," Macklin said, returning to the table and his lunch.

Caine started to take offense, but he shrugged it off. Macklin had no reason to like him or trust him and probably plenty of reasons not to. They'd have to discuss it if it started interfering with their business relationship, but this was neither the time nor the place. Instead he grabbed his plate and joined Aidan and the others at the bar. The server handed Caine a Tooheys Old. Caine wasn't all that adventurous a beer drinker, but he'd come this far. There was no backing down now. For a dark beer, it wasn't as heavy as Caine had feared, more ale-like than stout, much to his relief, and he found the taste more palatable than he would have expected. Maybe adapting to Australia wouldn't be as hard as he'd worried it would be.

"So what brings you to Yass?" Aidan asked, tapping their glasses together.

"My uncle was from outside of B-boorowa," Caine explained. "Well, my great-uncle really. My mom is his only remaining relative, but she's not cut out for life on a sheep station."

The men chuckled. "And you think you are?"

Caine shrugged. "Probably not yet, but I c-can learn. If anyone is willing to t-teach me," he added with a bitter glance over his shoulder at Macklin. The foreman sat slumped at the table, eating his food absently and glaring in Caine's direction every so often.

Aidan leaned closer. "I'll let you in on something. Aussies act like they're the most open, friendly people in the world because they don't get hung up on all that formality bullshit our Pommy ancestors considered so important, but underneath that, they're just as closed off. They aren't going to be willing to teach you anything, but that doesn't mean you can't still learn. Don't let them ignore you or shut you out. You don't have to piss them off, but stay in their faces just like a dog nipping at the heels of stubborn sheep until you're part of them without them realizing it."

"Why are you being so nice to me?" Caine asked suspiciously. "You don't know me from Adam."

"Because I like the way you play pool," Aidan said, "and because it takes a hell of a lot of gumption to do what you've done. If they run you off your station, look me up on your way south. I might be able to find you a place on a different station, one that won't make your life difficult just because you aren't from around here."

"Thanks," Caine said, taking the number Aidan jotted on the back of his bar coaster with a pen borrowed from the barman. "I hope it won't come to that, but thank you, really."

THREE

SPIRITS buoyed by his success at pool and in overcoming his instinctive shyness, Caine returned to the table where Macklin still sat, glaring at his lunch plate.

"I'm ready when you are," Caine said, the beer he'd drunk easing his nerves enough to smooth over his stutter for the moment. He knew it wouldn't last, but it was still a boost to his confidence to get the sentence out without a problem.

"Let's go," Macklin said, pushing back from the table and tossing some money down for the bill.

Caine shook his head and handed the bills back to the foreman. "You c-came all this way to get me. I'll shout you lunch." The Australian idiom felt odd on his tongue, but he was determined to follow Aidan's advice and do everything he could to fit in.

"A few Aussie phrases aren't going to make you any less of a Yank," Macklin said with a half sneer, raising Caine's hackles even more. "Don't pretend to be something you're not."

Caine's anger simmered to the surface, but he kept a lid on it for the moment, paying for their lunch and waiting until they'd returned to Macklin's Jeep to turn on the foreman. "What is your p-p-problem?" he demanded. "You d-don't even know me. Why are you acting like I've d-done something wrong?"

Macklin opened to his mouth to reply, closed it again, and snagged his hat off his head, running fingers through the shaggy blond strands that looked like they'd been cut with kitchen shears rather than by a barber's hand. "I'm sorry," he said, sounding sincere enough that Caine felt his anger start to fade. "I admired your uncle for a lot of different reasons, and losing him was hard. The thought of maybe losing everything he worked his whole life to build is even harder, but that's not your fault, and I shouldn't take it out on you."

Macklin started the Jeep and began the drive north to Boorowa. Caine sat in silence next to him for several minutes before continuing. "Uncle Michael and I wrote letters religiously when I was in middle school and high school," he said softly. "I wanted to come see him more than anything. He told me I could come for the summer or even for a year if Mom would agree. We'd started making plans, and then I got accepted to the Ohio University Summer Honors Academy. My s-s-st—" He couldn't get the word out, shaking his head fiercely. "My voice was covered by an education plan so they let me in despite it. I had a wonderful summer that got me excited for college, and I told myself and Uncle Michael I'd come another year. He understood, but it never seemed to work out after that. I sh-should have come then when I had the chance. Everything would b-b-be easier now if I had."

"We all have regrets," Macklin said when Caine had finished. "It probably would be easier now if you'd come then, but that's water under the bridge. We'll just have to make the best of it."

"I m-meant what I said before," Caine said. "I d-don't want to t-t-take over. I want to learn and work b-b-b—with you and the other hands." He cursed inwardly at having to fight his stutter so hard, but Macklin didn't seem to be judging him for that at least. For everything else, but not for that. "Lang D-downs is my future now too."

The silence fell between them again as they continued the drive. Caine stared out the window, watching the town fall away and the majesty of the bushland come into view. He'd seen it some on the bus, but the Hume Highway was a major road, nothing like the more intimate feeling of the Lachlan Valley Way that led them steadily north toward Boorowa. As they drove further north, the trees—Caine had no idea what kind they were, although they vaguely resembled the cypress trees he remembered seeing when he visited Florida as a child— thinned out, leaving great open spaces. "Is all this range land?" he asked.

"Most of it," Macklin replied. "There are smaller homes hidden between the hills, but for the most part, there's nothing out here but us and the sheep."

"I d-don't think I've ever seen so much open sky," Caine admitted. "I grew up in a city, went to college in another city, and then lived in a third city. This is amazing."

Macklin laughed. "We'll see how 'amazing' you think it is when the storms knock the power out and it takes days or weeks to repair."

"What d-d-do you do then?" Caine asked nervously. "No power for weeks?"

"We have generators," Macklin assured him. "Solar panels, windmills, and actual gas generators to keep essential systems running, but for the most part, we wait it out. The canteen is tied to the generators, the hot water heaters, and the heating systems for winter. Other than that, we don't need a lot."

"Lights?" Caine suggested. "Or maybe a computer? A TV?"

"Most nights we're too buggered to watch TV or get on a computer," Macklin said. "We work outside all day, we eat dinner, and then we sleep because we have to get up and do it all again the next day. I finally made Michael buy a computer two years ago because his handwriting got so bad I couldn't read his ledgers anymore, but that's about all we use it for. You sure you're ready for this?"

"No," Caine said, "but it's got to better than working in the mail room. *I'm* better than working in the mail room."

Macklin chuckled. "It won't be a mail room, that's for sure, pup."

Caine considered taking umbrage at the nickname, but it didn't seem malicious, not like the earlier attack, and next to Macklin, he was little more than a puppy following the more experienced dogs around. "I did some reading before I came," he said, "but it was all focused on North American sheep farming. I didn't know how much would carry over. Certainly not the dates when they cited certain things occurring."

"I can see that," Macklin agreed. "It would be spring in the States, right?"

"Yes, the snow had finally melted when I left home," Caine said. "So it was all about lambing and shearing right now."

"You're six months off from us," Macklin said. "We're in the middle of breeding and settling the sheep for the winter."

"What kind of accommodations do you have for them?" Caine asked.

"If it's a mild winter as far as snow is concerned, we leave them outside most of the time," Macklin said. "If we get enough snow to be dangerous for them, we have barns and sheds where we can shelter them until it melts enough for them to go outside again."

"Do you breed naturally or do you use insemination?" Caine asked.

"Naturally," Macklin said. "We have too many sheep to inseminate them and no reason to do it since about seventy percent of our ewes breed the first time out, and most of the rest do the second time. If they don't, there's usually something wrong with them."

"That must cut down on the work," Caine said. "That's g-good. I'm sure there's enough work as it is."

"We certainly aren't sitting around on our hands," Macklin agreed, sharing a quick grin with Caine. "We'll make it to Boorowa in another ten minutes or so. Tell me what you have in your kit so I know what we need to scare up for you."

"Not much that will suit for out here," Caine admitted. "I have a couple of pairs of jeans, nice ones, but not new. I don't mind if they get dirty. I have some sweaters, sweatshirts, T-shirts, but most everything else is stuff I wore to the office. Khaki pants, button-down shirts. I know they aren't practical for the station, but I didn't have anything else to bring."

"What about boots?" Macklin asked.

Caine shook his head. "A good pair of sneakers and some loafers, but nothing for hard work. I wasn't kidding when I told you I was a greenhorn."

"That you are, pup," Macklin agreed. "No worries. We'll get you sorted in Boorowa, but it won't be cheap if you insist on buying it all at once on your own penny."

"I'll buy what I need to get through the winter," Caine decided, "and I'll deal with the rest when it warms up in… when does it warm up? September? October?"

"September," Macklin concurred, "although that's always variable. I'm sure it does that at home for you as well."

"Lang Downs is home now," Caine insisted, "but yes, it was true in Philadelphia too."

Caine expected Macklin to challenge his statement, but to his surprise, the foreman let it pass without comment.

Boorowa was an even smaller version of Yass, with enough bustle to make it clear the town was in no danger of dying out while being anything but a city. Macklin pulled up in front of a country store that reminded Caine of the dry goods stores in the old Western novels he used to read as a boy. He kept the comparison to himself, quite sure Macklin would not appreciate it.

"So what d-d-do we need first?" he asked, nervous again now that they were back in public. Macklin seemed far less approachable when others were around than he did in the relative privacy of the Jeep.

"Relax, pup," Macklin said, obviously having picked up on the fact that Caine's stutter got worse when he was ill at ease. "Nobody's going to bother you here."

"I know," Caine said, "but I don't fit in."

"That hasn't bothered you before now," Macklin pointed out. "You didn't deal with those blokes in Yass like you cared if you fit in. You brought them to you instead. You came a long way to follow a dream. Maybe I wonder if you know what you're getting into, but you've got to respect a man for rolling the dice that way."

Caine took a deep breath. "So what do we need first?" he asked, relieved that his voice was steady this time.

"Moleskin jeans, some heavier work shirts so you don't ruin your fancy ones, two pairs of boots, and a hat, or you'll be so burned in a day or two you'll be sick with it."

"I thought it was fall," Caine said, looking around at the sparse foliage that had started to change color.

"It is, but that doesn't make the sun less of an issue," Macklin said. "The sun can burn you all year round."

"I guess it's a good thing I brought sunscreen," Caine muttered.

Macklin knocked him on the shoulder with his hat. "Buy a hat. Akubra's a good one."

Caine sighed and followed Macklin inside the store. The foreman obviously knew the shop owner, greeting him with a smile and a handshake and starting into a list of things he'd need for the "blow-in." Caine smiled politely and took the pile of clothes and gear the owner handed him. Thirty-seven, thirty-eight, and all the rest of the shirt sizes told him nothing when he was used to asking for a fifteen-and-a-half. He figured he'd just try clothes on and go from there. Of course if he hardened up anywhere to the degree Macklin was, he'd need new clothes by the time next winter rolled around. "Is there s-somewhere I can t-t-try them on? Since I don't know what size I need here."

The owner pointed toward a dressing room Caine could use. Caine kept his head high through sheer determination as he went to the back of the store, sure he could hear Macklin and the shopkeeper exchanging jokes at his expense. He pulled the curtain to assure his privacy and rested his head against the cool mirror on the wall. He'd been a fool to come. He couldn't do this alone, and Macklin, whom he'd hoped to rely on for pretty much everything, blew hot and cold, not giving Caine the rock to lean on he needed.

"Grow up," he muttered. "You might be a 'blow-in', but you aren't a stupid kid who made a spur-of-the-moment decision. You knew this would be hard. You aren't going to give up before the adventure even begins."

With that self-scolding fresh in his mind, he tried on the jeans and shirts Macklin and the shopkeeper had given him. He ended up with a size thirty-nine to be able to button it around his neck, but it hung loosely on his admittedly scrawny shoulders, making him wish he was built more like Macklin. The pants were even more confusing, with the waist measurement in centimeters and the length in a generic regular or long, neither of which fit his legs right. "I guess I'd better buy a sewing kit too," he added with a huff that would earn him a swat from his mother for sulking if she could see him, but she wasn't here to see his disgrace, fortunately. Setting aside the clothes that fit best, Caine put his own jeans and shirt back on and summoned a smile. "I'll need something to take up the hem of the pants," he said as he walked back out of dressing room. "I'm not quite the same shape as the average Australian man, apparently."

"You and half the men in Australia," the owner said with a grin.

"We have what you need at the station," Macklin added. "No need to spend your money on that. Now, what about boots, Paul? Do you have any Blundstones or RM Williams? No idea what size he'll need, but a pair of sneakers isn't going to cut it out in the paddock."

"We'll get him sorted," Paul promised. "Let me see those shoes you're wearing, son. I can try to find the right size from there."

Still feeling out of sorts but sensing that the mood in the room had shifted while he was trying on clothes, Caine slipped out of the sensible brown loafers he'd chosen to wear and handed one to the shop keeper.

"You said I'd need a hat too," Caine said, turning back to Macklin while Paul was busy with his shoes.

"They're over here," Macklin said, leading Caine to a display of hats under the label Akubra. The brand meant nothing to Caine, but the hats matched the one Macklin was wearing, if in better shape, so Caine figured they were good ones. He tried a couple on, not sure how they were supposed to fit, until Macklin nodded.

"That'll do, pup," he said. "That one fits you all right. It'll shade your eyes without falling in your face all the time."

Caine couldn't explain the surge of pride at getting Macklin's approval for something as simple as picking a good hat, but it was there nonetheless. If the man's attitude were a little more consistent, Caine wouldn't have worried so much, but the hints of hostility beneath the surface worried him a little. "Thanks. Anything else I need?"

"A drizabone," Paul said, coming back with several pairs of short-sided boots with elastic around the ankles. "And some thick socks. It doesn't snow much where you're going, but it can get cold, and there's nothing as miserable as frozen feet."

"What's a drizabone?" Caine asked.

"A coat," Macklin said, "a waterproof one. Try on the boots and then we'll find you one."

Caine tried on the boots, finding a pair that fit comfortably if a little tight around the ankles. He figured that would stretch as he broke them in, though. When he was done, Paul already had a pile of socks added to his growing stack. "Here," Macklin said. "This one should be about right."

Caine tried on the oilskin coat, finding it stiff and cold and not at all comfortable. "Are you sure this is the right size?" he asked. "It d-d-doesn't seem to fit right."

"Wear it around for a few minutes," Macklin advised. "It has to warm up to you. Once it does, it'll feel like a second skin."

Caine was somewhat dubious, but he left the coat on as he looked around the store for anything else he might need. He hadn't gotten an answer about how far Boorowa was from Lang Downs, so he didn't know how practical it would be to return to town for other necessities. He'd added a fresh tube of toothpaste and some other basic toiletries to his pile when he realized the coat had softened. He stretched experimentally, feeling it move with him instead of impeding his movement as it had done before. "Wow, this is pretty cool," he said, looking back at Macklin.

"Blow-in," Paul chuckled, but his kind expression took the sting from his words. "Stick with Macklin here. He won't guide you wrong."

"Anything else I need?" Caine asked Macklin.

"I don't think so, pup. Let's get this all packed up and then we can find a place to sleep tonight. I want you to see Lang Downs for the first time in the daylight."

Caine slid the coat off and paid for his new gear, blanching a little at the total, but it was an entire new wardrobe, and he wouldn't have expenses once he got out to the station. Even so, he'd maybe spread his spring spending out over a couple of trips instead of doing it all at once.

"So how far is it to Lang Downs from here?" Caine asked as they walked back out to the Jeep.

"It's only about an hour until we leave the main roads," Macklin said, "but then we have to cross Taylor Peak, and that's on dirt roads, and several hundred clicks. Once we get onto Lang Downs, it's another several hundred clicks to the main station, again on dirt roads. Not the best for driving at night unless there isn't another choice. It'll take four or five hours total, so we'll do better to leave after breakfast."

"Taylor Peak?" Caine asked. "Is that the neighboring station?"

"Yes," Macklin said. "Devlin Taylor owns it. We won't stop and say hello tomorrow, but I'm sure you'll meet him soon."

FOUR

THE Boorowa Hotel, an actual hotel this time as opposed to the one in Yass that had just been a pub, stood a couple of blocks south of what Caine had come to think of as the center of town. He had no idea if that was accurate since Macklin hadn't exactly given him a tour, but the courthouse and the big church were close together a few streets away, so Caine figured that was the heart of the area. Two stories tall and painted a fantastic butter yellow, the building was obviously maintained or restored from the late 1800s, giving it a rustic charm Caine appreciated. He kept his thoughts to himself, not wanting Macklin to think he was looking down on the elegant simplicity of the building. He did feel safe commenting on the lattice that surrounded the second-story balcony. "That's amazing work on the balcony," he said. "You don't see detail like that very often."

"It dates from the turn of the twentieth century," Macklin said. "The owners are very proud of it."

"And so they should be," Caine agreed.

Macklin got them two singles, much to Caine's relief. He could have shared a double if Macklin had insisted, but this way he would have his own space to retreat to at the end of the evening, especially if his jet lag caught up with him again and he wanted to go to bed early. Caine set his backpack on the bed and sorted through his new clothes. He would wear his new boots and jeans the next day, but he'd save the work shirts for once they got out to the station. It wasn't quite that cool yet, at least not during the day, and a sweater would be fine for driving if he needed more than a T-shirt. He put everything else back in the bags. He had no idea if Macklin would wear his hat down to dinner or around town, but Caine wasn't comfortable doing that yet. He'd do his best to fit in on the station, but he'd feel better in his own clothes while they were still in town. For tonight, though, he'd deal with being a "blow-in" because, really, that's what he was. He hoped someday he'd get past that label and be accepted as part of the local scene, even if not exactly a local, but that would take time and patience on his part. "This is what I want," he said softly as he grabbed his wallet to meet Macklin for dinner.

It seemed like they'd just eaten lunch, but when they took a table in the Marsden Café there in the hotel, the delicious smell of dinner brought Caine's appetite back full force. They ordered, Macklin getting a beer, so Caine did the same, then sat back to wait for their meals to arrive.

"Tell me more about my uncle," Caine asked into the silence between them. "I knew him from letters, and everything I read fascinated me, but I never met him."

"Michael Lang was one of a kind," Macklin said with such a fond smile that Caine's worries fell away for the moment. Whatever Macklin might think of Caine, that didn't carry over to Caine's uncle. "I was a kid when I showed up on Lang Downs, hungry and dirty and desperate for work of any kind. I figured he'd toss me off the station like everyone else had done, but he didn't. He had the cook feed me dinner and then asked me where I was from. I gave him some made-up bit of nonsense about not being from anywhere. He raised one eyebrow at me, told me if I'd tell him the truth, I could stay, and then waited me out. That was twenty-five years ago."

"So what was the truth?" Caine asked impulsively.

"If I tell you, I can stay?" Macklin retorted mockingly.

"I d-d-didn't mean it that way," Caine said. "I'm s-sorry. It's n-none of my b-business."

"No, it's not," Macklin said, his face as hard as Caine had seen it since they met, making him wonder what nerve he had hit by mistake. He resigned himself to another confrontation. "I've proven myself as Lang Downs's foreman, so you can either accept that or fire me and hope you find someone else with a fraction of my experience who won't rob you blind."

"I t-told you already I n-need your help," Caine reminded him. "I don't know how else to p-prove it to you. You have a p-place at Lang Downs as l-long as you want it."

"I'm sorry," Macklin said again, scrubbing at his sun-darkened cheeks with his hands. "It's been a rough few months, not knowing what was going on with the station and then hearing it went to a relative so far away.... Everyone was worried about what would happen, and you not knowing anything about sheep doesn't help. You could make any decisions you want, and we'd have no choice but to go along, even if they were bad ones."

"I get that," Caine said. He wanted to reach for Macklin's hand, to somehow impress his sincerity upon the older man, but he doubted that would be well-received. "I really do, but you have to give me a chance to prove that isn't my intention. If you toss my inexperience in my face every time I ask a question, how am I going to learn? If every question is met with the surety that I'm going to change something or make some bad decision, how will we ever find if there are ways we could be doing even better? I'm not saying I have any answers, because I don't, but I want to learn, and when I do, I might have something to add eventually. I want us to be a team, once I get to the point I can pull my own weight." *I want to get to the point that "pup" doesn't fit me anymore.*

"You can ask any questions about the station you want," Macklin said. "You've the right to do that, I suppose, but that doesn't carry over to people's personal lives. Those are still personal and that trust doesn't come just because you're the new owner's son."

"Uncle Michael always wrote about working on the station," Caine said, choosing to change the subject back to the one topic they seemed to be able to discuss without arguing, "but he was my mother's uncle, which means he would have been nearly ninety when he died. Did he still work with everyone?"

"Not as much the last few years," Macklin said, "and he complained about every minute he couldn't be out in the paddock. He hated paperwork, although he'd never let anyone else do it either until he couldn't write clearly anymore. He said working with the animals and the jackaroos kept him young."

"If he was still working the station in his eighties, I'd say he was right," Caine replied. "It's such a different life here from what I'm used to. Not just the sizes or the seasons. Intellectually I knew to expect those. It's the independence, I guess. All of my parents' friends are retired, and they're twenty years younger than Uncle Michael. They may still be active, but not like he was. And the idea of living out on a station, four or five hours drive from the nearest town, with power that could go out in a storm and everything else you've described to me... it just doesn't even connect to my experiences."

"Don't take this wrong, but if that's the case, why are you here?" Macklin asked.

"Because my life in Philadelphia was going nowhere," Caine admitted. Macklin might not want to talk about his past, and Caine would respect that, but maybe if he shared some of his own story, Macklin would come to see how serious he was about his commitment to Lang Downs. "You've heard me talk. When I get nervous, I stutter. I've been passed over for promotions at least once a year since I took the job straight out of college."

"Why didn't you go to a different company?" Macklin asked. "Or do something that didn't require you to talk a lot?"

"I was good in school, except for the speaking stuff," Caine explained. "Everyone assured me I'd outgrow the stutter or learn to cope with it or that it wouldn't be a problem. I believed them, and with the speech plan I had, I graduated near the top of my class and got a decent scholarship. College was a little harder since there was no speech plan at that level, but the professors were mostly willing to work with me. It never occurred to me I'd have a problem having a career, so I never learned a trade I could do instead. It's hard to get a job in construction if you don't know one end of a hammer from the other."

"I can see that being a problem," Macklin said, failing to hide his amusement completely. Caine didn't take offense. It was humorous unless you were the one living with the situation.

"The job I had paid the bills," Caine said. "It wasn't horrible, but it wasn't going anywhere. I wasn't ever going to get a raise or move up to a better standard of living. I had my own place, but I had to have a housemate to afford it, and since my housemate moved out a week before I found out about Uncle Michael, it just all seemed like a sign, a chance to learn something different, *do* something different, and maybe get out of the rut my life had become."

"No Sheila to keep you there?" Macklin asked. "A nice-looking guy like you, surely you had a girlfriend."

Caine laughed so hard he nearly choked on his beer. "No girlfriends," he said with a shake of his head. "A boyfriend, but he's the one who moved out. I'm apparently as bad in bed as I am in interviews."

An odd look crossed Macklin's face, too fleeting for Caine to pin down what it might have meant, but then he smiled. "Maybe that was the boyfriend's fault, not yours."

Caine rolled his eyes. "I appreciate the support, but I'm not getting my hopes up. So there you have it. My life in a nutshell. I sold my condo in Philadelphia and most of my furniture. My parents are keeping a few family pieces, but pretty much everything I own is sitting in that hotel room upstairs right now or in a box on the way here by mail. I don't know how else to convince you that I'm committed to this path, but there's no going back because there's nothing to go back to."

"Bloody hell, pup," Macklin said with a shake of his head. "You don't do things halfway, do you?"

"There wouldn't be much point in that, would there?" Caine retorted, but he relaxed under the approving tone of Macklin's voice. "Uncle Michael never talked about life in England in his letters, but I remember my grandmother talking about things and what they were like between the wars and then after World War II. My grandmother had it easy in a way because she married my granddad and moved to the US that way. She had him to rely on for shelter, food, and all. Uncle Michael didn't have any of that. He sold everything and took the ship to Australia, hoping it would lead to a better life. It did for him. I thought maybe taking a page from his book would be good for me too."

"I hope you're right," Macklin said. "I really do."

The fact that the entire station would suffer if it turned out to be the wrong choice was understood, but Caine appreciated Macklin's tact in not saying it aloud.

ALONE in his hotel room after dinner, Caine took a quick shower and flopped down on the bed, brushing his hair out of his face. He'd meant to get a haircut before he left Philadelphia, but he'd run out of time. After having spent dinner trying not to stare at Macklin too hard and failing miserably, he wondered if he ought to ask about finding a barber in the morning before they left. He didn't relish a five-hour drive back into town just to get a haircut, and he didn't want to end up looking quite as shaggy as Macklin did. The foreman could pull it off. On Caine, it would just look silly.

He was bone tired, but sleep proved elusive as he tried to make sense of Macklin's odd behavior over the course of the day. Caine could understand the foreman's concerns. If Caine had come in with an agenda or big plans for changing everything without knowing what he was doing, he could have ruined everything Uncle Michael had spent seventy years building. Caine would never be so self-involved as to do that, but Macklin had no way of knowing that. Furthermore, from the sound of it, Uncle Michael had ranked somewhere between grandfather and demigod on Macklin's list of people to be adored, not that Caine had a problem with that, but it probably rankled that Caine had gotten everything and Macklin had gotten nothing. Or maybe not nothing, since Caine had no idea what personal bequests Uncle Michael might have left, but certainly not the station.

"This would have been so much easier if you were still alive, Uncle Michael," Caine said to the empty room. He didn't get an answer, of course, but he hadn't expected one. It made him feel better to talk through his problems, though, and he felt a little less ridiculous talking to his dead uncle than he would have felt talking to himself. "You'd welcome me properly instead of making me feel like a blow-in, and you'd take me under your wing and teach me what I need to know, and maybe you'd even explain what the hell Macklin Armstrong's problem is."

He sighed and thumped his head against the pillow. "I need him to work with me, Uncle Michael. He doesn't have to like me, although it would help if he did, but I need him to accept me and teach me. If he doesn't, I've pulled up roots for nothing, and I'll have to go slinking back home to find another dead-end job and hopefully another place to live so I don't end up mooching off Mom and Dad for the rest of my life. It would almost be easier if he just hated me."

He closed his eyes and tried to put some order to his thoughts, as if he were really laying out the facts of the case to his uncle. "He was surprised to hear from me, I'm sure, when I sent him the first e-mail soon after Mom got the news about the station. I'm even surer he never expected me to move to Lang Downs. That's fine. I get that, but I'm here now. If he hated me plain and simple, I could probably even live with that because it wouldn't be confusing. But then he calls me pup and makes nice or funny comments, and I don't know what to do again."

He flushed slightly as he remembered Macklin's comment at dinner. "Is he gay?" he asked impulsively. "If I were at home and someone made a comment like the one he made about the bedroom stuff being John's fault rather than mine, I'd swear it was a pick-up line, but he can't seriously be thinking like that about me, can he?" If he were, Caine would be over the moon, but that wouldn't be realistic. A man like Macklin, all self-assurance and physical mastery, wouldn't want anything to do with plain, bookish Caine Neiheisel, who couldn't string a sentence together without stuttering half the time and didn't know what to do with his hands and feet the rest of the time.

FIVE

MACKLIN pounded on Caine's door at what Caine considered an absolutely ungodly hour, but Caine figured the man was used to getting up with the sun. He only hoped that meant they slept a little later in the winter. He wasn't going to hold his breath, though.

He put on his new jeans and boots along with a T-shirt and light sweater, stuffing the rest of his gear in his backpack and stumbling down to breakfast in the same café where they'd eaten the night before. Fortunately the coffee was strong and fresh, which helped perk Caine up a bit.

Macklin didn't try to make conversation, much to Caine's relief. He doubted he could have strung together a complete sentence anyway. When they finished eating, Macklin pointed toward the door. "I'll meet you in the car park in fifteen minutes. Will that give you enough time?"

"That's fine," Caine said with another yawn, wishing he had a travel mug so he could get a cup of coffee to go. He should have picked up a thermos or something at the store, but he hadn't thought about it. Maybe there would be an extra one at the station.

"Go on, pup," Macklin said, giving Caine a little shove in the direction of his room. "Get your kit so we can get on our way."

Caine nodded vaguely and climbed the stairs again, feeling even more worn out today than he had the day before. He thought the jet lag was supposed to get easier, but it only seemed to be getting worse, not a propitious start to his tenure in Australia. He checked the bathroom once more to make sure he hadn't forgotten anything and lugged his backpack and shopping bags down the stairs. Macklin took one of the bags from him without speaking, leading Caine back to the parking area and the Jeep. The silence stretched as they tossed Caine's belongings in the back next to Macklin's one small rucksack. Caine wondered if he should be embarrassed by the sheer quantity of his things next to Macklin's, but he reminded himself Macklin had only packed for a night, whereas Caine had packed—and purchased—for a lifetime.

They stopped at a gas station before leaving town, reminding Caine once again how far they had to go and how cut off they would be once they got there. "What do you do for gas at the station?"

"We have a petrol tank that we fill once or twice a year," Macklin replied. "We mostly use it for getting into town and for the generators when the power goes out. Most of the work is done on foot or on horseback and with the dogs. Too many places even a ute can't go."

"A ute?" Caine asked.

"A truck," Macklin clarified, "with a flat bed behind it."

"Oh, a pickup," Caine said.

"Blow-in," Macklin replied, but his voice was more teasing than critical.

"I'll learn," Caine swore. "Give me a few weeks and I'll have all your slang figured out."

"You know," Macklin said, heading out of town and back onto the highway, "I almost believe you."

It was the best compliment Caine had gotten since he arrived in Australia.

AN HOUR later, they pulled off the main road. "Last chance to back out," Macklin joked. "From here on out, it's nothing but you and the outback."

"What are we waiting for?" Caine asked, the relatively easy camaraderie of the morning having eased his fears from the day before. He was sure they weren't done with misunderstandings and confrontations, but as long as they had times like this morning spent in comfortable silence or pleasant conversation, Caine figured he'd live with the rest, and as they got to know each other better, maybe those moments of tension would come less often.

"Not a thing, pup," Macklin said, "except for you to open that gate so I can drive through."

"S-s-sorry," Caine said, not having realized Macklin would expect him to help. "I d-didn't know." He jumped out of the Jeep and opened the gate, waiting until Macklin drove through so he could latch it behind them. He ran back and climbed in.

"Don't give me that beaten-down look," Macklin scolded as he drove on. "I wasn't yelling at you. No reason for you to get upset. If you get upset at every correction or suggestion, you aren't going to last long out here."

"I'll learn," Caine said again, more fiercely this time, as he cursed his stutter silently. Nobody ever had to guess if he was nervous or upset because his voice gave him away instantly.

Macklin let it go at that, steering the Jeep across the open pastureland, a rutted dirt path the only indication now of where they were going. Caine grabbed the armrest on the door as they bounced along, the bumps jarring him even at the much slower speed. If he had this to look forward to for the next four hours, he was going to arrive at Lang Downs so sore he wouldn't be able to walk.

"This part of the road is used by the heavy delivery trucks so it gets torn up a lot faster than the roads deeper in the station," Macklin said, seeing Caine's distress. "Taylor doesn't bother maintaining it more because it's a lost cause. Once we get past the next gate, it won't be quite so rough."

Caine hoped that was true because he'd hit his head on the roof twice already, even with his seatbelt in place. "And on Lang Downs?" he asked.

"We'd never let a road get in this condition," Macklin said, his pride in his home so clear in his voice that Caine felt his heart beat a little faster.

"I'm glad. I know it's not my home yet, but it will be, and I want to be as proud of it as you are."

"Taylor runs his station as he sees fit," Macklin replied with a shrug. "Michael ran Lang Downs on a different set of priorities."

"And what set is that?" Caine asked curiously. "If I'm going to fit in, if I'm going to help you continue the tradition you're so proud of, I have to know what I'm upholding."

"He believed in working with the land instead of against it," Macklin said. "He believed taking pride in even the smallest job led to pride in the whole, and he was never afraid to get his hands dirty next to the jackaroos. He never asked anyone to do something he wasn't willing to do himself. Eventually he got to the point where he couldn't do some things because of his age, but there wasn't a job on the station he hadn't done at one time or another, from shoveling sheep shit to patching up roads to doctoring sick lambs."

"I can't say I know how to do any of those things," Caine admitted, "well, except maybe shoveling shit because how hard can that be, but I want to learn, and I want people to say the same thing about me when I'm Uncle Michael's age. Especially the part about taking pride in what I do. Even when I worked in the mail room in a job that nobody else cared about, I tried to do my best because if I didn't, I knew it, even if no one else did."

"With that attitude, you can learn the rest," Macklin said. He frowned suddenly and put on the brakes. "Stay here, pup."

"What's going on?" Caine asked, scanning the range and looking for whatever had caught Macklin's attention. He didn't want to disregard the foreman's order, but he'd just finished saying he wanted to be remembered as being willing to pitch in with whatever needed to be done. That said, his ignorance at the moment might be more hindrance than help, so he stayed where he was, watching in case another pair of hands became useful.

Macklin strode across the bush with such confidence and ease that Caine felt a stirring in his gut again. This was a man who belonged in the outback, who understood how the world around him functioned and knew his place in it. Eventually he slowed, bending down over something Caine couldn't see. A few minutes later, he stood again, waving his hat to get Caine's attention. Caine opened the door and stepped down.

"There's a tool kit in the boot," Macklin called. "I need a pair of wire cutters."

Caine had no idea what wire cutters looked like, but he figured something like a pair of scissors or snips, so he went to the back of the Jeep and rummaged around until he found something that looked likely. He picked his way across the bush far less confidently than Macklin had done, not sure what pitfalls—physical or animal—might be between him and his goal. When he reached Macklin's side, he offered the wire cutters and looked down at the sheep baaing in distress at their feet. "Can I help?"

"You'll have to," Macklin said. "I can't cut the wire and hold the lamb still at the same time." He pulled a pair of work gloves from his belt and handed them to Caine. "They'll be too big, but otherwise you'll tear your hands up working with the wire, and I doubt you're strong enough to hold this girl down. She weighs almost as much as you do, I'd wager."

Caine looked skeptical since the lamb didn't look all that big to him, but he pulled the gloves on and knelt down next to Macklin, studying the mess of barbed wire around the sheep's legs and torso. He wanted to get it off her as fast as possible with as few cuts as possible to minimize the chances of hurting her in the process.

"What are you waiting for?" Macklin asked after a moment.

"Nothing," Caine replied, forcing the wire cutters through the mess. The barbed wire snapped, freeing the lamb's leg, but it was still tangled around her belly. "She's a mess, isn't she?"

"I've seen animals in better condition," Macklin agreed. "Get her loose. We'll have to take her to Taylor. If we leave her out here like this, the dingoes will get her for sure."

Caine nodded and cut the wire a few more times, feeling each snip reverberate up his arm. Yet one more area where he wasn't as strong as everyone else, but he got the job done, and that was the important thing, as far as he was concerned. He'd get stronger with time.

When the last of the wire fell free, Macklin hoisted the lamb to his shoulders. "Get the wire. If we leave it here, something else will get caught and might not be as fortunate to have someone stumble across it."

Caine scrambled to do as he was told, gathering the scraps of wire and the wire cutters and hurrying after Macklin, silently wishing for the same ground-eating stride. He didn't think Macklin was that much taller than he was, but he walked like a man twice his size.

Macklin tossed the wire in the back of the Jeep with the toolbox, but he put the lamb in the back seat. "Climb in there with her, pup, unless you'd rather drive."

"I d-don't know where I'm going," Caine said. He didn't point out that the steering wheel was on the wrong side of the Jeep. On a private dirt road, he wasn't likely to run into oncoming traffic or have to worry about the rules of the road, but he still wasn't sure it was a good idea.

"You don't know anything about lambs either." Macklin tossed him the keys. "I'll tell you which fork to take."

Caine climbed into the driver's seat, sure this was a bad idea, but he wasn't going to tell Macklin that. The foreman already thought he'd turn tail at the first hard spot, and Caine wasn't about to do anything to support that misconception. Checking over his shoulder to make sure Macklin and the sheep were settled, he put the car in gear, praying he remembered how to drive a stick shift, and jerked forward over the rutted road. He heard Macklin mutter something in the backseat, but he was too focused on not stripping the gears—especially with the gear shift on the wrong side—to try to figure out what the foreman had said.

They bounced along painfully for long enough that Caine began to fear he'd missed a turn somehow when Macklin leaned forward. "Take the right fork ahead. It leads to the homestead at Taylor Peak. That's where we're most likely to find someone to take care of this poor girl."

As predicted, the road split ahead, not an intersection so much as two paths diverging. "Two roads diverged in a yellow wood," Caine mumbled with a smile at his own whimsy. He was a long, long way from New England, although he could certainly make an argument for taking the road less traveled by coming to Lang Downs.

"What was that?" Macklin asked.

"N-nothing," Caine said. "A quote from a poem I read a long time ago."

"What quote?" Macklin pressed.

"T-t-two roads d-d-diverged in a yellow w-wood," Caine said, the feeling of being on the spot sending his stutter into high gear. "It's from 'The Road Not Taken' by Robert Frost. He p-picks the less traveled one at the end of the poem."

"It doesn't ring a bell," Macklin said with a shake of his head. "Not a lot of American literature in Aussie schools, at least not when I finished twenty years ago. Maybe now, I don't know."

"We don't get a lot of Australian poets in our schools either," Caine said, not wanting Macklin to feel like Caine was criticizing him for not knowing the poem. "Some British literature, a bit of what they call World literature, American lit, of course, but unless you're an English major in college, most of it is in one ear and out the other."

"Not for you," Macklin pointed out.

"Just that one," Caine said, "and don't ask me to remember the rest of the poem. I know that one line, and I vaguely remember the sense of the rest, but I couldn't quote any more of it. I'm not even sure I could when we were studying it."

"I didn't mind the novels so much," Macklin said. "Some of those were pretty good, but I never could get my head around the poetry. Too much crammed into too small a space without enough to clue me in to where it was going."

"I know," Caine said with a sympathetic smile. He paused to force the Jeep back onto the rutted track, cursing under his breath. "Now give me a good adventure to sink my teeth into, and I could read and discuss for days."

"*Robinson Crusoe*," Macklin suggested.

"*Count of Monte Cristo*," Caine countered, "although I enjoyed *Robinson Crusoe* too."

"*Tale of Two Cities*," Macklin added.

Caine sighed. "Sydney Carton… now there was a hero."

"Or maybe an anti-hero," Macklin replied. "I couldn't get into a lot of Dickens's other books, but I loved that one. Oh, and same time period, but totally different feel… *The Scarlet Pimpernel*."

"I haven't read that one," Caine said. "I know the story, but that's because my French teacher made us watch the movie with Jane Seymour and what's-his-name in it. Oh, and Ian McKellen as the bad guy."

Macklin laughed. "You can't remember the name of the actor who played the hero, but you remember Ian McKellen?"

"Well, duh," Caine said. "He's hot as fuck, for one thing, and he's out and proud for another. Of course I remember him in stuff." The moment the words escaped, he regretted them. Not the sentiment, but he didn't know how Macklin felt about him being gay, and he didn't want to make the foreman uncomfortable. "Sorry, that was probably more than you wanted to know."

"It makes no difference to me who you find attractive," Macklin replied. "That's your business, not mine. You might not want to be quite that blunt with the jackaroos. They won't like it if they think you're coming on to them."

"I've known some straight guys I found attractive objectively," Caine said. He kept his voice measured because he didn't sense in Macklin's tone the ridiculous fear he sometimes ran across that his goal was to somehow turn every straight man he met gay—as if!—and he didn't want to come across as unduly defensive. "It's kind of like you looking at Nicole Kidman or someone and finding her attractive. Sure, she's nice to look at, but you know it's never going anywhere because she's never going to be interested in you. My number one requirement in pursuing someone is a chance of him returning my interest."

"Fair enough," Macklin said. "There's a gate up ahead. Usually I'd open it for you, but I'm not sure this girl's going to let me get out and back in without tearing up everything."

"I'll get it," Caine said, putting on the emergency brake and hopping out of the Jeep. He opened the gate and then had to remind himself to go back to the right side rather than the left to get back in.

He drove through, closed the gate behind them, and then drove on. As they continued, the road became considerably smoother. "I guess we're getting near the main house?"

"Yes," Macklin said. "Another twenty minutes, maybe. Just keep going."

Caine did as Macklin said, finding it easier to drive the Jeep as the minutes ticked by. The sheep in the back seat bleated occasionally, but it didn't sound to Caine like she was in constant or terrible distress. Not that he knew what that sounded like, but he figured if she were really badly hurt, she'd make more noise if nothing else. As they continued, the dirt road changed to gravel and rough-hewn buildings started to come into view.

"Head toward the barn all the way to the left," Macklin directed. "Even if Taylor isn't there, someone will be who can take the lamb off our hands and sort her out."

Caine slowed as they entered the busier paddock area. As he approached the barn, several men came out of the various buildings, watching their approach with stoic faces that betrayed no interest or emotion, only awareness. For no reason he could name, it made Caine nervous. "N-nobody's g-going to be upset that we're here, are they?"

"Don't panic on me, pup," Macklin scolded as Caine put the Jeep in park. "We're just helping out the neighbors. You can stay in the car if you want."

SIX

CAINE wanted nothing more than to stay in the Jeep as Macklin opened the door and pulled the lamb out, but he wouldn't help his case any by cowering in the vehicle like he didn't belong, or worse, like he'd done something wrong. He opened the door and scrambled down, trotting along behind Macklin as the Lang Downs foreman carried the lamb toward the biggest of the clapboard barns.

"Who's the kid, Armstrong?"

Caine waited to see how Macklin would answer, sure the foreman's response would govern his interactions with these men for some time to come, but Macklin ignored the question entirely.

"Where's Taylor?" Macklin said, setting the lamb down.

"Out in the bush," one of the hands answered.

Macklin scowled. "We found one of your lambs all tangled up in barbed wire. Tell Taylor he needs to clean up after himself better because if his trash gets on my land, I'm not going to be happy."

"Tell him yourself," the hand replied as another one took the injured animal into the barn. "It's not worth my job to say something like that to the boss."

Macklin's scowl deepened. He pivoted on his heel and stalked back toward the Jeep, leaving Caine scrambling once again to keep up. "Give me the keys," Macklin practically growled.

"They're in the ignition," Caine replied softly.

"Then get the wire out of the boot. I don't care if you toss it in their faces, but they can clean up their own bloody mess."

Caine hurried to do as Macklin said, opening the boot and pulling out the strands of wire he had cut off the sheep. In his haste, he forgot the gloves he still had on his belt from earlier, and one of the barbs jabbed deeply into his palm as he tossed the wire on the ground. He bit his lip to silence the curses that wanted to pour out, sure Macklin and the other jackaroos would never have done something so stupid. He shut the rear door and climbed back in the passenger side, remembering to go to the left side rather than the right. As soon as Macklin started the Jeep and pulled out of the yard, Caine let out the curse of pain he'd been holding back.

"Fuck."

"What now?" Macklin asked, his face still hard.

"Nothing," Caine replied, cradling his hand against his chest. "Let's get out of here, okay?"

"Nothing I'd like better, pup," Macklin said, not looking in Caine's direction. "You handled yourself well back there. Taylor's men are an unruly bunch of idiots. I don't know how he puts up with them."

"All I did was keep my mouth shut," Caine replied.

"With that lot, that's the best thing you could have done."

Caine shook his head and let it go. His hand had started to throb, making him a little sick to his stomach. He rested his head against the seat and closed his eyes, trying the same breathing exercises his speech therapist had taught him to help calm his stutter. He opened his eyes when he felt the Jeep slow, unbuckling his seatbelt so he could open the gate. The movement made his hand hurt worse, and he cursed again.

"What's the matter?" Macklin asked, turning to look at Caine this time.

"I hurt my hand," Caine admitted. "When I grabbed the barbed wire back there."

"Let me see," Macklin demanded.

Caine held out his hand to reveal the puncture in the center of his palm.

Macklin shook his head. "Wear gloves next time. I only have a basic first aid kit in the car. I'll patch it up as best I can, and then we'll have a real go at it when we get to the station."

Caine wasn't sure he liked the sound of that, but then he liked the thought of it getting infected even less.

"When was your last tetanus shot?"

"A c-couple of months ago," Caine replied. "I made sure everything was up to date before I came here."

"That's good at least," Macklin said, opening the glove compartment above Caine's knees and pulling out a first aid kit. "The doc comes to the station twice a year unless he has to fly in for an emergency. We try to avoid that."

"I'm sure," Caine replied. Macklin pulled out a tube of some kind of ointment, some alcohol wipes that made Caine shudder just at the sight of them, and a small bandage.

Caine bit his lip again as Macklin scrubbed at the wound until it bled slightly, not wanting to let on how much it hurt. "The blood will clean out the wound," Macklin explained as he put cream on the spot and then covered it. "Keep it covered until it's completely healed. It's easy for cuts to get infected out here and hard to get the medicine to clear it up."

Caine nodded, his fingers tingling as Macklin held them. "I didn't buy gloves in Boorowa."

"We'll find a pair for you," Macklin said. "We keep plenty of gloves on the station because we go through so many pairs. The leather might have a better chance against barbed wire than your skin, but it gets torn up too."

"My hand didn't stand a chance," Caine said, pulling back now that Macklin had finished with the bandage. "I'll get the gate."

He hopped out before Macklin could tell him not to because of his hand. Yes, it hurt some when he had to use both hands to lift the gate enough to start it swinging, but he didn't want Macklin thinking he couldn't pull his own weight. The Jeep drove through, and Caine latched the gate behind him, noticing as he did that the latch was loose.

"That gate didn't close very well," he told Macklin when he got back in.

"Not our problem," Macklin said. "It's Taylor's property on both sides of the fence. He has the gate to separate one pasture from another.

I spend enough time mending damaged fences where his property meets Lang Downs. The rest of them are his problem."

"You don't like him very much, do you?" Caine asked.

Macklin shrugged, his eyes on the road. He waited so long to reply that Caine had given up on getting an answer. "I don't hate him. I just don't have any use for him. You'll understand when we get to Lang Downs."

The answer he got gave Caine no more information than he'd had when he asked. He'd already decided that was par for the course where Macklin was concerned. Caine opened and closed two more gates before Macklin's posture suddenly relaxed. Caine looked around, trying to see what might have made the difference, but he couldn't put his finger on anything. Macklin didn't provide any explanation either, but when they reached the top of the next rise, he stopped the Jeep and smiled. "Welcome to Lang Downs."

Caine scanned the vista before him. He couldn't see anything that looked like it might be the main station, but he saw sheep scattered across the land in front of him, and, tucked into a dip between two hills, he caught sight of a small enclosure with a short chimney on top. "Does someone live there?"

"Not permanently," Macklin replied, "but we have drover's huts like that scattered over the property so there's shelter for the jackaroos on cold nights or in a storm when they're out with the sheep. Neil is probably already back at the station by now, and Ian is probably on his way, so no one is there now, but someone will be before nightfall. We can't prevent every problem, but we lose far fewer lambs than a lot of stations because we keep a closer eye on our mob."

"Do you have trouble keeping men because of it?" Caine asked. "I mean, it sounds like they have to work harder here."

"They do," Macklin agreed, "but we pay a fair wage, and they take pride in their work. The ones who don't rarely last more than a season. The ones who do end up making Lang Downs their home."

"It makes a difference when it's home, doesn't it?" Caine asked softly.

"It does at that, pup," Macklin said. "Ready to see the rest?"

"Ready when you are."

As Macklin drove on, he pointed out various things to Caine: improvements to the station, reasons for various husbandry decisions, interesting landmarks and formations. Much of it went over Caine's head where the actual sheep raising was concerned, but he appreciated the cessation in tension and Macklin's willingness to talk to him about the station. Whenever Caine jumped out to open a gate, he smiled to see the latch in pristine condition and the gate hung well so it swung easily on its hinges.

"That's the last one," Macklin said eventually. "We're almost at the main station now."

Caine leaned forward, eager for a glimpse of his new home. They topped another rise and the road dipped sharply down into a narrow valley. Buildings stood scattered along the floor of the ravine, neatly framed by gravel roads and well tended flower beds. "This isn't anything like the other station."

"No, it's not," Macklin agreed.

As they reached the outmost of the buildings, Caine saw people engaged in a variety of tasks, but everyone they passed paused and waved before returning to whatever they were doing. Macklin waved back occasionally, especially to a group of young boys who looked to be seven or eight. "Do they all live on the station?"

"Yes," Macklin said. "Their parents work here, they were born here, and so they're growing up thinking of Lang Downs as home."

"What about school? I mean, Boorowa isn't exactly a bus ride away."

"They take classes online through the School of the Air," Macklin replied, "and we make sure they learn everything else they need to know."

"That's amazing," Caine said. "I had no idea."

"We aren't complete savages out here in the wild," Macklin said.

"I didn't mean that," Caine protested. "I'm fascinated with the solutions to problems that hadn't even occurred to me to consider. Believe me, I'm not poking fun. So how many people live on the station?"

"About fifty year-round," Macklin replied. "More in the summer when we're shearing, lambing, and the like. Once the breeding's done, most of the seasonal ones will go home for the winter. A few might decide they like it here enough to stay on, a fair number like it enough to come back from year to year until they find something more permanent, and a few decide Lang Downs or sheep aren't for them and we never see them again."

Macklin pulled up in front of the main house. "I'll leave you here to get settled. Dinner is at seven in the canteen if you want to join us. Kami is probably already in the kitchen. Don't disturb him or dinner will be late, and you'll be very unpopular with the entire station."

"What do I need to do for my hand?" Caine asked, somewhat bemused by the sudden dismissal. "You said we'd need to treat it better once we got here."

"Wash it with soap and water, use some peroxide on it, more ointment, and a Band-Aid," Macklin said, his voice impatient as he dragged Caine's suitcases from the back of the Jeep. "The bathrooms should be stocked with everything you need. If not, ask Kami."

Before Caine could answer, Macklin had hopped back in the Jeep and driven off. With a sigh, Caine shouldered his backpack and picked up the bags from the shopping trip in Boorowa. He'd get those inside first and then come back for his suitcases. He traipsed up the path to the veranda of the only two-story building in the main area, obviously the station house. He felt odd opening the door and walking in without knocking, but there wouldn't be anyone to answer or care. He pushed open the door and stepped inside, blinking to help his eyes adjust to the dim interior. The front room was open and spacious with a rustic couch and chairs that had seen better days, and a big stone fireplace against the far wall. Caine smiled as he recognized the room his uncle had described to him in so many letters. Setting his backpack down, he took another step into the room until a honk and an angry shout outside reminded him of his suitcases. He rushed back outside. "Sorry," he called to the driver of the truck. "I couldn't carry everything at once." He grabbed both suitcases, lugging them out of the road. Once the truck had rumbled on, Caine carried one, then the other inside.

"So I guess I should figure out which room I'm going to use," he muttered. "Or maybe I should tell Kami I'm here first. I don't want him coming after me with a cleaver because he hears strange sounds in the house."

Deciding that was the wiser course of action, he wandered toward the back of the house in search of the kitchen. He found it, finally, at the end of what was obviously an addition to the original structure, a long, narrow hallway that opened out into a huge industrial kitchen. "Hello?" Caine called, peeking inside. "Kami?"

"What do you want?"

"I'm Caine Neiheisel, Michael's—"

"I know who you are," the cook interrupted, stepping into sight from the pantry, his arms full of potatoes. His pitch-black skin was wrinkled around the eyes, like he'd spent too many days squinting in the sun, although he didn't look that much older than Caine himself other than that. "I asked what you wanted."

"Just to let you know I'd arrived," Caine said, "and to ask if there was a room I should use."

"Any room but this one," Kami said, "and I knew you were here. I heard the door slam outside."

"Okay, then," Caine said, not sure how to act in the face of the apparent hostility. "I'll let you finish cooking. I'm going to unpack if you need me."

"What would I need you for?" Kami muttered, dumping the potatoes in the sink and beginning to scrub them.

Caine didn't have an answer for that, so he retreated, leaving the cook to his task. Regaining the living room, he peeked down the other halls and through the other doors, taking stock of the different rooms.

In addition to the living room, which dominated the first floor, he found a dining room and a small, modern office with a relatively new computer and printer. Climbing the stairs, he counted four bedrooms including Uncle Michael's. The closet in the master bedroom was as empty as the others, but Caine couldn't bring himself to invade Uncle Michael's space. He chose one of the smaller bedrooms instead.

Deciding the first order of business was to treat his hand, which had started throbbing again, Caine rummaged in the bathroom cabinets until he found everything he needed. The hydrogen peroxide stung even worse than the alcohol as it bubbled deep in his hand. Caine made himself clean it three times before putting more antibiotic ointment on it and covering it again. His jaw hurt from clenching it so tightly by the time he was done, but he was at least relatively certain it was clean. He went back downstairs and carried his bags up, then flopped on the bed and stared at them, trying to work up the will to unpack.

Before he knew it, he had fallen asleep fully dressed.

SHOUTS from outside roused Caine from his dozing. He blinked a couple of times before remembering where he was. Sitting up, he scrubbed at his face, wincing when the movement put pressure on his injured hand. He glanced around for a clock. Five thirty. He had time before dinner still. He could start unpacking and still have time for a shower. He didn't want their first impression of him to be half-muddled from sleep. He was starving, but after the conversation with Kami before his nap, he decided against looking for a snack now. He'd wait it out until dinner.

He slid his new boots off, rubbing at his ankles. The tight elastic had chafed even through his socks. Maybe he'd wear his tennis shoes to dinner instead of his boots. It would be one more thing setting him apart, but it had to be better than rubbing blisters on his ankles so badly that he couldn't wear his boots tomorrow when he went out to work with the others.

He hoped Macklin's dismissal of him this afternoon hadn't been a sign of how the foreman intended to treat him in the future. If so, they'd be having words again before long. Caine refused to be pushed aside like he had nothing to contribute to the station. He had a pair of hands and a level head. He could learn everything else.

"Stop jumping to conclusions," Caine scolded himself. "For all you know, he was eager to get back to his loved ones. You didn't even ask if he had a family on the station. He could have been eager to see his wife and kids."

Somehow Caine didn't think that was the explanation, but it gave him a plausible excuse for Macklin's dismissal. He spent the next hour sorting his clothes on the bed in his new room: winter clothes for work, winter clothes for around the house, summer clothes for work, summer clothes for around the house. If the piles were disproportionate toward clothes for around the house, Caine was nonetheless pleased to see he had clothes in all four piles. His T-shirts might not last more than a single summer, but he did have clothes he could work in when the weather was too warm for the long-sleeved shirts he'd bought in Boorowa the day before. He put the work clothes in the drawers of the big chest and hung the rest of his winter clothes in the armoire. He stuffed the summer clothes back in a suitcase and shoved it under his bed. He'd look for an attic or something later, but that would do for now. Grabbing his toiletries kit, he went to get ready for dinner.

SEVEN

BY THE time Caine finished his shower, the smell of dinner permeated the house, reminding his stomach he hadn't eaten since breakfast. It rumbled loudly as he dressed and went downstairs. "Can I help?" he asked from the doorway to the kitchen. "I can carry stuff if nothing else."

"Take that tray," Kami said, not looking up. "The big white one. Fill it with bread."

Caine took the tray Kami had indicated from the rack where it waited and set it on the counter. "Where is the bread?"

"In the oven," Kami snapped as if it were the most obvious answer in the world.

Caine suppressed another sigh at Australian men and their manners. He found a hot pad and opened the oven, pulling out trays of rolls. He put them on the counter to cool while he washed his hands so he could separate them and fill the tray as Kami had directed.

"You ever work in a kitchen before?" Kami asked as Caine worked.

"Only my m-mother's," Caine replied honestly.

Kami harrumphed but then barked another order at Caine, so Caine figured he hadn't been totally dismissed.

"What are you doing in here? I thought I told you not to disturb Kami." Macklin's voice cracked through the room.

"He's helping me," Kami snapped before Caine could protest the accusation. "He offered, which is more than most of your no-good jackaroos have ever done."

"Don't take that tone with me, Kami," Macklin said, but Caine noticed Kami didn't look at all cowed. "I specifically told him to leave you alone so dinner wouldn't be delayed."

"And he didn't bother me one bit," Kami replied. "He came down here ten minutes ago and asked if he could help. I said yes. Now, since *you're* disturbing me, you can carry that platter of bread out to the canteen for the men. Caine and I will be along with the rest of dinner in a minute."

"Th-thank you for s-s-standing up for me," Caine said when Macklin had left. "I d-don't think he likes me very much."

"I didn't say I liked you," Kami replied, but his eyes twinkled as he spoke. "I said you helped me. I'll decide if I like you once I get to know you."

"That's fair," Caine said. "So what else do we need to do?"

They got dinner ready to serve, heaping trays of meat and potatoes to go along with the bread Macklin had already carried out. The canteen where the hands ate was crowded, but not with fifty or more people like Caine had expected after his conversation with Macklin earlier in the day.

"This isn't everyone on the station, is it?" Caine asked, taking an empty seat next to Macklin because he didn't know anyone else.

"Some of the men spend the night out with the sheep," Macklin reminded him. "Others eat with their families. No one is required to eat here."

"You're taking everything I say the wrong way again," Caine said. "I'm just trying to understand the way things work."

"Look," Macklin said, pushing back from the table. "I know you want to help, but there's really not a lot you can do. Kami apparently likes you so why don't you help him out in the kitchen until you get your bearings? Once things aren't quite so strange to you, you can think about finding some other things to do too."

Caine stared in open-mouthed shock as Macklin grabbed his plate and left the bunkhouse.

"They found three dead sheep this morning. Nobody knows what happened to them."

Caine spun around to face the kid who had plunked his plate down on the other side of the table. If he had to guess, he'd put the boy's age at twelve or thirteen, older than the kids they'd seen running around earlier, but still only barely into adolescence. He quibbled for a moment about pumping the kid for information, but no one else seemed willing to talk to him. "Is that typical?"

The boy shrugged. "It happens, but not usually three at once. Mr. Armstrong was all put out about it."

That explained Macklin's temper. "I'm Caine," he said, offering his hand.

"I know who you are," the kid said, shaking it. "Everybody's buzzing with news of the blow-in. I'm Jason. My dad's one of the mechanics."

"Nice to meet you, Jason," Caine said. "Thanks for taking pity on me."

"It's not pity," Jason replied. "I want to hear about America. I love the way Yanks talk."

Caine chuckled. His nationality might be a strike against him with the adults, but maybe he could use it to his advantage with the kids. "Tell you what," he said. "I'll answer all your questions about America if you'll answer my questions about the outback."

"Really? My dad said you wouldn't have time for all my questions and I shouldn't bother you and really?"

"Really," Caine promised, "as long as you return the favor."

"Deal," Jason said. "Finish your tucker so I can show you around."

Caine finished the meal, leaving his plate with the others but stopping to thank Kami for the food. Kami waved him away with a dishtowel. When they were outside, Jason whistled softly and a black, gray, and white dog came trotting up. "This is Polly. She's an Australian shepherd. She's still too young to work with the sheep, but she's learning."

"May I pet her?" Caine asked, stretching his hand out for Polly to sniff.

The dog sniffed at his fingers, then looked at Jason, obviously waiting for his approval. Jason nodded and gestured her forward with his hand. That was the signal she had been waiting for, because she slid her head beneath Caine's hand and rested her jowl against his thigh. "She likes you. She's a good judge of people."

Caine smiled at Jason and knelt down to scratch Polly's ears a little more. Jason had said she was young, but she wasn't a small dog by any means. Her shoulder was nearly mid-thigh on him. "I'm glad to know I passed her test." He had a feeling there would be a lot of tests over the subsequent few months.

"So tell me about the station," Caine asked, looking up at Jason. "Were you born here?"

"No, I was born in Melbourne," Jason said, "but I came here when I was two. Dad lost his job in Melbourne and hired on here. Mum helps Kami out with the baking sometimes, when he'll let another person in his kitchen, and she helps with some of the cleaning in the bunkhouses. The jillaroos are okay, but some of the jackaroos don't take care of anything unless you make them." Jason leaned forward conspiratorially. "They don't get invited back next summer and have to go work for Mr. Taylor instead, but don't tell Mr. Armstrong I said that. He doesn't want people saying bad stuff about Taylor Peak even if it's true."

"It'll be our secret," Caine promised, but it wasn't news to him. Even without anyone saying anything, he had seen the difference between the two stations, and that was without the benefit of any knowledge about what might be going on beneath the surface. "So I've seen the main house, but that's the only building I've been in yet. Think I could get a tour?"

"Sure," Jason said. "Come on, Polly."

Polly moved obediently to Jason's side. "That's the bunkhouse for the girls," Jason said with a wave of his hand toward the other side of the valley. "I'm not allowed to go over there without Mum. I think she's afraid I'll see something I shouldn't. Like I care about girls. I'd rather teach Polly about sheep. Where are you from in America?"

"I'm from Cincinnati originally," Caine said as they walked down the gravel road toward the collection of buildings at the far end of the valley, "but I lived in Philadelphia b-b-before I came here."

"I've never heard of Cincinnati," Jason said, "but Philadelphia, that's American Revolution stuff, right?"

"It is," Caine agreed. "The Continental Congress, the Liberty Bell, the first presidential residence, although that's no longer standing, but they have this display where you can see what the floor plan was. It was really small by modern standards. So what are those buildings?" He pointed to a series of low-roofed sheds.

"Those are the pens we use for shearing and breeding and anything else we need to confine the sheep for," Jason explained. "They're empty right now. Dad says now that Mr. Armstrong is back with you, we'll start breeding in a few days."

"Why wait for me?" Caine asked. "I don't know what I'm doing."

"Dad said it was in case you decided to sell the station out from under us," Jason replied. "If you did, there was no reason to breed the ewes because they might all be going to slaughter anyway. If you didn't, waiting a few days wouldn't hurt."

Caine turned to face Jason, bending a little so he could look the boy directly in the eyes. "I d-d-don't know what the future will bring, but I p-p-promise I will n-never sell the station out from everyone. If it ever happens, it will be b-b-because everyone agrees it's what has to happen."

"You stutter when you get nervous or serious or stuff, don't you?" Jason asked.

"Yes," Caine said, not entirely sure how he felt about Jason's lack of reaction to his declaration.

"No worries, mate," Jason said. "It doesn't bother me."

Caine felt a surge of ridiculous relief at hearing Jason's casual acceptance. He doubted everyone would be as understanding, but with his new friend, he wouldn't have to worry about feeling self-conscious if he stuttered a bit. "Can we go inside them?"

"They stink," Jason said, "but we can go in."

Caine followed Jason across the slightly uneven ground and up the rise to the closest of the pens. The kid was right about the smell, but Caine figured he'd better learn to live with it. He was a sheep farmer now, and that meant dealing with the mess. "So how does it work?" he asked when they stepped inside and he could see the various smaller enclosures within the larger building.

"Breeding or shearing?" Jason asked.

"Breeding," Caine said. "That's what I'll have to deal with first."

"Breeding's easy," Jason said. "Bring the ewes in when they go into heat, leave them here with a ram for a few days, and then switch them out for the next batch. If it doesn't take this cycle, try again next time. Shearing is the hard work."

"I've seen pictures of shearing," Caine said. "I'm not looking forward to that."

"I like it," Jason insisted. "It's the start of the new season when all the new jackaroos come, and we have a big barbie when it's done. It's a regular holiday around here when the last sheep leaves the pen."

"Jason, your mother's looking for you."

Caine and Jason turned to see Macklin silhouetted against the door to the sheep pen. "I'm sorry you had to come looking for me, Mr. Armstrong," Jason said, his awe of the foreman clear in his voice. "I was just showing Caine—that is, Mr. Neiheisel—around a bit."

"I told you to call me Caine," Caine said, speaking to Jason but making sure his voice was loud enough to carry to Macklin. He didn't want Jason getting in trouble for something Caine had allowed. "I don't mind."

"Thank you, Caine," Jason said. "I'll see you tomorrow after I finish my schoolwork. I have history tomorrow."

"Good luck with that," Caine replied. "If you have to do economics, I can help you with that, but I was never very good at history."

Jason hurried out of the building, leaving Caine and Macklin alone. "He seems like a good kid."

"Yes, he is," Macklin agreed. He didn't seem in any hurry to leave, so Caine joined him at the door. "Economics?"

"I studied b-business in college," Caine explained, the sudden surge of attraction he felt this close to Macklin tying his tongue. "For all the g-g-good it did me."

"You never know when it might come in useful," Macklin said, starting toward the collection of small houses near the large bunkhouse. Caine wondered what brought about the sudden improvement in Macklin's attitude, but he decided not to question his good fortune. He'd take the cordiality when he could get it.

Caine fell in step beside him, not wanting the conversation to end. "Jason mentioned something about some dead animals. Do we need to be worried?"

"Don't know yet," Macklin said. "We couldn't tell what happened to them."

"What might have happened to them?" Caine asked. "Disease, old age, some kind of predator? Something else?"

"It probably wasn't disease or old age," Macklin said. "We cull the flock in the spring and autumn and only keep the healthy ewes. Once they reach a certain age, they don't breed well and their wool loses its luster, neither of which is profitable for us. One sheep might have broken a leg in a hole or succumbed to a snakebite, although that's rarer, but not three in the same pasture in the same day. By the time the men found them, they were pretty picked over by feral dogs and crows, so we couldn't tell if a predator got them."

They reached one of the smaller houses, and Macklin stepped up onto the veranda. "Do you want a beer?"

"Sure," Caine said, stepping onto the veranda as well. Macklin's mercurial moods confused him, but since the foreman seemed willing to talk, Caine went along with it. A beer might even make the man positively garrulous. "It's a nice evening. We could sit out here and drink it, and you could tell me what we need to do next as far as the sheep are concerned. I may not be able to help, but I really do want to know what's going on."

"I've got Tooheys and Carlton Cold," Macklin offered. "Have a seat."

"Tooheys is fine," Caine said, taking a seat on one of the two carved wooden chairs. While Macklin disappeared inside, Caine ran his hand along the grain of the wood, marveling at how smooth it was except where the knots still stuck out. He was surprised how comfortable it was for something so rustic.

"Cheers," Macklin said, handing Caine his beer and tapping the bottles together.

"Cheers," Caine replied, taking a sip of the beer. "So what do we do about the sheep you found?"

"There's nothing to do," Macklin said. "We buried the carcasses because there wasn't anything else to do with them."

"So if a predator got them, what's the next step?" Caine asked.

"It depends on what the predator was," Macklin said. "Eagles usually don't bother the full-grown sheep, but a pair of dingoes might. If that's the case, we increase the number of men and dogs out with the sheep and hope to scare them off. If it's feral pigs, we go hunting and have pork to tide us through winter."

"And if it was something else?" Caine asked.

"There isn't really anything else," Macklin said. "We've got our share of nasties in Australia—snakes and crocs and spiders and the like—but the crocs aren't around here, and the snakes don't bother the sheep because the sheep are too big to eat. I'd planned to give the flocks another couple of weeks before I brought them in closer for the winter to save our grass as long as possible, but if something is out there hunting sheep, we may not have a choice."

"If you have to bring them down early, what does that mean for the station?" Caine asked. "Do we have to supplement their feed over the winter?"

"We always have to supplement some," Macklin said, "but we try to keep it to a minimum. Hay gets expensive and more years than not, we run close to the line as it is. Adding extra weeks to that could put us in the red. Not exactly the impression I wanted to give your mum the first quarter after she took over."

"Don't worry about my mother," Caine said. "She doesn't have a head for business. If we tell her everything is going fine with the station, she'll accept that."

"That doesn't help when we can't pay the bills," Macklin reminded him.

"I'm not saying that," Caine insisted. "I'm saying we can look at expenses and income and take a longer view than one quarter. I've got a degree in business. I know how to juggle these kinds of things. If we need to spend a little extra money now in order to make more money later, I'm not going to freak about a balance on the credit card. Or however you pay for things."

"If you're in this for the money, you may as well go home now," Macklin said sharply. "Lang Downs isn't some honey pot you can skim cash from all the time if you expect to keep it running more than a year or two."

Caine's eyes widened in surprise at the return of Macklin's temper. He hadn't intended his comment the way Macklin had taken it, but apparently money was a touchy subject, and his neutral statement had come across as critical. "As long as I can scrape together enough money for a weekend in Sydney once a year, I'll have what I need," Caine said. "Mom didn't expect to inherit Lang Downs, so she isn't expecting any income from it for her own retirement either. I want to continue my uncle's legacy, maybe improve on it if there are ways to do that, but I want to honor him either way."

"That's what I want as well," Macklin said, his voice softening enough to give Caine hope they could have this conversation without it ending in a shouting match.

"So what are the sources of income for the station?" Caine asked. If he understood that, he could maybe figure out the rest.

"Lamb and wool," Macklin replied. "We sell the ram lambs and the ewe lambs we don't keep to replenish our own stock after they're weaned, usually in December, and we sell the wool in September."

"Do you sell lamb or mutton at other times of the year?" Caine asked. "I mean, I realize lamb is a very specific designation as far as the age of the animal, but there's year-round demand, so there has to be a way to meet that."

"We don't butcher here on the station unless it's for our own use," Macklin said. "Given how remote we are, we sell the stock to holding companies that handle all that, including housing the animals until it's time for slaughter."

Caine filed that away for future consideration. He would have to look into costs, but if they could take out the middleman, they might be able to earn some extra cash. "So how many lambs do we keep, and how many do we sell each year?"

"It varies depending on the winter and how many are born in the spring," Macklin said evasively.

"Okay, how many did we keep and sell last year?" Caine pressed.

"It was a bit of a rough year," Macklin said defensively, "even without Michael's death. The winter was hard, and we lost more lambs and ewes than usual to the weather, so we didn't sell as many in the spring."

"Macklin, I'm not questioning your decisions," Caine said gently. "I'm just trying to get a picture of the station. How bad is it?"

Macklin waited for so long to answer that Caine had decided he wouldn't. "If we have a good breeding season and a mild winter, we'll make it up next spring with extra lambs and plenty of wool, but if we have another winter like last winter, we'll have to start dipping into the reserves."

"Is there a mortgage on the property, or did Uncle Michael own it free and clear?" Caine asked.

"He owned it as far as I know," Macklin replied. "Why?"

"Because the station itself is huge in terms of collateral," Caine explained. "We could get a loan against the value of the station if we had to, not that I think it will come to that. Or we could look into some other ways to earn extra cash. Ecotourism or something like that. Give the tourist a real outback experience instead of the ones they get closer to Sydney."

"We're a working station, not some hobby farm," Macklin protested.

"My point exactly," Caine said. "We could provide the authentic experience other places can't."

Macklin didn't look convinced. "I think I'd rather wait until we have no other choice."

"And maybe that isn't the right option," Caine agreed, "but there may well be options Uncle Michael never considered. I just want us to keep an open mind to new possibilities."

EIGHT

CAINE spent the next several weeks going over the ledgers for the station, trying to get a better idea of the real financial and business situation. He hadn't used the skills he'd learned in college in the mail room at Comcast, but he hadn't forgotten everything either, and his personal interest in the success of the station gave him the motivation to work through the things that were outside his experience. He kept a running list of questions for Macklin. He had expected more resistance, given how reluctant Macklin had been to discuss the situation when it first came up, but the days ended peacefully on Macklin's veranda, drinking a beer and discussing Caine's questions and his understanding of the business side of the station. Caine chose to believe his obvious interest in the situation and his determination to keep Uncle Michael's legacy intact swayed Macklin's opinion in his favor.

"I'm not a legal expert," Caine said a month later, when he finally felt like he had a picture of the station as a whole, "or an expert on sheep for that matter, but I'm pretty sure we qualify, or come close to qualifying, as an organic station. It might mean some time and expense to establish that up front, but if we can get that certification, we can charge a premium for the lambs and maybe even for the wool."

"What would that entail?" Macklin asked warily.

"Here are the regulations," Caine said, handing Macklin the sheaf of papers he'd printed off the Internet. "I marked the ones I wasn't sure about, but from what I could tell, we already do a lot of it. We'd have to make sure to buy organic hay if we don't grow it ourselves. We'd have to make sure we're dealing with disease issues the way they want us to, but most of that—free range access, no pesticides, sufficient space when housed, natural breeding—is stuff we do already. It's a three-year process from pre-conversion to Grade A organic, but there are certain things that can take less time than that, and benefits that can accrue even as we go through the certification process."

"You've really done your homework on this," Macklin said, skimming through the pages Caine had marked up. "I'm impressed. I'm not sure how I feel about the lack of vaccinations, but if we didn't have that expense from the vet, we'd have some extra cash to buy organic hay and grain."

"Could we grow extra hay or even grain here on the station?" Caine asked. "It would mean changing the grazing rotations and all that, but one thing was clear in all the research I did. The more we do in-house, the easier it is to maintain our certification once we get it because we aren't relying on anyone else keeping their records in order."

"I don't know," Macklin said. "It's so easy to buy extra hay from Taylor or one of the other stations if they have any, or go in together for a big shipment if they don't. We'd have to look at all the regulations for grazing and rotation and compare that with our available land."

Caine's face fell at the discouragement.

"I'm not saying no, pup," Macklin said. "Just that I don't know. I've never thought about it in those terms before. We're moving the sheep down for the winter starting tomorrow. Why don't you come with me for the next few days instead of staying cooped up in that office? You can get a feel for the way things work, and we can look at everything through the lens of an eventual organic certification. What do you say?"

"You really don't mind if I go with you?" Caine asked excitedly. He hadn't asked sooner because he knew how Macklin felt about his ignorance, and he needed to look into the business aspect anyway, even if he hadn't come up with any new ideas besides the organic certification, so he'd know what to expect when it came time to start paying bills. That hadn't made it any easier to spend the days inside, knowing everyone else was out working with the sheep.

"As long as you do what I tell you, when I tell you," Macklin said. "I'll answer any questions you have tomorrow after dinner, if you're awake enough to talk with me after working all day, but when we're out in the outback, there may not be time to talk, and not doing what I say could lead to you or an animal getting hurt, and I can't have that."

"I'll do what you tell me," Caine promised.

"Dress warmly," Macklin added. "The wind is brutal outside the valley, and we won't have time to bring you back once we get out there."

"I will," Caine said, finishing his beer and standing up to leave. "Thanks for the beer. What time should I be ready?"

"Kami will have breakfast ready at four thirty," Macklin said. "We'll ride out at five. If you don't ride, you can drive one of the utes, but you won't be as involved in the actual herding that way."

"I can ride," Caine replied. "Nothing fancy, but I can handle a horse. The one useful skill I have."

"I don't know," Macklin said, holding up the papers in his hand. "If you're right about this, I'd say you've got more than one useful skill."

"Night," Caine said with a smile, pushing down the fear that, if he was wrong, he'd lose Macklin's respect entirely.

"Night," Macklin said as Caine walked back toward his house.

He was excited about the chance to go with Macklin the next day. The evenings he had spent in the foreman's company had served another purpose besides giving Caine a better understanding of the station's finances. They'd cemented Caine's fascination with the other man as well. Not that he actually expected to get the chance to do anything about it. Macklin was intensely private, steering the conversation away from anything remotely personal. Caine had no idea if the man had ever been married or in love or even seriously in lust. They said no man was an island, but Caine was pretty sure Macklin came close. The only time Caine saw any softening in that hard shell was with the station's kids. The foreman always had a smile, a hand clap, or a hug for the kids. Jason worshipped the ground Macklin walked on, and it was clear the other kids shared that adoration.

Caine shared it too. He just didn't get the same chance to express it, and he wouldn't unless he knew Macklin would welcome his attentions. Even if he hadn't assured the foreman he had no interest in pursuing someone who didn't return his regard, Caine wouldn't do anything to upset the delicate balance of their tentative friendship, and coming on to Macklin uninvited would surely shoot that all to hell.

He reached the main house and went in, shivering a little in the cool room. The days were still warm enough that he didn't turn on the heat, but at night the temperatures had started to drop. Kami had found a portable heater for him so he could heat his room without the expense of heating the whole house, but that only kept his bedroom warm. The rest of the house was definitely chilly. He hurried up the stairs and into his room, switching the heater on and standing directly in front of it until the room warmed slightly. While he waited, he went through his clothes, trying to decide what to wear.

Macklin had said to dress warmly, so definitely a long-sleeved work shirt and sweatshirt. He'd take his drizabone as well, just in case. He hadn't seen rain in the forecast when he checked that morning, but it would provide an extra layer of warmth even if he only had the wind to worry about. His boots still chafed at his ankles a little, but nothing like they had earlier in the month, and he knew better than to wear his tennis shoes. Gloves, his hat, and his heavy work pants completed his mental list. By that time, the room had warmed enough for him to get ready for bed.

He changed into pajamas and climbed between the cool sheets, wishing for a warm body to share the cold nights with. He'd have to look farther afield than Lang Downs if he had any hope of finding one, though. Other than Macklin, none of the men on the station piqued Caine's interest in the slightest. He'd learned that lesson in Philadelphia. No settling for what he could get because that was *not* better than nothing at all.

Shivering a little, Caine pulled the covers tighter around him and closed his eyes, hoping sleep would come quickly and that if he dreamed, he wouldn't remember it in the morning. Facing Macklin first thing after yet another erotic dream featuring the foreman as his lover would be a recipe for disaster.

CAINE stumbled into the canteen at 4:35, his hair still damp from his morning shower, but he'd awoken with a sticky mess on his stomach, so not showering wasn't an option. He might have dealt with Macklin rumpled from sleep or sweaty from the day before, but not smelling like sex. Fortunately no one else seemed any more alert than Caine was, staring silently into their coffee cups as they ate the hearty meal Kami had prepared, then packed sandwiches into rucksacks for the afternoon. Caine followed suit, not wanting to be caught unprepared. He had just finished eating when Macklin came in, his larger-than-life charisma drawing every eye in the room. A few of the men spoke to him. Others nodded and went about their business, but Caine swore every single one of them had noticed Macklin's arrival.

"I've got sandwiches p-p-packed," Caine said, joining Macklin as he sat down to eat his breakfast. Vague images from his dreams flashed through his mind, but he refused to let them interfere with the present. "Is there anything else I n-n-need?"

"First aid kit, water, and dry socks," Macklin said. "There's nothing more miserable than wet feet. And there's no reason to be nervous, pup. I won't let anything happen to you."

"I'm n-not nervous," Caine insisted. "I'm t-t-tired and that makes the stutter worse too." He hadn't been nervous until Macklin said something, but knowing the foreman was paying that close attention to him made him nervous now. He didn't want to betray his interest.

"You don't have to come," Macklin offered.

"No!" Caine said. "I want to c-come. I'll wake up eventually."

"Before we head out," Macklin warned. "Sleeping on horseback is not a good idea."

"I'll get more coffee," Caine said. "Do you want a cup?"

Macklin held out his empty cup in reply.

Caine filled both cups and returned to the table, handing Macklin his in silence. They sipped their coffee while Macklin finished eating. When Macklin was done, Caine followed him out to the barn.

"Take Titan," Macklin directed. "He knows what he's doing."

Caine took the gelding Macklin indicated from the hand holding the reins and swung into the saddle. He had more experience with English saddles than Western, but they were herding sheep, not roping cattle. Caine was sure he'd be fine.

An hour later, Caine wasn't so sure. The stock saddle fit his body differently than the English one did, but more than that, he wasn't in the same shape as the others, who seemed completely at ease on horseback as they climbed into the higher areas of the station. The temperature dropped steadily as the altitude increased, the weak winter sunlight enough to make Caine's eyes water but not enough to provide any warmth. By the time they reached the pasture where the sheep grazed, Caine was ready for a chance to move around and warm up a bit.

"Have some coffee," Macklin offered, riding up beside Caine as they all drew to a halt. He passed Caine a thermos. Caine took a sip gratefully, feeling the heat seep through his body.

"So what do we do now?" Caine asked.

"We start convincing the sheep to move back the way we came," Macklin said. "Between the horses and the dogs, it's usually pretty easy. Slow, but easy. The hard part is getting them all going in the right direction. There are always a few that want to go some other way."

Caine took another sip of the coffee and handed the thermos back to Macklin. "How do I help?"

"You don't know the signals for directing the dogs, not that they need much direction, so if you'd keep an eye out for breakaways as we get them started," Macklin said. "We don't want to miss any."

"I can do that," Caine said. "Is it all right if I get down and walk around for a bit while I'm watching? I'm a little stiff from riding so much."

"It's cold enough the snakes should have all gone to ground," Macklin said. "If you do stumble across one, just stay still until it goes away. You don't want to get bitten out here. Even with the antivenin we carry in the first aid kits, you'd be in a world of hurt."

"I'll be careful," Caine promised, dismounting stiffly and stretching to touch his toes a couple of times to release the tension in his muscles.

Macklin started shouting orders, the men and dogs going to work gathering up the sheep. Caine stood back and let them do it, leading Titan as he walked toward the upper edge of the field where he hoped to have a better view. The ground became rockier as he walked, escarpments jutting out in places, even creating small cave-like formations. Caine rounded one such escarpment to find a sheep stuck in the rocks.

"Macklin," he called, not wanting to make the situation worse, but the foreman didn't hear him. He climbed up on the rocks to call a second time, catching the Aussie's attention finally and waving him over.

While he waited for Macklin to arrive, he walked a little deeper into the crevice, trying to figure out how to get the sheep free.

"Caine, where are you?"

"In here," Caine called, pushing against a rock to steady himself. The rock shifted, falling to his feet and revealing a huge snake. "Oh, shit," Caine said, backing against the wall.

"Caine?"

"Um, w-w-we've g-g-got a p-p-problem," Caine said as Macklin appeared at the entrance to the crevice. "S-s-snake."

"Don't move," Macklin said, his voice as tense as Caine had ever heard it. "Whatever you do, do not move."

Caine froze against the rocks as Macklin edged closer to where Caine had uncovered the snake. After a moment, his shoulders sagged in relief. "Get over here," Macklin ordered sharply, grabbing Caine's wrist and hauling him closer when Caine didn't move fast enough. "It's an inland carpet python, but what the bloody hell were you thinking, pup?" Macklin demanded, shaking Caine by the shoulders as he yelled, an expression on his face Caine had no idea how to interpret. The anger was easy to read, but the rest... he couldn't be seeing what he thought he saw. Macklin couldn't possibly be afraid for him. "I told you there were snakes around. I warned you they'd gone to ground. If you'd uncovered a king brown snake or a tiger snake, you could be dead right now."

"I'm s-s-sorry," Caine said. "I saw the sheep. I wanted t-t-to help."

"That kind of help gets a man killed," Macklin repeated. "Don't make me go through that."

Before Caine could reply, Macklin's mouth covered his, kissing him hard and deep. Caine moaned into the kiss, shock warring with need as Macklin's stubble abraded his lips. The iron grip on his upper arms kept him from pulling Macklin closer, but he tipped his head in silent offering, hoping for more.

Macklin pulled back suddenly, stalking off as if the kiss had never happened, leaving Caine's mind reeling and his dick aching. "F-f-fuck," he muttered, scrubbing at his face as he followed more slowly behind Macklin. "Now what?"

Macklin didn't wait around for him to ask the question, though, shouting orders down the mountain for two of the men to come free the bleating sheep. Caine frowned and mounted Titan again. He'd bide his time, stay out of Macklin's way while they drove the sheep down to the winter pastures, then demand an explanation that evening when he went to discuss the day with Macklin.

As long as Macklin didn't slam the door in his face.

NINE

MACKLIN managed to avoid Caine for the rest of the day, not that Caine tried that hard to talk to him. This wasn't a conversation they needed to have where the men could overhear them. As they rode back into the valley that sheltered the main station, Caine wondered if they should even discuss it at Macklin's house. While the foreman lived alone, his house was near the others used by the families that lived at Lang Downs permanently, and if they ended up shouting at each other, it might be audible outside. He could try to get Macklin to come to the big house where they were more assured of privacy, except he doubted the foreman would agree, and Caine didn't want to make it an order. They had enough issues without adding a power struggle to the list.

Macklin didn't come to the canteen for dinner, adding to Caine's suspicion the other man was going to pretend the kiss had never happened. Caine spent the meal talking with Jason instead, who was excited about having participated in his first drive with Polly at his side. From everything Caine had seen, Jason had done a great job, and Caine made sure to tell him so.

"Really?" Jason asked.

"I'm not an expert," Caine reminded him, "but it sure seemed to me like you and Polly were where you were supposed to be, moving the sheep along with all the other men and dogs. I didn't see her running off to do something else or you goofing around instead of working. Maybe you still have stuff left to learn, but you helped today, and that's good."

"Mr. Armstrong said I could start helping around the station this winter," Jason explained. "I don't want to let him down."

"I'm sure you won't," Caine said, "and you can teach me all the things he lets you do while you're at it. I certainly have plenty to learn."

"Not a lot going on once the breeding's done," Jason said. "Make sure the sheep have enough to eat, make sure they have shelter if it snows, make sure the dingoes don't come in too close. We spend a lot of the winter fixing things that broke during the summer, and I spend it doing lessons."

"It sounds peaceful."

"It's bloody boring," Jason disagreed. "I have lessons to do. Mum said I could do them tonight because of the drive, but I can't get behind or she won't let me do the next one."

"Good luck," Caine said. He finished his dinner and then wandered casually—he hoped it was casually—toward Macklin's house. The door was closed, but he could see lights on inside so he knocked and waited. Macklin opened the door a moment later. "I missed you at dinner."

"I had things to do," Macklin said, not opening the door any wider or inviting Caine in.

"I figured," Caine said, keeping his voice steady by force of will alone, "but I didn't want to miss our b-beer."

"I don't have time tonight," Macklin repeated.

"Bullshit," Caine said, pushing past Macklin into the house. "You're avoiding me."

"I was out of line up there," Macklin said. "Just forget it ever happened."

"What if I don't want to forget it?" Caine asked. "What if I want it to happen again?"

"You've been here a month. You could be gone again in another month," Macklin said. "You're lonely, and you think I'd be a good substitute for the guy who dumped you in the States. You don't know me well enough to want me."

The speech left Caine momentarily flabbergasted. "You haven't heard a word I've said since we met, have you?" he said finally. "I'm not leaving. Even if you don't want me, even if the kiss really was a fluke, I'm not leaving. This is my home now, get it?"

"No," Macklin said. "I don't. I'm not saying I don't believe you, but I don't 'get it,' as you put it. I don't know how you can uproot your life the way you did and how you can claim such loyalty to Lang Downs after only a month, and because I don't understand, I'm having a hard time trusting it."

"That's fair," Caine said, weighing his words. "Why didn't you tell me you were gay?"

"Because it doesn't matter," Macklin replied, running his hand through his shaggy hair. "This isn't Philadelphia. It's the outback. Being gay isn't a choice."

"No, it isn't a choice," Caine agreed. "It's the way you are, just like it's the way I am. I've seen the way people around here watch you. You really think they'd care?"

"Maybe not," Macklin said, "but it doesn't matter since I've never met anyone out here I want to be with, and I don't want a lover who can't share my life."

"And now that you've met me?"

"You're… you're this beautiful exotic creature," Macklin said, obviously struggling to put his thoughts into words. "I can't stop staring at you, but you don't seem real."

Caine took a deep breath and stepped closer, catching Macklin's hand in his. "I'm real," he said, "and I'm just as fascinated by you." He brushed his lips softly over Macklin's to prove his point.

Macklin groaned, his grip tightening on Caine's hand while his other hand grabbed the back of Caine's head, hauling him close. Caine wrapped his free arm around Macklin's neck, holding on as the foreman kissed him with the same fierceness from that morning, like he was starved for touch and desperate for more. Caine gave it willingly, stroking the nape of Macklin's neck and opening beneath the onslaught of the kiss. Macklin's tongue invaded his mouth, possessing more than exploring, and arousing Caine faster than he'd imagined possible. Maybe it really was John's fault the sex had been boring, because there was nothing boring about the way he felt with Macklin!

Macklin lifted his head, eyes dilated and breath coming fast. "This isn't a good idea."

"It feels like a damn good idea to me," Caine said, rubbing against Macklin's body. He could feel Macklin's interest in the erection that matched his own.

"We have to work together," Macklin reminded him.

"So we'll work together," Caine replied, kissing along Macklin's jaw. "I wasn't planning on kissing you while we were working anyway."

"That's not what I meant," Macklin said. "If we sleep together and it doesn't work out, what are we supposed to do? Lang Downs is my home. I can't just go work somewhere else."

"And what if we sleep together and it *does* work out?" Caine demanded. "You could be tossing away a chance at happiness."

Macklin shook his head and disentangled himself from Caine's embrace. "Lang Downs is the only constant I have in my life. I can't take chances with that. You know the way out."

Caine watched in stunned silence as Macklin disappeared into another part of the house, leaving him alone and reeling in the living room. His body throbbed, demanding more of the pleasurable stimulation, a painful reminder of what had just happened. Slowly he turned and walked outside, staring up at the unfamiliar constellations as he tried to make sense of Macklin's swings in attitude. One minute the man had kissed him like he never wanted to let go, and the next he'd all but pushed Caine out the door. It didn't make sense.

Caine was tempted to pound on the door again and demand more of an explanation, but he doubted it would help. Macklin was a law unto himself, and trying to change his mind was like trying to channel the tides.

Caine kicked at the gravel beneath his boots as he walked back to the main house, all the aches from a day on horseback making themselves felt now that he didn't have the anticipation of talking with Macklin to drive them to the back of his mind. He was sulking and he knew it, but he'd just been rejected by the first man to catch his interest in months and the only man to ever make him feel like Macklin had with something as simple as a kiss.

Going into his house, he climbed the stairs and stared at the narrow shower. He wanted a bath, a long soak in a hot tub. He hadn't gone into Uncle Michael's room, not feeling like it was right to use that space, but he went in there now, hoping the bathroom would be larger than his. He found an old-fashioned claw-foot tub. "Oh, thank you, Uncle Michael," Caine said, turning the water on hot and plugging the drain so the tub could fill. He hurried back into his room to get everything he'd need for a bath. By the time he returned to the bathroom, steam filled the air. He stripped down and stepped into the water, sighing in relief as the heat seeped into his tired muscles.

He closed his eyes as the tub continued to fill, replaying his conversation with Macklin in his mind. He hadn't really expected to end up in the foreman's bed right away, but he'd hoped for a little more than a facile dismissal. Macklin hadn't kissed him like he was unaffected either time, which made the end of their conversation all the more puzzling. If Macklin returned his interest, why had he pushed Caine away?

Caine turned off the water and slid down lower so it covered his shoulders. It made no sense. People made relationships work even on remote stations like Lang Downs. There were several families living on the station year-round, so it was obviously possible, but they were all straight couples from what Caine could tell. Not that Macklin had actually said the fact they were gay was a problem, so maybe it really was his being convinced that Caine wouldn't stay or wouldn't take a relationship seriously.

"There's a solution to that," Caine said softly, staring at the ceiling. "I just have to convince him."

It wouldn't be easy. Macklin was determined not to believe Caine where staying was concerned, which meant he'd be even less willing to believe Caine was serious about him, but time was on Caine's side. He didn't have a deadline, a moment by which he had to succeed. He could keep working on Macklin, working *with* Macklin to prove his sincerity and his interest. Macklin might look like he was made of stone, but he had cracked today when fear and anger had gotten the best of him.

Caine didn't plan on provoking his temper, but he could provoke other things. With a bit of space and time to calm down, Caine could think back to their kiss in Macklin's living room and see the way Macklin had reacted. He wasn't uninterested. He was afraid. He was also desperate. Caine grinned. He wondered if Macklin would like a home-cooked meal for two. That would give him the privacy to touch as he pleased.

Just thinking about it made his body react. He'd spent far too short a time in Macklin's embrace, but the feel of work-hardened muscles was already imprinted on Caine's skin. He closed his eyes, reliving the sensation of Macklin's hands on his arms and the back of his neck, commanding him. He didn't think of himself as particularly submissive, but damn, there had been something about being *taken* the way Macklin had done the two times they had kissed. If sex with him was the same way, Caine figured he'd be a pile of ash by the time Macklin finished with him, because the kisses alone had been incendiary.

He ran his hand over his chest, trying to imagine what it would feel like if Macklin touched him there. Caine could still feel where Macklin had grabbed his arms after the incident with the snake, not quite bruised but definitely tender. Would Macklin's hands be as authoritative when making love? Would he press Caine back onto the bed and knead firmly? Caine imitated the caress he could picture with such ease, pulling on one nipple firmly, a hiss escaping at the sensation that arrowed down his stomach. He rolled it experimentally between his fingers, imagining the calluses of Macklin's hands in place of his own smoother fingers.

The jolt that went through him had to be from the thought of Macklin touching him, because Caine had never taken this kind of pleasure in touching himself before. He was as well-acquainted with his right hand as any man, but this felt different, more potent, almost as if Macklin were there with him, touching him for real instead of only in his imagination and his dreams.

Letting the fantasy spin out, Caine continued to play with his nipples with one hand while the other circled his cock, fully hard now. He stroked up and down the shaft slowly, trying to imagine Macklin doing the same, except that Caine had trouble envisioning it. Not that he thought Macklin would be a selfish lover, but somehow he suspected sex with Macklin would be as hard and fast as the kisses had been, that he'd be on his knees, his ass in the air, before he could blink. He groaned at the image, sliding his hand deeper between his legs so he could reach his entrance. This was where Macklin would focus his attention, Caine suspected, on stretching him to take Macklin's cock.

In the tub, he couldn't shift easily onto his knees to mimic the position he was sure Macklin would demand, but he worked a finger inside his hole, imagining Macklin was touching him instead. He found his prostate and flicked it, groaning as his cock jerked in the water. He pressed on the gland again and watched a fresh cloud of fluid seep into the water. Adding a second finger, he pumped slowly, not that he expected Macklin would go slow, but it had been a while since he'd last had anything inside him. Sex with John had been rarer and rarer over the past year, and what there had been of it tended to be a quick, uninspired blow job. Sex with Macklin might be quick at times, but Caine already knew it would never be uninspired. Not with the way the man kissed.

Feeling his guardian muscle relaxing, Caine started moving his hand more quickly, in imitation of the way Macklin would fuck him. He closed his eyes again and remembered the expression on Macklin's face when they had broken apart after their kiss in Macklin's living room. That and a particularly well-aimed pass across his prostate were all it took. Caine groaned as his cock spurted into the water, his release surging through him. He slumped against the back of the tub, his hand still resting between his legs. "Damn," he muttered. "Actually having sex with Macklin will probably kill me."

He let the water out of the tub and turned the taps back on. He'd need fresh water if he intended to actually get clean.

By the time he finished his bath, he was absolutely exhausted, the early morning, the hard riding, the scare with the snake, and the confrontation with Macklin combining with his orgasm to leave him completely wrung out. He flopped into bed, realizing as he was falling asleep that he hadn't asked Macklin what they were doing the next day. He thought about getting up and setting the alarm for early again, but the room was cold, his bed was warm, and his entire body felt numb. He'd hope he woke up in time, and if he didn't, he'd apologize for sleeping in by doing something for Macklin the following evening. He'd help Kami in the canteen and then make a special dinner for Macklin and himself.

Smiling as he imagined what that might lead to, he drifted into dreams of hot hands, hard lips, and an Aussie drawl.

TEN

MACKLIN and the others had already left by the time Caine stumbled bleary-eyed into the canteen the next morning. He got a cup of coffee, but he didn't bother Kami for breakfast. Breakfast had been served hours ago. Instead he grabbed a bowl of cereal and some milk. It would hold him until lunch.

"Mr. Armstrong wouldn't let you go out today either?" Jason asked, coming into the canteen and sitting down next to Caine.

"I forgot to ask him what time they were leaving this morning," Caine admitted. "I still have a few things to learn, I guess. Why wouldn't he let you go with them today?"

"He said it was supposed to storm and there would be ice up higher," Jason replied. "He promised my mum he wouldn't take me with them if it would be dangerous, and he seemed to think it could get nasty up there."

Caine blanched. "Then it's probably better I didn't go because I'd be no help at all and probably a hindrance. So what are you going to do today?"

"Schoolwork," Jason said with such a put-upon look on his face that Caine laughed.

"Do you think your mom would let you play hooky for a few hours and teach me some of the commands you use with Polly?" Caine asked. "I don't have a dog of my own, but if I don't even know the commands, I'll never be useful with the sheep. It'll help us both pass the time until the jackaroos get back, and if she says yes, I'll help you with your lessons later."

"Let's go ask her," Jason said, his face brightening.

"Let me refill my coffee," Caine said. "Even down here in the valley it's cold and damp today." He couldn't imagine what it would be like at the higher elevations. He'd definitely have to find a way to warm Macklin up tonight. The thought made him smile.

"There are thermoses in the kitchen if you want one of those," Jason suggested. "I can get one from Kami."

"Don't let him take your head off," Caine said with a laugh.

"He won't," Jason said. "He likes me."

True to his word, Jason returned a few moments later with a thermos. Caine filled it and pulled his drizabone tight around his shoulders and tugged his hat low on his head. "Let's go see what you and Polly can teach me."

BY THE time Jason was satisfied with the work they'd done with Polly, Caine's head was spinning with Away and Come, Stand and Look Back, and his feet were frozen solid. He wondered how the others were faring. It was nearing noon. If the day before was any guide, they'd be on their way back by now, the men and dogs driving the sheep before them in organized chaos. Macklin would be at the very rear of the procession, keeping an eagle eye on the entire proceedings, making sure everything went according to plan or that the jackaroos dealt with anything that didn't go as they expected.

It was not an image designed to foster Caine's peace of mind.

They stopped for lunch and to warm up, then Caine followed Jason home to help with his lessons as promised. Fortunately the math was basic algebra and the history was World War I, so even with the different perspective, Caine was able to help some. They finished by three and Caine started to get worried. They still had a couple of hours until sunset, but the day before, they had already been back to the station by this time. "Should we be worried about them?" Caine asked Jason.

Jason shrugged. "Not yet. They'll be cold and miserable when they get here, the way it's been drizzling all day, but if they were in trouble, Mr. Armstrong would have radioed in or sent someone riding back if the radios were out."

"We should make sure there's plenty of coffee and tea for them when they get back," Caine said. "They'll need to get warm. Macklin lectured me days ago on the dangers of staying cold and wet in the outback."

"Kami will have it all ready for them," Jason said. "He knows the drill."

The sound of baaing echoed down the valley. Caine looked up and saw the first sheep beginning to pour over the crest of the hill. "Run tell Kami they're here," Caine said. "I'll go see what I can do to speed up getting them inside where it's warm."

Jason ran off toward the canteen as Caine headed toward the barn to open the gate for the riders as they came in. The other jackaroos who hadn't accompanied Macklin that morning joined Caine there as well. "Can you take care of the horses and the dogs so I can get the others inside and warmed up?" Caine asked the men who waited with him.

"No worries, mate," Neil, one of the year-rounders who had gone out with Macklin the day before, said.

As the men came in, Neil and the others relieved them of their mounts, and Caine steered them toward the canteen. Macklin came in last, no surprise to Caine. "Leave your horse with Neil," Caine said, coming to where Macklin was leading his horse into its stall. "He'll take care of it while you get warm."

"I'll see to him," Macklin insisted.

Caine rolled his eyes at the stubborn reply and followed Macklin into the stall. "Then let me help get him untacked and settled. You have to be frozen through."

"I'm fine," Macklin said, but Caine swore the foreman's lips were blue. He grabbed Macklin's saddle, setting it outside the stall for Neil or one of the others to pick up, and returned to help rub Macklin's mount down.

"Come on," Caine said when they finished. "Everyone else is already inside warming up."

"I'm fine," Macklin insisted.

Caine grabbed one of Macklin's hands and pulled off his glove. The skin beneath was chilled to the touch. "You aren't fine. You're cold and wet. You're the one who lectured me about the dangers of hypothermia. Go home and change clothes. I'll get a cup of coffee from the canteen and bring it to you. Even better, go home and take a hot shower. You can have your coffee when you get out."

Caine let Macklin go with that despite the temptation to follow the foreman home and into the shower. Instead he detoured by the canteen and poured a thermos of coffee for Macklin. They could share it after Macklin changed clothes while they discussed what else needed to be done. He didn't bother knocking when he reached Macklin's house, expecting the foreman to be in the shower. He found him making a cup of tea in his kitchen.

"You should have told me you wanted tea instead of coffee," Caine said. "Kami has both ready. Why aren't you in the shower?"

"Because there's still work to be done," Macklin said. "I'll shower before bed tonight."

"At least change clothes," Caine said, running his hand across Macklin's shoulders. "Even with your drizabone to protect you, your shirt's wet, and I'm sure your feet are as well."

Macklin hesitated still.

"Go!" Caine ordered. "Or I'll start undressing you right here, and somehow I don't think you want me to do that."

Macklin's eyes darkened at Caine's comment, giving him enough courage to take a step closer, but before he could reach for the button on Macklin's work shirt, the foreman pivoted on his heel and disappeared into the other room. Caine let him go, checking on the tea and turning off the electric kettle when he saw it had started to boil. He added the ball of tea leaves and set it aside to steep while Macklin changed. He considered looking for a mug for his coffee, but he didn't want to invade Macklin's privacy too much. He'd drink from the thermos for now and ask for a mug when Macklin returned.

It didn't take long. Macklin obviously hadn't showered, but he was wearing dry clothes at least, and that was Caine's primary concern. "Your tea is steeping. I didn't know if you wanted sugar."

Macklin didn't answer directly, opening the cabinet and pulling out a mug. He dumped two heaping teaspoons of sugar into it before adding the tea. Getting out a second mug, he handed it to Caine, still in silence. Caine resisted the urge to fill the silence with aimless chatter. Macklin wouldn't appreciate it, and that would defeat the purpose of being there. He wanted Macklin to enjoy his company, not wish he were anywhere else.

Macklin joined him at the small table and sipped his tea slowly. "Two more days and we should have all the sheep in winter pastures," Macklin said finally.

"That's good," Caine said. "Then we can start the breeding, right?"

"Yes," Macklin replied. "We'll separate the ewes out into groups according to the rams we want to breed them with and then let the rams in and let nature take its course."

"It sounds labor-intensive," Caine observed.

"Time-consuming," Macklin said, "but not hard. The biggest issue is keeping the bloodlines from getting inbred. We replenish our breeding stock by keeping the most likely lambs from one year to the next, which means that the sires of those ewes are here on the station. We don't want to breed a ewe to its sire."

"That makes sense," Caine said. "So you obviously keep records."

"We have a breeding book," Macklin said. "Not really a book anymore—it's all on the computer—but all the ewes have a tag, and we keep track by number of who their sires are so we can breed them to some other ram."

"It sounds like you need a biology degree to keep it all straight," Caine said with a smile.

"Or a lot of hands-on training," Macklin replied. "Would you like to see the records?"

"I'd love to," Caine said.

"I'll get my laptop."

A knock on the door interrupted them. "After I see who that is," Macklin added.

"Sorry to disturb you, boss," Neil said, "but Devlin Taylor is here asking to see Caine."

"We'll come to the big house," Macklin replied.

"Our neighbor?" Caine asked. "What does he want?"

"To stir up trouble, I'm sure," Macklin muttered. "Bring your coffee, pup. He can talk a man's ear off, so we might as well be comfortable while we're listening."

"You don't have to come if you don't want to," Caine offered. "Neil said he wanted to talk to me."

"I don't trust him not to sell you some load of sheep shit," Macklin replied. "He wants Lang Downs, and I don't know what stories he'd invent or bad information he'd give you to get it."

"He can say whatever he wants," Caine said. "I'm not interested in selling, so it doesn't matter what he says."

"It does if he gives you bad advice and we end up in trouble because of it."

"Macklin," Caine said, grabbing Macklin's arm and stopping him before he could open the door, "you're my foreman, not him. Your dedication to Lang Downs is not in question. If I need advice, I'll ask you, and if Taylor's told me something different, you're the one I'm going to listen to. Attraction aside, you're the one I trust."

"Don't mention that to Taylor," Macklin warned, pulling free of Caine's grip and opening the door.

"I'm green, not stupid," Caine retorted, grabbing his hat and following Macklin outside.

If Caine hadn't already met Macklin, Devlin Taylor would have been the epitome of an Australian grazier, as far as Caine could tell when he caught sight of the man standing on the veranda of the main house. Sun-darkened skin, sun-bleached hair, whipcord body, hipshot stance, but Caine had met Macklin first, and so when he looked at Taylor, he saw all the little ways he was less. His boots were similar to Macklin's but without the scuffs that came from hard work. His shoulders were broad, but not quite as solid. His hips were trim, but Caine could see a slight paunch above his belt. Devlin Taylor might live in the outback, but he was no Macklin Armstrong.

"Introduce me to your new boss, Armstrong," Taylor said with false joviality. "My boys tell me you dropped by last month, so I thought I'd return the favor. Being a good neighbor and all."

Caine gritted his teeth at the overly hearty slap on the back Taylor gave him.

"C-caine N-neiheisel," Caine said, not wanting for Macklin to answer. He wanted Taylor to deal with him, not with his foreman.

"Neiheisel," Taylor repeated. "What kind of name is that?"

"Cincinnati German," Caine replied, hackles rising at the implied insult.

Taylor shook his head. "So you're old man Lang's great-nephew, is that what I heard?"

"That's right," Caine said. "My g-grandmother was his older s-s-sister." He opened the door and gestured for Macklin and Taylor to go inside.

"This must be quite the shock for you, all the inconveniences of the outback after living in the city all your life," Taylor said as they went inside.

"Not at all," Caine replied. "It's a thrilling adventure. Would you like something to drink? Coffee? Tea?"

"A cup of tea if you have one."

"I'll be right back," Caine said.

Caine left the two men alone in the living room and headed to the small kitchen reserved for his personal use to turn on the electric kettle. He could have checked with Kami in the big kitchen, but he didn't want to bother the cook this close to dinner. He started back toward the living room when he overheard the two Aussies talking.

"He'll never make it, Armstrong. He's a city boy through and through, and from what I dug up, a faggot on top of it. The jackaroos will never listen to him, and if you take his side, they won't listen to you either. Help me convince him to sell out. I'll pay him a good price. We'll combine the stations and with the number of sheep we'll be able to run, we'll both be rich men."

"I wasn't interested the first two times you made the offer," Macklin snapped. "What makes you think I'll be interested now?"

"You hadn't met him the first two times I suggested it," Taylor replied. "How do you hold your head up, knowing you're working for a poofter?"

"I hold my head up knowing I'm working for Michael Lang's nephew," Macklin answered.

Caine slunk back to the kitchen, not sure what to make of everything he had overheard. He hadn't expected his sexuality to be a source of tension this early in his tenure. If he met anybody, sure, but he'd expected to have time to prove himself first, to be a known quantity to the men before it became an issue. He wasn't hiding it— he'd told Macklin the first day because it came up logically in conversation—but he wasn't advertising it either. Pouring two cups of tea, he carried them back to the living room, making sure to make enough noise that Macklin and Taylor heard him coming.

"So what brings you by today, Mr. Taylor?" Caine asked politely.

"I wanted to meet my new neighbor, like I said," Taylor replied, "and to tell you I'd be happy to help out in any way I can. Advice, extra men, anything you need, you just send someone over to Taylor Peak."

"That's a very generous offer," Caine said, "but I'm sure it's one we won't have to take you up on. Macklin keeps everything running tight here."

"I'm sure he does, but your uncle and I were good friends, and in his memory, I'd like to help you out. We've been seeing packs of feral dogs up at the higher elevations. You'll need to be careful about that so you don't lose sheep."

"We'll keep an eye out for them," Caine said, not about to discuss Macklin's decision to move the sheep down to lower elevations or the dead animals they'd found the month before. He didn't think Taylor would do anything as underhanded as killing their sheep to convince Caine to sell, but he didn't want to put ideas in the other man's head either.

Even if all his comments did was reveal the differences between their management decisions and Taylor's, Caine preferred not to give the man the opportunity to offer unwelcome advice. If it had just been differences in management style, Caine might have listened, but Taylor had ulterior motives, and Caine didn't trust that at all.

"You must be lonely out here in the outback by yourself," Taylor said.

"I'm hardly all b-by myself," Caine said with a forced laugh. He could already see where this was going, but he refused to give Taylor the satisfaction of trapping him into admitting something that was none of the other man's business. If Taylor had the balls to ask outright, Caine might have answered, but he wasn't going to dignify Taylor's probing with a reaction. Macklin might read his nervousness in his stutter, but Taylor didn't know him that well. "There are a good fifty people living here."

"That's not company," Taylor scoffed. "That's jackaroos."

"No," Caine replied, "that's Macklin and Kami and Jason and Neil and all the others. Or are you one of those b-b-bosses who thinks you can't be friends with your employees?"

"Kind of hard to fire someone if you're friends," Taylor pointed out.

"If you're f-friends, they'll work hard enough for you that you d-don't have to fire them," Caine countered. He turned to Macklin. "When was the last time you had to f-fire someone from Lang D-downs?"

"We've had people choose to leave," Macklin said, "or not come back after a season or two, but I haven't fired anyone since I took over as foreman. I haven't needed to. My people work too hard for that."

Caine looked at Taylor smugly. "There, you see, Mr. Taylor? There's no harm in being friends with the people who work on the station."

"There's friends and then there's company," Taylor tried again.

"This is also t-t-true," Caine agreed, "but I need to g-get settled in my new life before I worry about c-c-company. Are you married, Mr. Taylor?"

"Divorced," Taylor said, flushing beneath his tan. Caine hid a smile. Score one for the poofter. "My wife had a hard time coping with being so far from the city. She said Boorowa didn't count."

"I suppose that would d-d-depend on your definition of a c-city," Caine replied. "I enjoyed the day I spent there, although I do hope to visit Sydney again when I'm not jetlagged."

"You can come with me next month," Macklin offered. "I go to Sydney for a week in the middle of winter. It's my yearly vacation."

The offer surprised Caine, especially with Taylor there and in light of what Taylor had said about Caine's sexuality. Maybe it was Macklin's way of telling Taylor it didn't matter. He smiled at Macklin, hoping that was the case, but even if it wasn't, a week in Sydney with Macklin sounded like heaven. "Thank you. I'd l-like that. I don't mean to be rude, Mr. Taylor, but I have some work I have to do before d-d-dinner, so if there isn't anything else, I'll say good-bye."

"No, nothing else," Taylor said, clearly surprised at the dismissal. "Although if you ever change your mind about staying, look me up. I'm sure we could work something out."

"If I ever change my m-mind, I'll r-r-remember your offer," Caine replied. Not that he would change his mind, but Taylor wouldn't believe him if he said it, so he left it at that.

Caine showed Taylor to the door, closing it firmly behind him rather than going out on the veranda to see the man off. His mother would fuss at his lack of manners, but Caine was ready to be rid of the man. He turned back around to find Macklin standing practically on top of him, all but pinning him to the door.

"Do not even think about selling to Devlin Taylor."

Caine smiled and draped his arms around Macklin's neck. The foreman reared back, but Caine held tight. "Didn't I tell you I was staying?"

Macklin shrugged free of Caine's embrace, and Caine let him go. "Yes, but you told Taylor you'd remember his offer."

"Just because I remember it doesn't mean I'd take it even if I did decide to leave," Caine pointed out, "and after what I overheard while I was making tea, I wouldn't sell to him if his was the only offer I had. How do you put up with his attitude?"

"His attitude is pretty typical," Macklin said. "Why do you think I go to Sydney once a year? And I don't put up with his attitude. I don't put up with him at all unless I have no other choice. How much did you overhear?"

"Him trying to convince you to talk me into selling and then his tirade about me being gay," Caine replied. "He doesn't know about you, I take it?"

"Nobody except Michael did," Macklin replied, "and he didn't care. He supported me completely."

"I'm glad to know that," Caine said. "It makes it easier to know he wouldn't have a problem with me being here now."

Macklin snorted. "He never told you, did he? I suppose that makes sense since he didn't really know you. He was gay, too, pup. He and his foreman Donald were partners in every sense of the word. Donald died soon after I got here, so he wouldn't have been in any of Michael's letters about the station itself, but I assumed you knew."

"No, he never told me," Caine said. "I don't even remember him mentioning that name. Did everyone know?"

"It wasn't something anybody spoke of, but I can't imagine that they didn't know," Macklin said. "The station wasn't as big then, so there wasn't a separate foreman's house, just the big house and the bunkhouse. Donald and Michael lived here, the rest of the men lived in the bunkhouse. By the time the station grew big enough to build the extra houses, Donald was ill, and so the explanation was that Donald needed more space and care than the bunkhouse could provide. Most of the men here now arrived after Donald's death. I've never asked them if they knew. Like I said, it's not something people talk about."

"So the men don't know about you either, then, do they?" Caine asked.

"It's not something people talk about," Macklin repeated. "There was no reason to tell them. I don't have someone like Donald."

"You could."

"You really want to give Taylor more ammunition for his attacks on you, pup?" Macklin asked.

"I don't give a damn about Taylor," Caine replied. "I have to live my life. We could be good together, Macklin."

Macklin's face tightened. "I already told you it couldn't work."

"No, you told me you were afraid to try because it might go wrong," Caine insisted. "It might go wrong. There are no guarantees, but it might go right. Uncle Michael and Donald made it work. Maybe we could too."

"Bloody hell, you're tenacious, pup," Macklin said. "This is a bad idea."

"It's not a bad idea," Caine said, approaching Macklin again and resting his hand on the other man's forearm. "Take a chance on me, Macklin. Let me prove to you I'm worth it."

"I'll think about it," Macklin conceded.

That was enough for Caine. As long as Macklin was thinking about it, Caine could keep wearing away the foreman's resistance.

ELEVEN

THE database that held the breeding records was simple in its layout but incredibly complex in the amount of information it held. Macklin had computerized the records back to Lang Downs's inception so that they could trace every sheep back generations. Caine had taken one look at it and handed the computer back to Macklin.

"Tell me how we keep from breeding the wrong ewes and rams."

"Each sheep has an ear tag," Macklin explained. "We tag them in lots so a particular range of numbers all came from the same ram. Then it's a question of checking those numbers against the database to make sure we don't put them in with their sire this year. It takes time to check, but it keeps the bloodlines safe for future breeding and for selling the lambs for food."

Caine nodded. "So do you take a printout or how do you consult the database when you're out herding sheep?"

"We have it on a PDA," Macklin said. "The sheep come in, we check the number against the database, and route them accordingly."

"There are a lot of things I still don't know how to do," Caine said, "but surely I can figure that out."

"It's not hard," Macklin agreed. "I'm sure you can handle it."

It was boring, cold, dirty work, standing in the fields as the men brought the mob in a few sheep at a time. They'd call out the number from the ear tag, Caine would look it up and identify the sire, and Macklin would order the ewe into one pen or another according to a system Caine still hadn't figured out.

Caine had guzzled two thermoses of coffee by lunchtime, and he was still frozen through. The other men were moving, herding the sheep while Caine stood still at the center of the enclosures and waited for the men to come to him.

As they headed in to lunch, he sought out Macklin. "Can I s-switch with someone after lunch? I'm f-f-freezing, standing on one p-place the whole time. Jason has b-been t-teaching me to work with the d-dogs."

"Are you stuttering because you're cold or because you're really that worried I'll say no?"

"C-cold," Caine said, glad it was the truth. Macklin still made him nervous at times, but not where the station was concerned. He might say no, but Caine had come to trust that Macklin wouldn't automatically refuse him as a blow-in.

"Stick with Neil," Macklin decided, handing Caine more coffee. "I'll see if Jason wants to take your job. I told him he could help this afternoon if he finished his lessons this morning."

"He'll want to work with P-polly," Caine said. "I don't want to keep him from helping."

"He's a hard worker and Polly's learning fast," Macklin replied, "but the first lesson any jackaroo has to learn is that you do the job you're assigned. Even if it's shoveling shit, and there will be plenty of that to do this winter, so don't you forget it either."

The twinkle in Macklin's eye was the only clue he was teasing Caine, but Caine saw it and smiled. "Yes, sir, Mr. Armstrong, sir. Whatever job I'm assigned."

"Get some tucker," Macklin chided with a shake of his head and a shove in the direction of the food Kami had prepared. "You'll need it if you're going to herd sheep this afternoon."

Jason came in while Caine was eating, obviously excited about the afternoon. His face fell a little after he talked to Macklin, but he nodded and came to sit with Caine. "Mr. Armstrong says you're going to help with the sheep this afternoon. You should take Polly with you. You know her better than any of the other dogs."

"Are you sure you don't mind?" Caine asked. "She's your dog."

"I'd rather be helping too, but Mr. Armstrong reminded me that everybody is helping even if they aren't herding the sheep themselves. Even Kami, who isn't anywhere near the pens, helps."

"He certainly does," Caine agreed. "I'd have a lot harder time going back outside if he hadn't filled me up with that chicken curry."

"My favorite is his pad thai," Jason said, "but he doesn't make that as often in winter. In the winter, he does stews and curries and thick sauces that stay with you and help keep you warm."

"I'm sure his pad thai is as good as everything else, but I'm glad for the curry. I can feel my toes again finally."

"Wear an extra pair of socks," Jason said.

"I'm wearing two already," Caine replied. "Next time I'm in Boorowa, I'm going to look for fleece-lined boots."

"Good luck with that," Jason said. "Eat fast. Mr. Armstrong is already heading back outside. You don't want to make him wait."

Caine used the naan to wipe the last of the curry from his plate and hurried outside after Macklin. "Come on, Caine," Neil called when Caine reached where the other men waited. "Let's get started."

Neil whistled for his dog, a grizzled old shepherd Caine didn't know. Caine turned to look for Polly when Jason came running up. "Go with Caine, girl."

"Come on, Polly," Caine called. "Let's show these jackaroos what a couple of pups can do."

The afternoon passed far more quickly than the morning, with constantly moving after the sheep, cutting them off from the flock a few at a time, and then separating them the way Macklin ordered. Caine and Polly didn't work as seamlessly as Neil and his dog, Max, but Caine was pleased with how well they did. Neil only had to send Max to correct them once, and Caine figured if the sheep he and Polly moved weren't quite as orderly or tightly bunched as the ones Neil handled, it still wasn't bad for a first day's work.

"We'll make a jackaroo out of you yet," Neil praised when they finished for the day and headed in for dinner.

"You did great today!" Jason gushed when he came in to the canteen a few minutes later. "You look like a real jackaroo out there!"

"Polly did a great job," Caine demurred. "All I did was tell her what to do."

"But you obviously told her the right things," Jason insisted. "Will you tell Mr. Armstrong I taught you? Maybe he'll let me help tomorrow."

"I'll tell him," Caine promised, "but I can't promise it'll make a difference in what he has each of us doing tomorrow. He assigns the jobs, not me." Maybe someday Caine would have the confidence in himself and the trust of the men enough to help with the decisions, but for now, he'd be satisfied with Macklin explaining his own decisions as he did each evening while they talked about the plan for the next day. His comments had given Caine insight into the personalities and abilities of the crew.

Macklin still hadn't come into the canteen when Caine finished dinner, so he filled a plate for the foreman and headed toward Macklin's little house. He found the foreman in the living room, poring over the breeding records. "You didn't come to dinner."

"I was still full from lunch," Macklin replied, not looking up when Caine walked in.

"I brought dinner anyway," Caine said. "I'll put it in the kitchen. You can have it for a midnight snack if you want. Do you want a beer or some tea?"

"Beer," Macklin answered absentmindedly.

Caine rolled his eyes and carried the plate into the kitchen, sticking it in the refrigerator and getting two beers. He opened them and carried them back into the living room. "So what's so important in that book that you didn't even look up when I came in? It's no different than it was last night."

"I'm looking at the record of the ewes that didn't lamb successfully last year," Macklin explained. "The ones we brought in today were the youngest ewes, the ones we haven't bred before. For the older ones, if we had miscarriages or the breeding didn't take at all, I want to try breeding them with a different ram. We might have better results."

"And are those ewes going to start coming in tomorrow?" Caine asked.

"They're all mixed in with the rest of the mob," Macklin explained. "We keep the yearling ewes separate after they're weaned, but the rest mingle at will during the summer. I want to flag them in the database now so I'll remember them over the next few days."

"Can I help?" Caine took a sip of the beer and settled on the couch next to Macklin.

"It's pretty much a one-man job," Macklin said, "but I wouldn't mind the company."

"Then I'll stay," Caine said. He hadn't planned on leaving anyway, but the acknowledgement warmed him. He liked the idea that Macklin wanted him around.

They sat together in comfortable silence, Caine almost dozing as Macklin worked. Eventually Macklin closed the computer, the movement jostling Caine awake. "Sorry, I haven't been very good company tonight."

"You worked hard today," Macklin said. "You should be tired. Why don't you get some rest?"

"I'll go in a few minutes," Caine said, stretching slowly. "I'm not quite ready to say good night yet."

"Why not?" Macklin asked. "Something on your mind?"

"Someone," Caine corrected, tugging on Macklin's hand until the foreman scooted closer. "I've wanted to kiss you all day."

"Caine," Macklin said, his voice discouraging, but Caine didn't relent, leaning forward until he could kiss Macklin lightly.

As with their previous kisses, Macklin took charge instantly, the kiss turning hard and rough and passionate. Caine gasped beneath the onslaught, letting Macklin claim his mouth, but eventually he pulled away. "You always k-kiss me like you'll d-die if you don't get m-more of me right now."

"Is that bad?" Macklin asked. The vulnerability in the question struck Caine to the very core.

"Not bad at all," Caine replied quickly. "It makes me feel incredible, but it's nice not to rush sometimes too."

Macklin flushed beneath his tan, making Caine feel bad for bringing it up, but it was too late to take it back. He'd just have to show Macklin what he was missing. "I suppose there isn't a lot of t-t-time for slow and tender if you've only g-got a w-week a year, but things are d-different now. We don't have to rush, r-r-remember?"

"Nervous, pup?" Macklin asked.

Caine shook his head, pushing on Macklin's shoulders until he relaxed against the back of the couch. "T-t-turned on." He straddled Macklin's thighs, not sitting down yet so he could lean over Macklin and brush their lips together lightly. "It's hard t-to concentrate when you're this c-close."

"Do you need to concentrate?" Macklin asked, leaving control of their kisses in Caine's hands.

"If you w-want m-me to t-talk, I do," Caine replied, moving his lips across Macklin's cheek to his ear. "Or I c-can just k-kiss you."

Macklin's arms wrapped around Caine's back. "Just kiss me."

Caine didn't need to be asked twice, nibbling on Macklin's earlobe before blowing lightly along the delicate whorl, probably the only delicate spot on the man's entire body. It made the shiver that ran through him all the more arousing to Caine. He followed the line of Macklin's jaw, rough with a day's growth of whiskers, to the strong chin with its intriguing cleft. He licked the slight indentation, tasting the lingering soap from Macklin's shower. The moment their lips touched again, Macklin grabbed the back of Caine's head, holding him in place and devouring his mouth.

Caine relaxed into the kiss, settling onto Macklin's thighs as the foreman kissed him until he could barely breathe. Head spinning, he took the initiative again, pushing up so Macklin's head tilted back to maintain the kiss. Instead of passively allowing Macklin's invasion of his mouth, Caine sparred with him now, his tongue vying with Macklin's for dominance. To his surprise, Macklin retreated, allowing Caine to deepen the kiss and explore his mouth for a change. Impossibly aroused, Caine lifted his head, his breath sawing in and out of his chest as he stared down at the man beneath him. "You m-m-make me c-c-crazy," Caine panted.

Macklin tugged on Caine's hips until he settled across Macklin's thighs again, feeling the foreman's erection against his own. "The feeling's mutual."

Caine bucked his hips against Macklin's. Macklin met him thrust for thrust, pulling him back into the kiss. Caine offered his mouth willingly, already envisioning his fantasies becoming flesh, when the lights suddenly flickered and went out.

"Bloody hell," Macklin cursed, stilling Caine's hips with his hands. "We have to get the generators running."

"Can't someone else do that?" Caine asked, reluctant to move now that Macklin had actually let him close.

"We keep the sheds locked so the kids won't get in there and mess with them," Macklin said. "You and I are the only ones with keys. If we don't go out there, Neil or one of the others will come knocking on that door in a matter of minutes."

Minutes wasn't long enough for what Caine wanted. With a frustrated curse, he flopped to the side. "Let's go. The sooner we get them on, the sooner we can come back here."

"Not tonight, pup," Macklin warned. "Once the generators are running, we have to check the power lines to see where the problem is. We don't want a downed line causing a fire."

"Start the generators," Caine said. "I'll saddle the horses."

Macklin nodded as he retrieved a flashlight from the closet next to the door. Dusk had not quite given way to darkness, but Caine was glad of the light anyway. He didn't know the station yet as well as Macklin did. Macklin opened the generator shed and took another flashlight from the shelf inside. "Take this one to the barn with you. You'll need it to get the horses ready because the barn lights aren't hooked to the generators."

"I'll see you in a few minutes," Caine said, taking the light and heading to the barn. Several of the other men were already inside, getting horses ready. Caine saddled Macklin's horse and then got Titan's tack. He fully expected Macklin to argue about Caine accompanying them, but Caine refused to be left out.

"What are you doing?" Macklin demanded.

"Saddling Titan," Caine replied, surprised he managed to keep his voice steady. His arousal had faded with the lack of stimulation, but Macklin's voice sent it spiking again.

"Like hell you are," Macklin retorted. "You're going back to the big house and going to bed."

Caine would have liked to reply that he wasn't going anywhere near a bed without Macklin, but he didn't know who else was within earshot, and he didn't want to ruin things between them by revealing their relationship to the hands without discussing it first. "Why? You're going out."

"I am," Macklin agreed, "and so are Neil and a couple of others who know the station as well as I do. Everyone else is staying safely inside."

"I'm coming with you," Caine insisted. "This is m-my station now, and it's my responsibility to make sure everything is s-s-safe."

"You'll do no such thing," Macklin growled, stalking closer to Caine as if the sheer force of his physical presence could force Caine to change his mind, but Caine refused to be cowed.

"Then neither will anyone else," Caine said. "If it's not safe, then no one should do it, and if it has to be done anyway, then I should be willing to take the same risks as everyone else."

"You don't know where you're going. You don't know what you're looking for, and you don't know what to do if you find it," Macklin shouted, startling the placid Titan into shifting nervously, knocking Caine into Macklin.

"You're s-s-scaring Titan," Caine said, his heart pounding anxiously.

"I'll show you scared," Macklin muttered. "All right, fine. Come with us if you insist, but you stay directly behind Ned, and you do exactly what I tell you."

"What you tell me when you tell me," Caine promised, already familiar with the drill. That had been Macklin's demand every time they left the main station since Caine had arrived. After the encounter with the snake, Caine had been careful to listen.

Macklin stomped off and returned a few moments later, leading Ned. Caine followed them outside and mounted Titan. Macklin shouted orders, sending Neil and two other hands along the power lines to the south. "We'll take the northern lines," Macklin told Caine. "We'll keep in touch with the radios, and Kami will radio from here if the power comes back on."

"It's not storming," Caine said as they rode out, following the power lines that connected Lang Downs with Taylor Peak in the south and Cowra in the north. "What else could cause the power to go out?"

"A transformer might have blown," Macklin said, "or a tree may have come down on a line. It's not storming, but the winds are blowing hard. And it may not be a problem on Lang Downs's land, but we have to check. I hope you dressed warmly underneath your drizabone, pup. It could be a long night."

"I'll be fine," Caine said, although he could already feel the cold seeping into his feet again. Two hours later, Caine wished he hadn't been so insistent on coming with Macklin. Even with the drizabone, the cold had moved up his legs and arms, leaving him shivering.

The radio on Macklin's belt crackled to life. "We found the problem, boss. There's a transformer out near the Taylor Peak fence line. No lines down."

"Good work," Macklin said. "Head back in if you can. Stop at one of the huts if you need to and ride back in tomorrow morning. Don't take unnecessary risks."

"Yes, boss. See you in the morning."

"We can head back," Macklin said, looking at Caine for the first time since they'd left the main station.

"G-g-g-good," Caine said, his teeth chattering. "The s-sooner the b-b-better."

"Of all the stupid, bloody, idiotic…. Come on, pup," Macklin said. "There's a drover's hut about ten minutes from here. We'll spend the night there, and the next time I tell you to stay home, you'll bloody well listen."

"I bloody well won't," Caine replied, turning Titan to follow Macklin, "because you won't, and I won't have you doing something I'm not willing to do myself. I'll just dress warmer next time."

Macklin led them to one of the drover's huts. It had a lean-to against one wall for the horses. Macklin pulled the saddles off and tossed blankets over their backs. "Get inside and start a fire," Macklin ordered. He pulled the radio from his belt to call back to the station and let them know his and Caine's plans for the night.

Caine stumbled inside, using the flashlight to locate the pile of wood next to the fireplace. Fortunately, his parents had a wood-burning fireplace, and he'd learned how to set a fire when he was growing up. He got the wood ready and was searching for matches when Macklin came in.

"Where's the fire?"

"Where's the matches?" Caine snapped back. "This is the first time I've been in one of the huts. I don't know where things are."

Macklin grabbed the matches from the drawer by the stove in the kitchen. "I'll do it."

"No, you'll give me the matches and I'll do it," Caine insisted. "I'm not helpless. I just hadn't found the matches yet."

Macklin tossed him the box of matches and stood there glaring with his arms crossed as Caine knelt down and worked on the fire. Caine ignored him, striking the match and putting it to the tinder carefully. He fed tiny twigs to the tentative flames until they licked their way up the larger logs and finally caught. When he stood up and turned back around, Macklin's face betrayed his surprise. "Not bad for a blow-in."

"Not bad at all," Macklin agreed. "It'll be a few minutes before the fire takes the chill off. There are blankets on the bunks, but I don't know how clean they are."

"We'll take them back with us in the morning and wash them," Caine said, picking one up and wrapping it around his legs as he sat back in front of the fire. "Maybe I'll just sleep here. That way I can add wood to the fire during the night."

"You'll be more comfortable on a bunk."

"I'll be warmer by the fire."

"Help me move the table, and we can put the bunks right next to the fire," Macklin suggested. "That way we can be warm and comfortable."

TWELVE

THEY got the bunks arranged and the fire built up, but even then, even under the blankets, Caine couldn't seem to stop shivering. He tried to stay as still as possible in the firelight so he wouldn't disturb Macklin, but apparently he didn't do as good a job as he thought he was because Macklin rolled over and sat up. "Still cold, pup?"

"Y-yes," Caine said.

"Let's try this." Macklin pushed his bunk right up against Caine's and spread his blanket over both bunks. "Come here."

Caine hesitated only a second before scooting back against Macklin, the foreman's larger body spooning against his and surrounding him with warmth. Caine sighed and relaxed, feeling the heat begin to seep through his clothes. "How are you so warm?" Caine asked.

"Thick blood," Macklin replied. "The cold just doesn't seem to bother me the way it does a lot of people."

"Lucky," Caine said, snuggling closer and pulling the blankets tight to keep the heat in.

"Don't move around too much, pup. You'll give me ideas."

Caine pushed back deliberately this time, feeling the growing bulge of Macklin's half-hard erection. "Maybe I want to give you ideas," he said huskily.

"Caine."

"You brought it up," Caine pointed out, not at all perturbed by the discouraging tone of Macklin's voice. "If you didn't want me thinking about sex, you should have just let me fall asleep, which I would have done in about two minutes if you hadn't mentioned it." He turned in Macklin's arms so they were facing one another. "Now that you've mentioned it, you have to follow through."

"I *have* to?"

Caine licked the cleft in Macklin's chin again. "Or I can seduce you into it if you'd prefer."

"Fuck," Macklin groaned.

"Not without condoms and lube," Caine said, "but I'm sure we can think of something." He slid a hand between them and cupped Macklin's cock through his jeans.

"I'm sure we can," Macklin said, his voice gratifyingly hoarse. Caine kissed along his jaw, aiming for his ear again, as he squeezed lightly.

Macklin caught his hand and pinned it to the bed as he rolled toward Caine, adjusting them until he lay fully on top of Caine. He captured Caine's mouth, invading it with his tongue. Caine relaxed into the thin mattress, relishing the feeling of Macklin's weight pressing down on him. Macklin's broader shoulders and heavier frame dwarfed Caine, surrounding him with much welcome heat and adding to the desire that had spiked again when Macklin mentioned ideas. Even knowing they couldn't have sex without condoms, the position screamed intimacy in a way lying side by side did not, and Caine yearned for that. Ever since Macklin had told him about Uncle Michael, Caine had been unable to dismiss the hope that history would repeat itself, and lying beneath Macklin this way seemed a perfect way to start. Keeping the blankets wrapped around them, he slid his arms around Macklin's shoulders and then down his back so he could cup the other man's ass and urge him to move. They might not be able to fuck, but that didn't mean they couldn't make each other feel good.

Macklin rutted against him, so Caine figured he could move his hands for other things. He worked open the buttons on Macklin's shirt, burrowing beneath the heavy fabric to find a long undershirt underneath. He worked his way beneath that as well until he found skin. He explored Macklin's treasure trail first, following it up rather than down, curious to see whether Macklin's chest was smooth or hairy. He found a light mat of hair widening out from his ribs to his nipples on either side.

"What are you doing?" Macklin asked, breaking the kiss.

"Making you feel good, I hope," Caine said, rubbing his thumb over one nipple. "Don't tell me no one has ever touched you like this." Macklin didn't answer, but that was an answer in itself. "It's too cold here, but when we get back to the main station, I'm going to spread you out on a bed and show you what you've been missing."

"I'll hold you to that promise, pup," Macklin rumbled, opening Caine's shirt as well to find skin beneath. "No wonder you're frozen! Where's your long underwear?"

"What long underwear?" Caine asked seriously. "If I didn't buy it when we were in Boorowa, I don't own it."

Macklin scowled. "We obviously need to make another trip. Until we do, I'll lend you some of mine. They'll be too big, but it's better than freezing your bollocks off." He slid a hand between them and cupped Caine's groin. "I don't want anything happening to them."

"N-n-neither d-d-do I," Caine groaned, the surge of arousal tying his tongue. "D-d-do th-th-th—" He couldn't concentrate enough to get the words out, but Macklin understood him anyway, massaging his balls through his clothes. Caine thrashed on the bed, wishing it was warm enough to get rid of the clothing and the covers so there was nothing but bare skin and the freedom to enjoy it. "F-f-fuck," he managed to get out as his body clenched in preparation for release.

Macklin's lips closed over his, forestalling any further attempts at speech. Caine didn't resist the kiss, diving into the connection with desperate need. His body thrummed with passion, but his heart ached for more than that. He could find release alone in his house; with Macklin, he wanted more. He wanted a lover.

He teetered on the verge of release, his sac drawing up, his cock tenting his pants as he rocked against Macklin, but it wasn't enough. He broke the kiss to breathe and try to beg for more, but before he could force the words out, Macklin stroked his cheek, the tenderness of the gesture giving him the final push he needed. With a wordless cry, he toppled into his climax. Macklin grunted against him, his hips stuttering and then stilling. He panted against Caine's neck, his breath hot in the still cool room.

When Caine could move again, he wrapped his arms around Macklin's shoulders, keeping the other man close. Macklin hadn't said so outright, but Caine suspected his previous sexual encounters had ended after he'd found release. Caine had no intention of letting that happen tonight. He'd use the excuse of staying warm if he had to, but he hoped it wouldn't come to that. He hoped Macklin would stay because he realized he could have more with Caine if he would just take Caine up on his offer.

Macklin rolled to the side, but he pulled Caine with him, keeping their bodies close. "There's no hot water in the drover's huts, but if you let me up for a few minutes, I can warm up a cloth by the fire," Macklin offered. "You might get a bit uncomfortable otherwise."

"In a m-minute," Caine said, burying his nose against Macklin's shoulder and simply holding on. "D-don't want you to move yet."

"I'm not going anywhere, pup," Macklin promised. "Even if I get up for a minute, I'll come back and keep you warm tonight."

"It's not t-tonight that worries me," Caine said. "W-will you still b-be here t-tomorrow night?"

"Tomorrow night you'll be snug and warm in your own bed."

And where will you be? Caine was tempted to ask, but he didn't want to send Macklin running for the hills because Caine had gotten too clingy or demanding. "You're welcome to join me there," he said instead.

"You did offer to show me what I've been missing," Macklin said. "We'll see what tomorrow brings. Let's clean up a little so we can get some sleep."

Caine let him go, watching in the flickering light as he wet a rag from the sink with water from a bottle in the pantry. Caine shuddered a little at the thought of how cold that water would be, but Macklin brought the cloth back to the fire, holding it close to flames for several minutes. "It's not warm exactly," he said, coming back to bed, "but it's not freezing anymore. Let me clean you up."

Caine nodded, his breath catching in his throat as Macklin undid his pants and pushed them down along with his boxers. The cloth was only lukewarm, sending a shiver through Caine when Macklin wiped it across sensitive skin, but the care in the touch outweighed the discomfort from the temperature as Macklin cleaned Caine as best he could. "I can't do anything about your boxers, but that should be a little more comfortable."

Caine squirmed until he could kick off his pants and boxers, pulling his pants back on with no underwear. "Commando is better than sticky," he agreed. "My turn."

"I'm fine," Macklin said, backing away. "Turn over and go to sleep."

"I th-thought you s-s-said you were g-g-going to keep me warm."

"Don't look at me that way, pup," Macklin protested. "I'm just going to put more wood on the fire. I won't be a minute."

That didn't make the feeling of rejection any less, but Caine refused to let Macklin see him hurting any more than he already had. He rolled to his side so he faced away from the foreman and waited in silence as Macklin added wood to the fire. The telltale rustling of clothing was salt in Caine's wounds. Macklin wasn't "fine"; he just didn't want Caine touching him.

He almost resisted when Macklin crawled back beneath the covers and spooned behind him, but Macklin's arms pulled him closer, and his lips nuzzled the nape of Caine's neck. Relaxing a little, Caine rested his hands on Macklin's arm.

Macklin's bare arm.

Caine sucked in his breath, surprised at the feeling of bare skin. Tentatively he ran his fingers up Macklin's arm, expecting to encounter cloth at his elbow or his bicep, but he reached as far as he could still touching skin. He started to turn in Macklin's arms to keep exploring, but Macklin tightened his embrace. "Go to sleep, Caine. We have work to do in the morning."

Caine settled against Macklin, but he did reach behind him to rest his hand on the foreman's thigh. He found cloth there, but the smooth silk of his long underwear rather than the heavy moleskin of his jeans. Smiling, he closed his eyes and tried to sleep.

CAINE woke slowly the next morning, vaguely aware of Macklin having gotten up during the night to put more wood on the fire and very aware of the arm still around his waist and the hard body—and hard cock—pressed along his back. He shivered in anticipation, hoping Macklin would be more willing to allow Caine's attentions than he had been the night before.

He turned slowly, trying not to disturb Macklin, but the green eyes opened immediately, dashing Caine's hopes of waking Macklin up by making love to him. He watched confusion, awareness, and then unease flash across Macklin's face. "We should get back to the station," the foreman said immediately.

"In a minute," Caine replied, leaning in for a morning kiss.

Macklin didn't quite dodge the kiss, but he didn't return it either, not like he had the night before. Instead he held himself rigidly still in Caine's embrace, so obviously uncomfortable that Caine relented and let him go. He felt the sting of the rejection, but he reminded himself that Macklin had probably never had a morning after before and had no idea how to handle it. Caine could afford to back off a bit rather than send Macklin running for the hills. "Is there anything in the pantries we could have for breakfast?"

Macklin stood and turned his back as he pulled on his trousers. Now Caine smiled for real, amusement taking the place of hurt. As if turning his back could keep Caine from knowing he'd woken up hard. "There might be some Vegemite and some bread or biscuits, but I don't know how fresh they'd be."

Caine made a moue of distaste. He had learned to appreciate any number of things since coming to Australia, but Vegemite was not a taste he had acquired. "Maybe I'll wait until we get back to the station."

Macklin chuckled, turning around as he buttoned his shirt, hiding the long underwear and glimpse of skin beneath. "And here I thought we were making an Aussie out of you."

"It'll take more than a couple of months in the outback before Vegemite will be on my list of preferred food choices," Caine said, "especially when the kitchen and Kami's cooking are just an hour or two's ride away."

"Speaking of Kami, we should get back," Macklin said, looking pointedly at Caine where he still lay snuggled beneath the blankets.

Caine stood, shivering when his sock-clad feet hit the cold floor. He reached for Macklin again, ignoring the look of discomfort that crossed the other man's face. Macklin was going to have to learn how to deal with intimacy outside of bed, and Caine figured the best way to do that was to give him no other choice. "After we say a proper good morning."

"Caine."

"What?" Caine asked. "You certainly liked kissing me last night. What's wrong with kissing me this morning?"

"Last night was…."

"Exactly," Caine said when Macklin didn't finish his sentence. "Last night was. Stop trying to pretend it didn't happen or that you didn't enjoy it as much as I did. I'm not asking you to marry me, Macklin. I just want a good morning kiss."

The panic on Macklin's face might have been funny if Caine hadn't been hoping for the opposite reaction. He sighed. "Why is this so difficult?" he asked gently.

"We don't have time to discuss this," Macklin replied. "We need to get back to the station."

"Why?" Caine asked. "Not why at all, but why the rush? What's so important that you can't answer my question first?"

"Why is it so important that we discuss it now?" Macklin countered.

"Because we're here now and you're acting strangely now and if you d-don't give me an explanation now, maybe you never will."

"Maybe it's better that way," Macklin muttered.

"Macklin, stop avoiding the issue."

Macklin sighed and pulled away, pacing the small hut restlessly. "Because I've never done this before, right? I've fucked, but that's it. I don't know what you want from me, and that makes me antsy as a sheep surrounded by dingoes."

He ran his hands through his messy hair as he spoke, turning to glare at Caine as if the entire situation was his fault. The admission, however awkward, softened Caine's frustration. He crossed to Macklin again. "What I want right now is a simple good morning kiss," he said again. "What I want more generally is up to us to decide. That's the beauty of a relationship. It's not what I want. It's what we want."

"And if you could have whatever you wanted?" Macklin asked slowly.

"What Uncle Michael had with Donald," Caine replied immediately. "But they didn't build that relationship in a day or a month. Relationships take time and work. They take fighting and negotiating and sometimes even stepping back a bit. And sometimes they don't work, and then you just have to accept that and move on."

"That's what worries me," Macklin admitted. "If it doesn't work, I'll be the one who has to move on."

"If it doesn't work, I'll leave," Caine offered. "You don't need me to run the station. I can g-g-go back home. This is your home. Even if we d-didn't make it, you wouldn't do anything to damage the station or its reputation."

"You're making it awfully hard to resist, pup."

Caine smiled. "Then don't," he said, lifting his head for a kiss. This time, Macklin gave it to him. It was as deep and demanding as the kisses from the night before, but Caine didn't mind, not when Macklin was finally kissing him. He relaxed into the embrace that accompanied the meeting of lips, wrapping his fingers in the ends of Macklin's hair.

The caress seemed to be the reminder Macklin needed that not every kiss had to be hard and fast. His lips gentled on Caine's, the tenderness from the end of their encounter the night before coming to the fore. Caine sighed happily into the kiss, sure he could kiss Macklin like that all day and never get enough.

The radio squawked to life on the table behind them, startling both men, but when Macklin would have pulled away, Caine drew his head back down for one more, swift kiss before letting him go.

"N-now you c-can answer them." He didn't even mind the stutter. He wanted Macklin to know how their kisses affected him. Maybe it would help convince the other man of the depth of his investment.

Caine busied himself putting his boots and coat back on as he waited for Macklin to finish checking in with the main station, assuring them he and Caine had weathered the night and were on their way back. He gave orders to continue separating the mob for breeding.

"But I don't know which ewes to put with which rams," Ian said.

"As long as you don't put them with their sires, it'll be fine," Macklin said. "I'll adjust my plans when I get back and see what you've done."

"So I guess this means we should head home," Caine said when Macklin set the radio back down on the table.

"In a minute," Macklin said. "After I get a kiss to keep me warm for the ride back."

Caine was sure he'd never moved so fast in his life as he did getting to Macklin's side now, his joy at Macklin's comment warring with the thrill of the foreman's mouth against his, gentle as before but with just a hint of teeth to give the promise of more to come. When Macklin lifted his head and smiled down at Caine, Caine's happiness was complete.

THIRTEEN

A WEEK later, Caine was ready to throttle Macklin again. While the foreman invited him in for a beer every evening and kissed him readily whenever they were in private, he had not invited Caine beyond the living room and kitchen of his house, and any time Caine hinted at more, he drew back, closing himself off or finding an excuse to end their evening together. Caine had tried reminding himself that Macklin was new at relationships and that he needed time to adjust to the idea, but Caine was getting tired of waiting.

"Aussie men are too stubborn for their own good," Caine muttered as he walked into the canteen. They had separated the last of the ewes into their breeding pens that afternoon. They would put the rams in with the ewes in the morning, and then the summer workers would head back to Boorowa or Cowra, leaving only the full-time residents at the station for the winter.

Kami had made a special send-off dinner, and everyone had gathered in the canteen, even those who usually ate in their own homes. Caine appreciated the festive atmosphere and the desire of the station hands to send everyone off in style, but as dinner turned into drinking and everyone sitting around chatting, he despaired of getting a chance to talk to Macklin alone. He wanted to know what was going on in the other man's head, but barring that, he needed his good-night kiss, and he wasn't going to get it in a canteen full of jackaroos. Everyone needed to realize it was late and go back to the bunkhouse or their homes so he and Macklin could go sit in Macklin's living room again.

Finally, as it neared midnight, people began to drift off. Caine stayed as close to Macklin as he dared, shaking the hands of the jackaroos who would be leaving in the morning and thanking them for their hard work on the station. It felt a little odd, but he was the closest thing to the owner of Lang Downs at the moment, and he wanted to reinforce that with the ones who were staying as much as with the ones who were leaving. When the last people had left, Caine turned to Macklin with a smile. "I was starting to worry we wouldn't have time for our beer."

"You mean you didn't have enough beer tonight, pup?" Macklin teased.

Caine's smile broadened. "I wouldn't say no to one more."

"Come on then, pup," Macklin said with a shake of his head.

They crossed the distance between the canteen and Macklin's house in silence, walking close but not touching. More than once, Caine had been tempted to reach for Macklin's hand, but he wasn't sure of his welcome, and the last thing he wanted was for Macklin to send him away in a fit of pique again. Despite the absence of a repeat of their night in the hut, he and Macklin seemed to have reached a balance, not snapping at each other or putting each other on edge. The evenings they'd spent on Macklin's couch, drinking beer, kissing, and discussing the requirements for applying for organic certification had been remarkably stress free as long as Caine didn't bring up adding any new intimacy to their relationship. Given that he was about to add enough stress by asking why Macklin hadn't done more than kiss him since they got back to the station, Caine didn't want to make matters worse by putting Macklin on edge before they even started their conversation.

They walked inside, and Caine followed Macklin into the kitchen, catching his hand as he reached for the refrigerator door. "I don't need another beer. I need you to come kiss me."

Macklin pulled Caine against him, kissing him hard and fast, quite the contrast to the majority of their kisses over the past week. "I've been waiting to do that since you walked into the canteen tonight."

Caine's eyebrows rose in surprise. Macklin hadn't refused to kiss him since the morning in the hut, but this was the first time since then he'd admitted to wanting it. "I wouldn't have minded if you did it then."

It was the wrong thing to say.

"You know we can't do that."

"No, I don't. I know you say we can't do that, but I really think you're overreacting. Okay, the men don't know me as well as they know you, but they all worship the ground you walk on. They'd be surprised, but they wouldn't say anything. Not to you."

"You'd be surprised how deeply their prejudices run."

Caine pursed his lips. "Fine. I won't argue, but I still think you're wrong. Let's talk about something else."

"Like what?"

"Like what's been running through your head all week," Caine suggested. "Like why you haven't taken me back to bed."

"I've had a lot on my mind," Macklin replied defensively.

"Like what?" Caine asked. "What's bothering you?"

"I usually go to Sydney after I take the summer staff down to Boorowa," Macklin said. "I stay for a week and... relax for a few days before picking up winter supplies on the way back in."

"You mean you go to bars and pick up twinks who will let you fuck them and leave them," Caine surmised.

"I don't make them any promises," Macklin said.

"I never said you did," Caine replied, "but it's still what you do. Are you going this year?"

"I thought maybe you'd go with me," Macklin said.

"What? Why?" Macklin had mentioned Caine possibly going with him when Taylor was there, but he hadn't said anything since then, and with all the tension between them, Caine hadn't expected anything else to come of it.

"So we could have some time alone somewhere safe," Macklin replied. "Somewhere where people don't know us and won't care."

Caine considered the invitation for a moment. It had obviously cost Macklin to make it, to ask Caine to go with him, not as a partner in the hunt but as his eventual lover. In some ways it might be easier to start their relationship away from the station and the prying eyes of the people who worked for them, but if they did that, if they started a life together shrouded in secrecy, breaking that later would be even harder. Caine was willing to do many things to have a life with Macklin, but hiding wasn't one of them. "What if I d-don't want s-safe? I want a life with you, or if I c-c-can't have that, I want a life with someone, a p-partner who will stand at my side and support me the same way I support him. Sneaking off to Sydney once a year isn't the life I want."

Macklin ran his hand through his hair. "You don't know what you're asking for."

"Was I unclear?"

"Bloody hell, you're determined to misunderstand me."

"Then make me understand what you're saying," Caine said. "I'm not trying to be difficult, but I'm obviously missing something that's clear to you. Help me out here."

"You aren't in Philadelphia anymore. Being gay out here in the outback isn't something anyone admits to," Macklin said, struggling to explain. "I'm not saying people aren't gay, but they don't talk about it because if they do, they'll spend the rest of their lives fending off jokes and comments if they aren't fending off fists."

"So therefore we should hide," Caine concluded. "From what you told me, Uncle Michael didn't hide. Maybe he didn't talk about it, but he didn't hide it either."

"And no one here but me and Kami remembers Donald," Macklin said. "He died over twenty years ago. Besides, things were different then. The station was smaller and they excused their living situation through necessity."

"So how do you picture things working between us if we can't be open about being together?" Caine asked seriously. "I want to sleep like we did in the hut with your arms around me and your body keeping me warm. I want a *life* together, not just the occasional furtive fuck."

Macklin sighed. "I don't have the answers, Caine. I don't know how to give you what you want and still have anything left of the rest of our lives. If word gets out, the jackaroos may not come back next summer. Where would we be then?"

"If those jackaroos don't come back, can we hire others?" Caine asked. "Can we find people who will accept us as a couple?"

"Maybe," Macklin said, "but who knows whether they'd know anything about sheep. We could end up with a totally green crew and have to teach them everything. We could end up with no winter crew because the year-round people decide to leave too. We could end up with nothing."

"The economy isn't exactly great at the moment," Caine reminded him. "Do you really think people would leave without some assurance they could find another job? And even if they do, you don't think we'd find people who will take a job despite our orientation because it's better than no job at all?"

"I don't know," Macklin replied. "I just know it's a huge risk to take."

"Taylor already knows about me, which means it's probably only a matter of time before word gets around anyway," Caine pointed out. "We could be facing all of that anyway without the benefits of being together. If we're damned if we do, damned if we don't, I'd rather be damned for being with you than simply be damned for being me. Don't go to Sydney next week. Stay here and be with me instead."

"I don't know if I can," Macklin replied honestly. "The only person besides you I've ever actually told was Michael."

"You didn't exactly tell me either," Caine said, smiling at the memory of their first kiss. "You just kissed me and then ran from me." He took Macklin's hand. "Maybe it's time to stop running."

"Bloody hell, pup, ask for something difficult, why don't you?"

"Being out is a leap of faith," Caine said. "Faith that the world around you will find it in them to accept you, that the people around you will support your choices, that you can lead your life honestly instead of hiding in the shadows the whole time. You have a station full of men and women who believe in you. Maybe it wouldn't hurt to believe in them too."

"Okay, pup," Macklin said, raising his hands in conciliation. "You've made your point. One way or another, I have to go as far as Boorowa tomorrow for supplies, and I can't make it there and back in one day. Will you come to town with me, not because we're hiding but because you want to be with me instead of being here alone?"

Caine nodded. "And when we get back, you'll stop keeping me at arm's length so much." A pained look crossed Macklin's face. "I'm not going to walk up and kiss you in the barn or in the middle of a mob. The men don't need to see what we do when we're alone together. I just don't want to hide the fact that we are alone together."

"We're not exactly hiding that now," Macklin pointed out.

"No, but if any of them cared to look, right now they'd see me go home every night. Maybe after we get back, I won't always. Or maybe you'll come to the main house some evenings instead. Maybe you'll even stay," Caine replied.

"Maybe I will," Macklin said slowly. "I told you before, I have no bloody idea what I'm doing when it comes to relationships. Be patient with me. I'm trying to make it worth your time."

That flash of vulnerability, a side of Macklin Caine suspected no one else ever saw given how rarely he saw it, erased all the frustrations of the week. Macklin might be a good ten years older than Caine, but when it came to navigating the rocky shoals of a relationship, Caine was the more experienced. He rather liked that idea. "Stick with me, old man. I'll t-teach you what you need to know."

"You think you can teach an old dog new tricks?" Macklin teased.

"I already have," Caine replied smugly. "You only knew one way to kiss when we started."

Macklin chuckled and kissed the smirk off Caine's face. "So now that we've gotten all that out of the way, do you want a beer?" he asked when he lifted his head again.

"No," Caine said. "It's late, and we have an early morning if we're going to get the breeding done and then drive to Boorowa. And since I wasn't planning a trip, even an overnight one, I have to pack still. I should probably go so we can both get some sleep."

"You could sleep here."

"Are you sure?" Caine couldn't keep his surprise out of his voice. After everything Macklin had said, he'd been sure Macklin would accept his departure as he had every other night this week.

"To sleep, pup, not to go at it all night," Macklin clarified. "It will be an early morning, and even earlier for you since you'll have to pack before breakfast. If you'd rather not stay, I understand."

"No!" Caine said quickly. "I want to stay. I just want you to be sure."

"Stay," Macklin repeated. A slight tremor in his voice betrayed his uncertainty, but Caine chose not to mention it. Macklin had invited him to stay. Nothing else mattered now.

Caine answered the request with another kiss, keeping it soft and loving since the offer was only to sleep. Tomorrow night, when they had time and didn't have to get up early, he would see if he could talk Macklin into having sex. Tonight, it would be more than enough to sleep in the other man's arms again.

Macklin returned the kiss, tucking Caine beneath his arm and holding him close but making no move toward the bedroom. "I thought we were going to sleep," Caine prodded gently.

"Be patient with me, remember?" Macklin said. "I haven't ever done this before."

"It's not hard," Caine said with a soft smile. "We walk into your bedroom, we get undressed, and we climb under the covers and go to sleep. Just like if you were by yourself."

"Easy for you to say," Macklin muttered.

"Come on," Caine urged, tugging on Macklin's hand. "Unless you've changed your mind?"

"I'm not changing my mind." Macklin took a deep breath. "Okay, time for bed."

Macklin's room was similar in size and design to Caine's, but without the portable heater Caine used to keep his room at a temperature he was used to. He shivered a little, glad he would have Macklin in bed with him to keep him warm.

"I'll, um, I'll just go get ready," Macklin said, gesturing toward a door Caine assumed led to the bathroom.

Caine stopped him for a quick kiss. "I'll be waiting."

When the door closed behind Macklin, Caine stripped off his shirt, shivering in the thin T-shirt he wore beneath. He wanted to take that off, too, but he didn't want to make Macklin uncomfortable, and he had no idea what the other man slept in. Given the temperature of the room, Caine doubted Macklin slept in the nude, at least not in the winter, although it was an enticing enough image to make Caine want to suggest a heater. He'd simply have to convince Macklin to sleep in the main house with him next time.

Caine folded his shirt and jeans, setting them neatly on the dresser since Macklin's room was spotlessly clean. If they had been franticly making love, clothing scattered everywhere might not have mattered, but as it was, folding his clothes gave Caine something to occupy his time while he waited for Macklin to emerge from the bathroom.

The door opened just as Caine started to wonder if Macklin had changed his mind and was going to sleep in the bathtub. He wore red-and-blue plaid flannel pajamas, the kind Caine had always associated with his grandfather. He had to smother a smile, not wanting to offend Macklin, but he was not as successful as he'd hoped, judging by the scowl on Macklin's face.

"What? They're practical on cold nights. It's not like there's ever been anyone here to see them."

"They look very warm," Caine said soothingly. "It is cool in here."

"You have to be freezing," Macklin said, looking at Caine in his T-shirt and boxer briefs. "Get in bed."

"I was waiting for you," Caine replied.

"Well, I'm here now." Macklin turned down the heavy down duvet on the bed. "Get in."

"Which side is yours?"

"Just get in," Macklin said, his voice a low growl. Caine crawled beneath the covers and scooted to the other side of the bed so Macklin could get in next to him. When Macklin had pulled the duvet over both of them, Caine fingered the buttons on the pajama top.

"I don't suppose you could get rid of this since we'll have a little extra body heat tonight?"

"I thought we were going to sleep."

"We are," Caine promised, "but skin to skin is so much nicer. Give it a try. If you get cold, you can put it back on."

"Only if you take yours off too."

Caine sat up, swiftly pulling his T-shirt over his head. His nipples pebbled in the cold air as he lay back down and looked at Macklin expectantly.

Macklin's eyes fixated on the tight nubs, making them tingle even more. "P-please," Caine whispered, arousal surging through him.

Macklin lowered his head, flicking his tongue across one nipple, then the other. Caine gasped and leaned into the caress for a moment before tugging on Macklin's hair. "If we're g-going to sleep, you n-need to s-stop now."

To Caine's surprise, Macklin nodded and sat up, unbuttoning his pajama shirt and lying back down. He pulled Caine into his arms and kissed him gently. "How do you sleep best?"

Caine didn't answer aloud, turning in Macklin's arms so the other man lay spooned behind him. He pulled one arm around his waist and sighed in contentment. The slight hum of arousal from Macklin's mouth on his chest lingered, but it added to the sense of rightness rather than detracted from it. They didn't have to rush. This was a big enough step as it was. Maybe tomorrow night, they'd take another one, and maybe they wouldn't. Caine found he didn't mind waiting to have sex as long as Macklin kept holding him like he never intended to let him go.

He fell asleep with a smile on his face.

FOURTEEN

MACKLIN'S alarm went off early the next morning, startling Caine out of a deep sleep. The foreman rolled over and turned it off, then rolled right back against Caine, nuzzling his neck. Caine smiled and pressed back into the kiss and into the erection he could feel nudging his backside. He turned in Macklin's arms, sliding a hand between them to caress the other man through his pajamas.

"Don't start something we don't have time to finish," Macklin groaned.

Caine gave the hard cock a last, lingering stroke before leaning up to kiss Macklin. "Tomorrow morning, when no one is expecting us at breakfast, I'm going to give you a proper wake-up call."

"And what would that be?" Macklin asked, his voice husky.

Caine licked his lips, easily imagining running his lips over Macklin's chest and down to the waistband of his pajamas and beyond. "What do you think?"

"Bloody hell," Macklin groaned. "I'm not going to be able to stop thinking about what you'd look like with your mouth on me."

"Good," Caine said with a triumphant smile. "It'll keep you warm when we're outside today."

"And what will keep you warm?" Macklin replied.

Caine's grin widened. "The thought that I'm wearing a pair of your long underwear beneath my clothes. Oh, and the knowledge that tonight I'll have you all to myself." He ran his hand down Macklin's side. "I plan to take terrible advantage of you."

Macklin groaned again and rolled away from Caine. "If you keep that up, I'm going to walk funny all day and someone's going to notice."

Caine relented, not wanting to push Macklin too far. "We can't have that, can we? I could always leave the long underwear here. I'm not going to stop imagining tonight."

"Don't be a Galah," Macklin said. "There's no reason for you to be cold. I'll just think of other things."

"A Galah?" Caine asked, not familiar with the term.

"It's a kind of bird," Macklin replied. "The expression means don't be silly or stupid. You shouldn't be cold just because the thought of you wearing my clothes makes me hard."

"I guess we should get up, shouldn't we?" Caine said with a sigh.

"If you're going back to your house to change and pack, yes," Macklin agreed. "You don't want to miss breakfast."

"And I don't want to be walking out of your cabin as everyone else is going to breakfast," Caine said. "No need to provoke a crisis just yet."

"Thank you," Macklin said, kissing Caine quickly. "I'll get you that long underwear."

He pulled on his pajama shirt and padded barefoot across the floor. Caine shivered just looking at him as he put back on his T-shirt and waited for the long underwear. The floor was icy when he stood up to put them and his own clothes back on. He gave Macklin one more kiss. "I'll see you at breakfast."

"I'll be there."

Caine didn't see anyone as he walked back to his house. He didn't make a conscious effort to come in discreetly, but he also didn't call out to Kami to let him know he was there like he usually did. He'd worry about that when or if Macklin started spending the night there or if Kami asked specifically where Caine had been the night before.

Going upstairs, he showered quickly, pulling on clean briefs before putting Macklin's long underwear back on underneath the work clothes for the morning. If they had time, he'd shower and change again before they left for Boorowa because he didn't really want to smell like sheep for the long drive. He tossed a change of clothes and some toiletries in his backpack, wishing he had lube and condoms, but he hadn't expected to need them when he moved to Australia. Maybe Macklin would have some. Packing done, he went down for breakfast.

"What do you mean you're coming back tomorrow?" Kami's demand was the first thing Caine heard as he walked into the kitchen. "What happened to your annual trip to Sydney?"

"I decided not to go this year," Macklin replied, nodding to Caine as he came in. "I thought with a new boss on the station and with the storms we've been having, it might be a good idea to stay close to home. Caine and I will drive to Boorowa tonight, pick up the supplies in the morning, and be home tomorrow evening."

"It's your choice, I suppose," Kami said, "but don't take it out on me when you're grumpy because you didn't get laid this winter."

Caine coughed to hide his smirk. Macklin would be getting laid a whole lot more often than one week a year if Caine had anything to say about it.

"I'll be sure and not mention it," Macklin promised, his eyes twinkling as he looked at Caine. "Come on, pup. Let's leave Kami to finish breakfast. I want to run a thought by you about the organic farming idea."

"Sure," Caine said, following Macklin out into the living room. The moment they were alone, his laughter escaped. "Oh, G-g-god, if K-kami only knew," he wheezed between fits of laughter.

"If you don't talk a little softer, he'll know anyway," Macklin said, but he was smiling, so Caine didn't worry about trying to contain his laughter.

"So what was your thought?" Caine asked when he finally stopped laughing.

"That I wanted to get you alone so I could kiss you," Macklin replied, suiting actions to words. Caine returned the kiss, smiling when they parted.

"You keep saying you don't know anything about relationships, but you're doing just fine this morning."

"Good to know," Macklin said. "Let's eat so we can get the rams moved into the pens and get on the road. It gets dark early, and I want to be in Boorowa before that if we can."

"Ready when you are," Caine said. "I packed before I came down this morning."

They ate breakfast with the rest of the hands, heading out immediately afterward to start moving the rams in with the flocks of ewes. The big males weren't nearly as biddable as the ewes, fighting the dogs and the men, trying to go anywhere but into a pen with a hundred other sheep. Finally, though, they managed to get all of them in the pens where Macklin wanted them.

Macklin thanked the summer jackaroos, shaking hands with each of them in turn and wishing them well. Caine waited to the side, adding his own thanks to those who stopped to speak to him before leaving. When only the year-round residents remained, Caine glanced at his watch. "We should pack sandwiches for lunch so we can eat on the way."

"Good idea, pup," Macklin said. "I'll ask Kami to put something together for us while we load the ute."

"He'll tell us to make them ourselves," Caine warned.

"He won't tell me that," Macklin said.

Caine looked at him skeptically, following Macklin into the kitchen. "Kami, could you make us a couple of sandwiches for the road?"

"Bread's in the bread box, meat's in the refrigerator," Kami said without pausing in his chopping.

"Told you," Caine mouthed to Macklin. "I'll do it," he said aloud. "You load the ute. It won't take me long, and then we can toss my pack in before we leave."

"Bloody foreman," Kami muttered when Macklin left. "Always assuming everyone will do whatever he says just because he says it."

"He is the foreman," Caine pointed out.

"And?" Kami demanded. "This is my kitchen. I decide what happens in here, not him."

"He said something about getting supplies for the winter," Caine said, not about to get into that argument with Kami. He and Macklin could duke it out between themselves. "Did you give him a list? And if not, is there anything in particular you need? I can make sure we pick it up while we're in town. I'd hate for you not to have what you need for the winter."

"You're a good boy to think of me, Caine," Kami said. "Your uncle would have been proud of you."

The compliment surprised Caine so much he couldn't think of a reply. "Thank you," he said finally. "I'm glad you think so. Do you have a list?"

"I gave it to Macklin a week ago," Kami said. "He's a good boy too. Makes me hope history will repeat itself."

That was even more of a surprise. "I… I d-d-don't know what to s-say."

"Don't say anything," Kami replied. "I'm a sentimental old fool."

"N-no, that isn't what I m-meant. I m-meant—"

"Don't say anything," Kami repeated. "Macklin will tell me what he wants me to know when he's ready for me to know it. This was just between you and me."

Caine nodded and finished making sandwiches for Macklin and himself. He tossed them in a rucksack along with a couple of bottles of water and some chips, enough to tide them over until they reached Boorowa, although Caine was sure they'd be ready for dinner when they got to the hotel.

Leaving the sack by the front door, he hurried up to his room to get his backpack. Macklin was waiting for him in the living room when he came back down. "Ready, pup?"

"Ready," Caine said, grabbing their lunch and following Macklin outside. Macklin tossed Caine's backpack in the back of the truck with his own gear and gestured for Caine to climb in.

Caine waited until they had passed through the first gate and out of the main station before leaning his head back against the headrest. "You said Kami knew Donald too, right?"

"Yes," Macklin said. "Kami was already cooking here when I arrived. I don't know his whole story, but from what I've pieced together, Michael took him in much the same way he took me in, about ten years before I arrived at Lang Downs. Why do you ask?"

"Just something he said, that's all," Caine replied, not wanting to say too much. "It made me wonder what he knew. He also said Uncle Michael would have been proud of me."

"He's right," Macklin agreed. "I didn't think you'd make it a week, much less months. I expected you to give up before you had a chance to toughen up. I was wrong. We'll make a grazier out of you yet."

Caine smiled. "I know I'll never be as comfortable with it as someone like you or Jason who grew up with it, but I want this to work. I want the people of Lang Downs to be proud of me."

"We are," Macklin assured him. "You won me over, and I was determined to keep my distance."

"You just want to fuck me," Caine teased.

Macklin's breath hissed out at the provocative words. "Not saying I don't, but that alone wouldn't have been enough to change my mind," Macklin insisted after a moment. "There have been plenty of good-looking jackaroos coming through the station over the years, and I never acted on any of that. Your appearance wouldn't have swayed me if you'd been a different caliber of man."

Caine's heart melted a little at the words. "I'm glad. You are going to fuck me, though, right?"

"Right here in the ute if you don't stop pushing me," Macklin threatened.

"Is that supposed to discourage me?" Caine asked with a grin.

"Yes, because there's not enough space to do it properly."

"I'm sure you know where the closest drover's hut is," Caine said.

"Of course I do, but that's hardly any better. Narrow bunks and no heat," Macklin retorted. "Behave yourself until we get to Boorowa, and then we can discuss what we will and will not be doing to each other tonight and tomorrow morning."

"Or we could discuss it while we drive and then do it when we get to the hotel," Caine suggested optimistically.

"If we discuss it, we won't be driving for long," Macklin said. "Tell me where we are with the organic certification."

They spent the rest of the drive discussing the ins and outs of beginning the process of organic certification. By the time they hit the main road, they had worked out the remaining details. It would take another month or two to finish putting everything in place, but Caine was hopeful they could begin the certification process in the spring.

They spent the final hour talking about what Caine could expect on the station over the winter. He was a little concerned that the weather had gotten cold earlier than usual, but they would deal with whatever happened as best they could.

"So what's first on our agenda?" Caine asked when they reached the outskirts of Boorowa.

"We let Paul know we're in town so he can put together our order for pick-up tomorrow," Macklin said. "Then we check in to the hotel so we have our rooms for tonight, and then we can think about dinner."

"Rooms?" Caine said. "Do we need more than one?"

"Only if you want one of your own."

"After last night, do you really have to ask that?"

"Yes, I do," Macklin replied seriously. "I don't want to assume I know what you're thinking and end up arguing because of it. I know what I'd prefer, but you have a say in this as well."

"We only need one room," Caine said.

"Then we'll check in to our room and then think about dinner," Macklin amended. "But one room or two, we have to talk to Paul first. I faxed him a list a week ago, but I didn't have the definite date we'd be picking things up, especially since always before, I've gone to Sydney for a week before picking up the supplies."

"We'll take a trip to Sydney," Caine promised, "but because we want a week in the city rather than because we need to hide what we're doing. I've always wanted to see a performance at the Opera House."

"You're an opera fan?" Macklin asked as he parked the truck.

"Not especially, but I've heard such amazing things about it that it seems like it would be worth it."

They went inside the store, Macklin calling out a greeting to Paul.

"Well, well, if it isn't the blow-in," Paul said when he saw them. "Ready to give up yet?"

"Absolutely not," Caine said, "although I do have a few more things I need to buy while I'm here besides the supplies Macklin ordered. It's colder than I expected up at the station."

"I'll have your supplies ready next week like usual then?" Paul asked Macklin.

"I'm not going to Sydney this year," Macklin said. "Too much to do at Lang Downs. We'll load up in the morning if you can have everything ready by then. The day after at the latest."

"I can have them in the morning," Paul said. "I've been putting the order together already to make sure I had everything you needed. Let me just take care of your blow-in and I'll finish the rest."

"My name is Caine," Caine insisted. "Not blow-in."

"Let me just take care of Caine, then," Paul said, his voice betraying his surprise at Caine standing up to him that way.

"He needs long underwear," Macklin said. "He's freezing his arse off without them."

"I'm sure we have something that will suit," Paul said. "They're over on the back wall."

Caine found the area Paul indicated and selected several sets. He paid while Macklin discussed business with Paul, and then they were done and on the way to the Boorowa Hotel. The receptionist at the hotel didn't blink an eye at them checking in with only one room, but Caine figured she thought they were simply sharing a room to save on expenses. Now that he knew Macklin better, he would have suggested it even if he didn't have hopes for the evening, so she wasn't completely off base.

They left their bags in the room and went back to the hotel restaurant for dinner. As much as Caine wanted Macklin naked in that bed, his stomach was demanding dinner. If they ate first, they wouldn't have to worry about interruptions later.

FIFTEEN

CAINE couldn't have said later what he ate or what they talked about. He went through the meal on autopilot, his whole body buzzing in anticipation of the night to come. If Macklin shared Caine's nerves, it didn't show, but then Macklin rarely let anything peek out from behind the stoic mask he wore. It made the rare glimpses of emotion that much more precious.

By the time dinner was over and they headed back to their room on the second floor of the hotel, Caine was practically vibrating with his need to hurry. Only the necessity for discretion kept him from grabbing Macklin's hand and dragging him up the stairs. The moment the door closed behind them, he threw himself in the other man's arms, diving into a reckless kiss designed to drive them both wild as quickly as possible.

Macklin returned it willingly, but after several long moments, he lifted his head. "Slow down a bit, pup. We have all night. You have some promises to keep."

"L-l-like?" Caine asked, already stuttering from arousal.

"I think you said something about showing me what I'd been missing," Macklin said. "I don't really know what that means, but I'd sure like to find out."

Caine swallowed hard, remembering his promise from the night in the drover's hut when he'd realized how little experience Macklin had with anything except fucking. "T-t-take off your sh-sh-shirt."

Macklin unbuttoned his work shirt and tossed it on the chair before pulling his undershirt off. He turned back to Caine, waiting in tense silence. Caine took a moment to appreciate the sight in front of him. Macklin's face might hint at his age with the lines around his eyes and the weathered skin, but he had the body of a much younger man, his shoulders broad and strong from a life spent working, his waist trim, the entire ensemble covered in hard muscle and a fine dusting of hair, enough for Caine to run his fingers through without crossing the line to hirsute.

"Well?" Macklin said after a moment.

"Well, you l-look good enough t-to eat," Caine said, urging Macklin to lie down on the bed. "I c-could stare at you all n-n-night."

"I hope you'll do more than just look," Macklin said with a soft laugh.

"D-definitely," Caine replied, climbing onto the bed next to Macklin. He traced the pattern of hair from the lower edge of Macklin's collar bone out around the edge of his chest and along his ribs to where it arrowed into the waistband of his jeans. There would be time to peel back the denim and follow that line of hair lower later. Some lucky man had probably given Macklin his first blow job years ago, but if Caine wasn't the first to take his time with Macklin's chest, he was one of only a very few, and that was more than good enough for him. The others had been fucks. He was Macklin's lover, or he would be if things continued the way they had the past two days.

"Why don't you take your shirt off too?" Macklin suggested.

Caine shook his head. If he did that, he'd end up distracted by Macklin touching him, and then he wouldn't be able to keep his promise. "L-l-later."

To keep Macklin from arguing, he bent swiftly and licked one of the roseate nipples partially hidden by the hair on Macklin's chest. Macklin arched off the bed with a soft curse. Caine smiled and did it again, sucking lightly this time as he pushed Macklin back toward the mattress and found his other nipple with his fingers. He tweaked and plucked at it in time with his sucking, determined to show Macklin the benefits of a real lover. Not that Caine had all that much experience, but at least he knew how to take his time making love.

Macklin tugged on Caine's hair, pulling him up into another kiss. "The guy in Philadelphia who said you were boring in bed was a complete Galah. One touch, and I go up in flames."

Caine smiled and kissed Macklin again. "The f-f-feeling is m-mutual. He n-never made me f-feel as g-good as you do."

"We're a pair, aren't we?" Macklin said with a chuckle.

"Yes, but a p-pair of what?"

Macklin grinned and rolled Caine to his back, unbuttoning his shirt and pushing it off Caine's shoulders. Caine lifted up so Macklin could pull the undershirt over his head as well. "Let's see if I've learned the way of it, shall we?"

Caine hadn't expected Macklin to leave him in charge for long, but he hadn't expected it to happen quite that fast. He wasn't complaining, exactly, but he hoped he'd get another chance to get his hands and mouth on Macklin's chest. He wasn't done exploring. He wasn't going to get that opportunity now, though. Macklin had him pinned to the bed again, his heavier body holding Caine's thighs still while his hands and lips moved over Caine's torso with surprising gentleness. Given the tenor of most of their kisses and the speed of their first encounter, Caine hadn't expected gentleness without some coaxing, but Macklin seemed to have picked that up on his own, keeping his teeth well clear of Caine's nipples as he licked and sucked on them one at a time. His fingers kept up a steady stimulation on the opposite side, enough to bring Caine to full hardness but without ever crossing the line to being rough.

As hot as Caine's fantasies had been, he found this even more arousing because Macklin obviously cared enough to be careful, and that was a far more potent aphrodisiac than sheer lust. Not for the first time, he silently cursed the stutter that made it almost impossible for him to talk when he was turned on. He wanted to tell Macklin how good it felt to be touched again, to feel as cherished as he was desired, but the fight to get the words out wasn't worth it right now. He settled for wordless moans and groans, hisses and sighs, hoping they would convey his pleasure clearly enough. Macklin certainly didn't show any sign of stopping, so Caine hoped he was getting his message across.

When Macklin's hands started working on his jeans, relief surged through Caine. Whatever else happened—God, he hoped Macklin had condoms!—it would at least involve them getting naked together. He lifted his hips and forced his voice to work. "P-p-please t-tell me you have c-c-condoms."

"No," Macklin said with a groan. "I always buy what I need when I go to Sydney. I was hoping you would have them."

"John and I were exclusive for six years. We s-stopped using them," Caine explained. "It d-doesn't m-m-matter. We'll d-d-do something else instead. I d-did promise you a b-b-blow job."

"You promised to wake me up with one," Macklin said. Caine's dismay must have shown on his face because Macklin said, "No worries, pup. I'm not going to leave you hurting."

Caine breathed a sigh of relief when Macklin undid his jeans the rest of the way and pushed them and his boxer briefs down to his knees. His hand, hard and hot despite the cool room, closed around Caine's cock, stroking firmly without being rough. Caine's hips surged upward into the caress, desperate for more stimulation. He had the passing thought that he should try to reciprocate, but he couldn't make his body cooperate any more than his voice.

Then Macklin leaned down to whisper in his ear, and Caine lost even the train of coherent thought. "Look at you," Macklin murmured. "Greedy little bottom, pants around your knees, begging to be touched."

Caine had always hated it when John tried to talk dirty during sex. It had always seemed forced and uninspiring. Maybe it was Macklin's accent that made this different or maybe it was the way Macklin touched him, but Caine wanted more. More of Macklin's hands on his body. More of Macklin's voice in his ear. More of Macklin in his life.

He'd never be able to get all of that out, though, so he settled for turning his head and kissing Macklin hungrily. Macklin responded in kind, keeping his touch light on Caine's cock as he ravished Caine's mouth.

When they broke their kiss, Macklin's hand delved between Caine's thighs, cupping his sac and then probing lower. "Makes me wish I'd picked up some lotion."

Caine rolled out of bed, stripping his pants off so he wouldn't trip, and dug through his bag until he found a small bottle of lube he hadn't tossed before he moved.

"L-l-l-lube."

Macklin's grin made Caine weak in the knees as he patted the space Caine had vacated. "Come back here and let me finish what I started."

Caine all but jumped back onto the bed, but instead of lying back down, he opened Macklin's jeans and pushed them down. "T-t-take them off."

To Caine's surprise, Macklin hesitated.

"W-what's wrong?"

"I'm not used to being naked with anyone," Macklin admitted. "In a back room or an alley, you open your pants enough to pull your dick out, but you don't strip all the way down. There isn't enough time or privacy for that."

Caine nodded, heart hurting as he imagined the emptiness of Macklin's life with a week of anonymous encounters each year and nothing in between. "You d-don't have to if you d-don't want to, but I'd l-like to t-t-touch you too."

Macklin nodded slowly and pulled his jeans off. Caine caught his breath at the sight of Macklin, hard and uncut, the tip just peeking out from beneath the foreskin. Tentatively, he stroked the almost hidden slit.

"Don't do too much of that, pup," Macklin said, catching Caine's wrist, "or this will be over before we start."

Caine thought watching Macklin come apart beneath his hands sounded like a marvelous idea, but he could wait until later if it would put Macklin more at ease. He let his hand fall to Macklin's rock-hard thigh, appreciating the strength beneath his fingers, and waited for whatever Macklin wanted to do next.

To Caine's delight, Macklin squeezed some lube onto his fingers, rubbing them together until they were completely coated. "Tell me if it gets too dry," he said, circling a finger around Caine's entrance. "I don't want to hurt you."

Caine couldn't formulate an answer, but he figured he could say "ow" if it hurt.

Macklin teased him for several long minutes until Caine was moaning constantly and pressing up into Macklin's hand, his body begging for more even if he couldn't say the words. Finally Macklin gave him what he wanted, breaching him with the tip of one finger. Caine came halfway off the bed, his body seizing at the intimate touch after so long.

"I'm not hurting you, am I, pup?"

Caine shook his head vehemently. "D-d-d-don't s-s-stop."

Macklin pulled Caine the rest of the way to sitting and into a hard kiss, his tongue tasting every inch of Caine's mouth. "Not stopping," he promised. "Not until you come apart for me."

That wouldn't take long if Macklin kept playing with Caine's prostate. The foreman found the sensitive gland on the first pass and exploited it mercilessly, his finger flicking across it with unerring precision. His other hand circled around Caine's cock again, stroking in time with the flicks of his finger so that Caine was stimulated from within and without. He rocked between Macklin's hands, harsh sobs escaping as he raced toward the summit. When he swore he couldn't take anymore without exploding completely, Macklin's hands stopped moving. They didn't withdraw, merely froze on his cock and in his passage.

"Not yet," Macklin said. "Breathe for me until you're a little more in control."

Caine opened his eyes and looked at Macklin skeptically, but he took a few deep breaths, feeling his climax recede. Macklin leaned over and kissed him tenderly this time, gentling Caine with an assiduity Caine had not expected, given what Macklin had revealed of his past experiences. Caine sighed and relaxed into the kiss. The moment he did, Macklin's hands moved again, far faster and more demanding than before, catapulting Caine into release. He climaxed with a hoarse shout, every bone in his body feeling like liquid. He struggled to catch his breath, wanting to return the pleasure Macklin had given him when he heard Macklin grunt harshly. Forcing his eyes open again, he watched in helpless fascination as Macklin tugged on his cock a few times before splattering Caine's stomach with his release.

"I wanted to d-do that."

"I'm sorry, pup. I couldn't wait," Macklin said, lying down next to Caine. "Watching you, touching you… it was too much."

"That's t-twice you've t-taken care of yourself instead of l-letting me d-do it," Caine said. "No m-more. You make me feel selfish."

"Wake me up like you promised and we'll be even," Macklin said.

"I will," Caine agreed. He snuggled closer to Macklin, heedless of the sticky mess on his belly. As his pulse returned to normal, he relaxed enough to speak more easily. "Where did you learn that trick? That's not something you pick up from fucking around in bars."

"I took my first trip to Sydney at twenty," Macklin said. "Michael insisted I go to relax a little, as he put it. I was still a scrawny kid then, not exactly top material even if that's what I wanted to be, but the guys who were looking for tops weren't looking at me. I figured my only choice was to leave with one of the older men. He wanted me to go home with him. In hindsight, it was a stupid move, but I didn't know any better. Fortunately, he wasn't after any more than I was willing to give. I spent the week with him before I came back to Lang Downs, and he taught me all about sex. I just haven't had much chance to use it before now."

"I thought you'd never had a lover."

"He wasn't a lover," Macklin insisted. "He wanted a sweet young arse to fuck. I was willing to be that arse for him for the time I was in Sydney. Foreplay consisted of him fingering me until I came and then fucking me until I came again, or fucking my mouth until he came. It wasn't cruel, but it was just sex, and we both knew it. And that was over twenty years ago. I had enough sense to make him wear a condom, but that's about it. You're the only lover I've ever had."

Hearing Macklin call him his lover reassured Caine. Whatever bumps in the road they'd have ahead, Macklin wasn't thinking of their encounters as a fling. "I'd say I was sorry you haven't met anyone in all that time, but if you had, we might not be here now, and I can't regret that."

"Some things are worth waiting for, pup," Macklin said, kissing Caine gently. "Now get some sleep. We've got things to do tomorrow and a long drive home."

Caine nodded and kissed Macklin one more time before rolling onto his side and pressing back against Macklin's front. With no clothes between them, Macklin's cock settled perfectly between Caine's buttocks, pressing tightly against his entrance. Caine hissed at the intimate sensation.

"I'll buy condoms tomorrow," Macklin promised, his voice hoarse.

"Good." Caine's voice trembled with renewed need, but he forced his body to relax. They didn't have to rush, even after they had condoms. "Don't forget the lube either. That tube's almost empty, and spit or lotion isn't going to cut it."

"Greedy little bottom," Macklin teased, but he stroked Caine's arm tenderly as he said it, his hand coming to rest above Caine's heart.

"Only for you," Caine replied.

"Really?"

Caine shrugged. "I told you what John thought about sex with me. He never actually said it, but it was pretty obvious neither of us was overly passionate about the other. We went through the motions because we were a couple and expected to have sex, but I never felt like I'd die if I didn't come right then, the way you made me feel tonight."

Macklin tugged on Caine's arm until he rolled to his back. Macklin rolled on top of him, pressing Caine down into the soft hotel mattress. "There is nothing... *nothing* boring about sex with you, Caine. Nothing." He rocked against Caine, his cock already half-hard again, to prove his point. "You're handsome and passionate and being in bed with you is more exciting than all the fucking I've ever done. Maybe it was his fault, maybe it was just that you weren't good as a couple. Either way, you forget what he said or made you feel because I can't get enough of you."

"I don't suppose Boorowa has a twenty-four-hour store that sells condoms." The feeling of Macklin growing hard against him left Caine aching to prove everything would be as good with Macklin as their first two encounters had been.

"Not likely," Macklin said with a groan. "I should have gone before dinner."

"Or I sh-should have," Caine replied, stroking his hands down Macklin's back to cup his buttocks. "G-g-god, I've n-n-never g-gotten hard again this f-fast."

Macklin chuckled. "I'm a good ten years older than you and you've got me hard again. *Not* boring in bed, pup."

SIXTEEN

"TH-THIS time you have to l-l-let me m-make love to you," Caine insisted, squirming out from beneath Macklin. "I want to touch you too."

The flicker of unease Caine had seen several times before passed across Macklin's face, but Caine didn't back down. "P-please? I'll s-stop if you say to, but I want to make you f-feel as g-good as you made me feel."

"I'll try, pup," Macklin said, "but I'm used to being in charge, at the station, in bars, wherever. It's hard to let that go."

"Surely you can handle a hand job," Caine joked.

"It's not that easy," Macklin said. "Fucking around is one thing. Being with you is something else entirely. Being here, just lying here in this bed with you, scares the hell out of me, pup. You've been at Lang Downs for a couple of months. You still don't know what it's really like, year in and year out. Every man who comes to the station thinks he's hot stuff, tough as nails and strong enough to move mountains. They respect me, they listen to me because I'm tougher, stronger, harder than they are. Without that, I'd lose all control over them."

"You're the boss. They have to listen to you."

"No, they had to listen to Michael. They might have to listen to you, but I'm foreman because they know I'll kick their arses if they don't do as I say," Macklin insisted.

"And how is me giving you a hand job different than you giving me one?" Caine asked, still not following Macklin's argument.

"It's giving someone else the upper hand," Macklin explained. "Aside from that one week when I came to Sydney the first time, I've never let anyone have the upper hand in anything, and even that was just fucking. This is different."

"So you're somehow less gay if you give me a hand job than if I give you one?" Caine asked incredulously. "That doesn't make any sense. It's a hand on your dick. You're a guy. You're going to react to that no matter whose hand it is. Putting your hand on me is far more indicative of your sexuality than letting me touch you."

"But I'm still the one in control," Macklin explained.

"F-fuck that," Caine said. "You can b-be as in control as you w-want out in the outback. I'll be the first to admit I n-need you in control out there, but in p-private, when it's just us, I don't need someone who just wants a b-body to fuck when it's convenient. I need a p-partner who's going to share my life, not r-run it for me. I thought m-maybe that would be you, but if you can't even let me t-touch you, how will you ever let me l-love you?"

Furious, Caine climbed out of bed, shivering as he looked around for his underwear. He swiped at the drying mess on his stomach, hating its presence now as much as he had reveled in it minutes before. He grabbed a clean pair from his bag and pulled them on before turning to look for his shirt. Macklin intercepted him before he could reach it.

"Did you mean it?"

"Mean what?" Caine snapped, pulling away and grabbing his shirt. He couldn't stand there half-dressed anymore, not when he felt so vulnerable.

"What you said about loving me," Macklin said softly.

Oh, shit, did I really say that?

"It doesn't matter now," Caine said, keeping his back to Macklin. "You won't let me."

"I warned you I didn't know what I was doing," Macklin reminded him, his hands coming to rest on Caine's shoulders. "And you told me relationships were about negotiation and fighting sometimes until you could find a way to make it work."

"You aren't trying to make it work," Caine retorted, shrugging Macklin's hands off and pulling his pants on. "You're trying to make me just another fuck. I won't do it, Macklin. It's all or nothing. I won't be your piece on the side."

"You couldn't be farther from that," Macklin swore. "The things we've done together…. Bloody hell, Caine, I've never touched anyone the way I've touched you. I've never wanted to. The kisses, sleeping together last night, spending the night together tonight. I've never shared that with anyone but you, so whatever fucked-up idea you have in your head, get rid of it. I'm struggling here. I haven't the slightest idea how to give you what you want because I've never done it before, but the fact that I'm trying, the fact that I *want* to give it to you in the first place, should tell you how different this is from anything in my past. You're asking me to change overnight, and that's not an easy thing to do."

"So what happens now?" Caine asked slowly. "We seem to have reached an impasse."

"I don't know," Macklin replied just as carefully. "You can get dressed and go downstairs, check into another room, and forget this ever happened, although I hope that won't be your choice. Or you can stay and we can try to find a way forward we can both live with."

"Do you really think there is a way forward?" Caine asked.

"I don't know," Macklin said again, "but I know I want there to be one."

"My grandmother always said, 'Where there's a will, there's a way.' I guess we keep searching until we find it."

"Don't scare me like that again, pup," Macklin demanded, pulling Caine into his arms. "I can deal with dead sheep, bloody snakes, power outages, and everything else the outback can throw at me. I can't deal with you walking out on me."

"Then don't give me a reason to," Caine replied, fighting the urge to sink back into Macklin's embrace. It would be so easy to give in and pretend everything was better now, but that wouldn't actually fix anything.

"I didn't think I'd given you one tonight until you got ready to storm out," Macklin said. "I'm not saying you were wrong to be upset, so don't look at me that way. I'm just saying it's not as easy as you telling me not to give you a reason to walk out. I'm trying to be as honest with you as I can. I'm making a huge change in my life, in my way of thinking, in everything. That doesn't happen overnight."

Sometimes it does, Caine thought, remembering his decision to come to Australia, but unlike Macklin, he'd had nothing left to lose. Macklin had nearly everything. Caine would have to be worth that risk. "So what do we do now?"

"I hope you'll come back to bed and sleep in my arms again," Macklin said. "It felt good having you with me last night. I know that isn't what you want, but it's something, I hope, and then we'll see how tomorrow goes."

Tomorrow was supposed to start with Caine waking Macklin up with a blow job, but after tonight, Caine wasn't sure how likely that was to happen. He wanted it more than ever, as a chance to prove to Macklin how good it could feel to let someone else be in charge occasionally, but Caine was afraid that was wishful thinking. He'd try, but he wouldn't get his hopes up for success. Still, sleeping with Macklin was better than sleeping alone. Being asked to sleep with Macklin was even better. He would have to remind himself to celebrate the tiny steps rather than assume they would simply move through them.

Not for the first time, he felt like he had entered an entirely different world than the one he'd left behind in Philadelphia. "Sleeping in your arms is good," he said, realizing Macklin was still waiting for an answer. "Waking up in your arms will be even better."

"Then get rid of those clothes and come to bed," Macklin said. "I'm freezing."

Caine smiled and stripped back down, climbing beneath the covers and snuggling against Macklin. "Turn over," he said. "I want to hold you for a while."

Macklin tensed, but Caine nudged his shoulder. "I'm not going to do anything you aren't ready for. I just want to have you in my arms too."

Macklin nodded and rolled slowly onto his side with his back facing Caine. Caine scooted up behind him, adjusting the pillow and their arms and legs so he could spoon behind Macklin. It was a bit awkward with the slight difference in their heights, but Caine eventually got comfortable. "There," he said, pressing a kiss to Macklin's spine. "This isn't so bad, is it?"

"I could get used to it," Macklin replied.

"So could I."

THE sky outside the hotel window was still pitch black when Caine awoke the next morning, startled from sleep by the rumble of a passing truck. Macklin had rolled onto his back during the night, still in Caine's arms, but no longer spooned together. Caine smiled. The perfect position for a little morning fellatio.

Moving carefully so Macklin wouldn't wake up soon enough to protest, Caine slid beneath the covers, seeking Macklin's groin by touch alone. His cock, when Caine found it, was already at half-mast, making Caine wonder what Macklin was dreaming about. Caine hoped it was him.

Shifting around to find a comfortable position, he lifted up over Macklin's belly and closed his mouth over the tip of the other man's erection, sucking lightly as it swelled against his tongue. At that angle, he couldn't take the entire length in his mouth, so he gripped the base with his hand, working the entire shaft. He wanted Macklin to come awake to such pleasure that he wouldn't protest Caine touching him.

The groan above him suggested he'd been successful.

"Caine."

Caine didn't stop what he was doing, reaching for Macklin's hand instead to reassure him. Now that Macklin was awake, Caine moved a little more so he could take more of the shaft into his mouth and throat, nearly touching the curls at the base of Macklin's cock with his lips.

"Bloody hell!"

Caine took that as a sign of approval and did it again before pulling back to run his tongue beneath the foreskin and along the slit that was covered in salty fluid. Macklin cursed again, pushing the covers down. Caine shivered in the cool air, but he didn't protest. If Macklin wanted to see him in the slowly lightening room, Caine was fine with that. Anything to reassure his lover.

"Too much," Macklin gasped when Caine's tongue swiped through the slit again.

Caine backed off, bobbing his head so his lips ran up and down the fully hard shaft again.

"Turn around," Macklin said. "I want to touch you too."

It wasn't exactly what Caine wanted, but it was better than Macklin telling him to stop. Careful not to break contact with Macklin's cock—he was afraid if he did, Macklin wouldn't let him start again—he shifted his hips until his knees bumped the headboard and his groin rested near Macklin's head.

Macklin pushed Caine's hips to the bed, rolling until he straddled Caine's head. Caine moaned as the new position allowed Macklin's cock to slide easily into his throat. He rested his hands on Macklin's hips, urging him to move if he wanted. He didn't immediately, keeping his hips at a height that put the tip of his cock directly against Caine's palate. A moment later, Caine felt wet heat surround his own neglected erection. He moaned around his mouthful, stroking Macklin's side in encouragement.

When Macklin shivered, Caine stroked again, sliding his hand between their bodies so he could find Macklin's nipples. He tugged at one lightly, winning a groan from his lover that sent the most delightful vibrations through his cock. Macklin lifted his head enough to speak. "If you keep that up, I'm going to end up fucking your mouth, pup."

Caine tweaked his nipple again in silent invitation, lifting his head as he did so more of Macklin's cock disappeared into his mouth.

Macklin's hips jerked downward, filling Caine's mouth completely. He managed to swallow so he didn't choke on the sudden invasion, but he dropped his head back quickly, letting Macklin set the pace rather than trying to dictate it himself. He'd end up gagging for sure if he did. He was tempted to slide his hands over the tempting swell of Macklin's ass bobbing in his face, maybe even fondle the sac that kept smacking his nose, but after Macklin's reaction the night before, he decided not to take the risk of Macklin pulling away. He'd play with Macklin's nipples instead and save the rest for later. One of these days, though, he was going to get his mouth on that pink pucker that kept flashing into view as Macklin's buttocks flexed and released.

Macklin's mouth returned to Caine's cock after he'd established a rhythm with his hips, but the contact was tentative, as if he didn't really know what he was doing. The thought made Caine want to smile. Macklin might not be willing to come out yet, but he was making changes for Caine, letting Caine into his life in ways he'd never done for anyone else. That made the challenges ahead easier to contemplate. It might take time, but Macklin wasn't refusing to consider other options. He just needed to reach each step at his own pace.

Macklin's thrusts sped up, the rhythm faltering. "Close," Macklin gasped, pulling out to the very tip so Caine had a chance to pull away if he wanted to. He grabbed Macklin's hips with one hand, pushing them back down toward his face as he tugged on Macklin's nipple again with the other, giving silent permission for Macklin to find his release in Caine's mouth.

It only took a few more thrusts before the salty flavor of Macklin's release exploded on Caine's tongue, filling his mouth and running down his chin even as he tried to swallow. Macklin groaned through his climax, his head resting against the inside of Caine's thigh as he shook with the force of his orgasm. "Don't move," he ordered when Caine started to shift from beneath him. "I'm not done with you yet."

Caine certainly hoped not. He hadn't intended to pull away so much as move to the side so Macklin could lie down if he wanted to, but the foreman had other ideas, his mouth returning to Caine's cock as his fingers probed between Caine's cheeks. Caine spread his legs wider, inviting the caress. He had no idea when Macklin had found the lube, but the fingers that slid inside of him, two to judge by the stretch, were slick, moving easily inside him as Macklin found his gland again and teased it as he had the night before. Caine tossed his head on the mattress, caught between Macklin's tentative mouth and masterful fingers. The contrast nearly brought him undone right then.

It was probably the most awkward, bumbling blow job Caine had ever received, but Macklin's fingers in his ass kept him fully engaged and on the verge of release, and the determination in Macklin's stance as he kept trying to take Caine deeper into his mouth endeared him to Caine even more. It would be so easy to fall in love with the man as he was right now. The problem was the way he acted the rest of the time.

"C-c-close," Caine gasped out when a particularly well-aimed thrust of Macklin's fingers left him struggling for control. Macklin lifted his head, his hand pumping Caine's cock hard and fast, tipping the balance in the favor of release. If a part of Caine was disappointed that Macklin had pulled back, he reminded himself how long it had taken before he had been comfortable letting someone come in his mouth.

The fact that Macklin had given him a blow job at all was a huge step. Caine just needed to hold on to that fact when he started doubting how serious Macklin was about their relationship.

When Macklin suddenly got up and disappeared into the bathroom, Caine told himself not to panic. Macklin hadn't left. He'd gone to get a washcloth to clean them up. When he heard the water running, he relaxed, waiting for the return of the tender lover who had cleaned him so carefully the night in the drover's hut. When the door didn't open immediately, he remembered Macklin's hesitations and made himself wait patiently while his lover attended to his own ablutions before returning. His patience had nearly reached an end before the door finally opened and Macklin came back out, washcloth in hand, to tenderly wipe Caine's stomach clean.

"Sorry it took me so long," Macklin said. "I needed...."

"Did I freak you out again?" Caine asked. "I was hoping it felt too good for that."

Macklin shrugged sheepishly. "It did feel good. It was only after the fact that I lost it a little. I'll get better."

Caine took the washcloth from Macklin's hand and tossed it aside, patting the space on the bed beside him. "If you get any better, you'll kill me."

"I pulled back before you came."

"If you'd stopped and left me hanging, I'd complain," Caine said, "but it took me a long time before I could let someone come in my mouth. It's not a competition, Macklin. If you make me feel good and I make you feel good, how we do it isn't the issue. Although you didn't have to get up to clean me up, you know. I'd have loved it if you licked me clean."

"That's a little too much too fast, pup," Macklin said, "but for you, I might manage it next time."

Caine didn't stop to think about Macklin's taste lingering in his mouth. He simply reached for his lover, pulling him into a deep kiss because that declaration of willingness was tantamount to a declaration of love as far as Caine was concerned. If Macklin didn't feel something for him, something that had the chance at being real and abiding, he wouldn't have said anything at all. He would have stopped with "too much too fast."

The odd look on Macklin's face when they parted, the way he rubbed his tongue across his lips like he had tasted something odd or unexpected, finally registered with Caine. He leaned forward and kissed Macklin again, close-mouthed this time. "That's what you taste like," Caine said. "I'm hoping you'll give me another taste soon."

"If you keep looking at me like that, it won't take long," Macklin said.

As tempted as Caine was to suggest a second round, the sun was above the horizon now, and they had work to do and a five-hour drive ahead of them. "Tonight," he said instead.

"Tonight," Macklin agreed.

SEVENTEEN

BY THE time they loaded the truck with the supplies from Paul and Macklin slipped off to buy condoms, it was nearly lunchtime, so they ate in Boorowa before heading north to Lang Downs. They made decent time, but even so, with unloading the supplies and getting everything put away, it was dinnertime, and Caine hadn't gotten so much as a kiss since they left the hotel room that morning. He bided his time, not wanting to provoke another confrontation with Macklin when a little patience would bring the end of the meal and a chance to have their usual evening beer.

As the men filed out after the meal, Caine followed Macklin toward his cabin, not speaking so he wouldn't draw attention to them but not hiding either. The moment the door closed behind them, he threw himself into Macklin's arms for a fast, hard kiss. "All day is way too long to go without being able to kiss you."

"What are you going to do when we have to spend all day out in the paddocks with the mob?" Macklin asked, his voice rife with amusement.

"Pull you behind one of the piles of rock and kiss you there," Caine replied, stealing a second kiss.

"You didn't get enough of piles of rocks when you ran into that snake?" Macklin teased.

"I'll be more careful next time," Caine insisted. "Unless you have a better suggestion?"

"Right now my suggestion involves less clothing and more privacy," Macklin replied, nudging Caine toward the bedroom. "I swear that box of condoms is haunting me."

Caine grinned even as his stomach curled at the thought of making love with Macklin again. Would he be on his hands and knees, his ass in the air like in his fevered imaginings, or would Macklin prefer some other position? He couldn't wait to find out. "What are we w-waiting for?"

Macklin's grin matched Caine's. "Turned on already, pup?"

Caine flushed at having given himself away with his stutter, but he could hardly deny it. "You have that effect on m-me."

"Good," Macklin replied, his voice so smug Caine smacked him in indignation. "What? Why is it bad to be glad I can turn my lover on with a few words?"

"I d-don't like it when I s-s-stutter," Caine said defensively.

Macklin kissed him so tenderly that Caine melted into the foreman's embrace. "I'm sorry you stutter because I know it makes you uncomfortable, but I'm not sorry I can make you so aroused that you can't control it the way you usually do. Come to bed?"

Caine nodded his agreement, not even Macklin's reassurances enough to make him truly comfortable trying to talk when he knew he wouldn't get a sentence out without stuttering.

Macklin led him down a short hallway to the bedroom where they had slept so peacefully two nights before. Caine didn't expect tonight to be nearly as peaceful, not at first anyway.

Unlike the last time they had come to Macklin's bedroom together, there was no shyness this time, no awkward hesitation as to how the next few minutes would go. Macklin pulled Caine close, hands moving swiftly over his clothes, stripping him to bare skin in seconds. To Caine's surprise, Macklin stepped back after that and let Caine return the favor.

As tempting as it was to rush, Caine ignored the bite of cold air on his skin and took his time pulling Macklin's clothes off, licking, kissing, caressing the skin he revealed, paying special attention to Macklin's nipples and then, as he sank to his knees, to Macklin's cock.

"I thought we were going to use those condoms," Macklin said hoarsely.

"W-we are," Caine promised, "b-b-but I c-can d-d-do this f-first, c-can't I?"

"Not for long," Macklin warned, staring down at Caine with glittering eyes. "I couldn't see you this morning. The sight of you on your knees, your lips stretched around my dick, is almost too much."

Caine didn't try to answer that comment, holding Macklin's gaze as he guided Macklin's cock to his mouth, sucking it as deep as he could.

"Fuck," Macklin ground out, grabbing Caine's arms and all but tossing him onto the bed.

Caine looked back at Macklin over his shoulder and pushed up onto his knees, wiggling his ass in teasing invitation.

"Greedy little bottom," Macklin said again, kneeling on the bed behind Caine. "Do you know what happens to people who tease me?"

"Th-they g-g-get f-f-fucked?" Caine asked hopefully.

"Eventually," Macklin replied, "but first they get teased in return." His hand slid between Caine's legs, fondling his sac and then moving forward to stroke his cock.

Caine dropped his head to his forearms, uncaring of the wanton picture he made, ass sticking up in the air in silent supplication. It was hardly a secret he wanted Macklin to fuck him, and the longer the foreplay went on the better, as far as Caine was concerned. The more aroused he was, the easier it was for him to relax into being topped. He had the random thought that this was maybe the reason he and John had stopped fucking. Caine wasn't ever turned-on enough to enjoy it.

That wouldn't be a problem with Macklin's voice whispering in his ear and Macklin's hand jacking him slowly. He was already leaking onto the quilt, and they'd hardly gotten started.

Then Macklin's thumb pressed against Caine's entrance, and Caine let out a wordless sob. The digit filled his entrance without going deep enough to find his prostate, making him focus completely on his guardian muscle and the stretch of penetration. He lifted his hips more, trying to find a comfortable position. Macklin's thumb followed him, staying right there. "Relax," the raspy voice murmured in his ear. "Get used to the sensation."

Caine tried to do as Macklin said, but his body didn't want to cooperate.

"You're still tense, pup. Turn over," Macklin said, his finger slipping free for a moment.

Caine rolled onto his back. Macklin nudged his legs apart, settling between them and smearing more lube on his fingers. Then his thumb was back, that same awkward feeling of fullness without the additional stimulation, except that this time, Macklin bent his head and licked along Caine's cock. The distraction worked. Caine's muscles relaxed, and the discomfort faded to a tingling awareness instead.

When Macklin lifted his head again, he looked at Caine, his face serious. "How long has it been since someone last fucked you?"

Caine shrugged. "A y-year, m-maybe a l-little more."

"Galah," Macklin muttered. "He had you in his bed and didn't make love to you every chance he got? His loss."

My gain, Caine thought as Macklin leaned up and sucked on his nipples in turn. He tossed on the bed, trying to get Macklin's thumb deeper, but the need to expel the intruder had passed, leaving him aching for more, for Macklin's thick cock.

More came first in the form of a finger joining Macklin's thumb, widening the stretch but hitting Caine's sweet spot at the same time. He cried out at the dual sensation, coming halfway off the bed.

"Okay, pup?" Macklin asked, urging him back onto the mattress and kissing him thoroughly until he relaxed. Macklin's lips moved lower, across his jaw and down over his collarbone. Caine arched into the caress, body thrumming. Macklin tongued one nipple, winning a moan from Caine. Then he took the taut nub between his teeth, the pinch sending another frisson of need down Caine's back.

"Not too rough?" Macklin asked as he released Caine.

Caine shook his head, so Macklin repeated the caress on the other side, his finger and thumb moving in a constant, slow rhythm inside Caine's body. Suddenly a second finger joined the others, pressing hard on his prostate. Caine cried out again, but Macklin soothed him with gentle hands. "Easy, pup. Am I hurting you?"

Caine shook his head vehemently. He appreciated Macklin's diligence in checking with him, but Caine wanted to stop thinking and let go. He wanted Macklin to carry through on the promise of their earlier encounters and take him out of himself and into release. "J-j-j-just f-fuck me already," Caine gasped out.

Macklin shook his head. "No fucking, but I'll make love to you."

The words charmed Caine despite his hurry. Macklin might still be struggling with their relationship, but he wasn't putting it on the same plane as the anonymous encounters in his past. "J-just d-d-do it!"

"Greedy little bottom," Macklin teased. "You're still too tense. Come for me, and I'll give you what you want."

Caine bit back a shout of frustration. He didn't want to come without Macklin. Grabbing Macklin's wrist, he pulled the other man's fingers free. "N-now!"

Macklin looked like he would keep arguing, but after a moment, he put on a condom and moved between Caine's legs. "Do you want to turn over?"

Hands and knees with his ass in the air had been Caine's fantasy, but staring up at Macklin now, he realized this was even better. He shook his head and reached for Macklin, guiding him into place. Macklin moved willingly, pressing against Caine's entrance until his muscle gave and the tip popped through. Caine bit his lip at the intrusion. Macklin's fingers had stretched him, but this was different. Immediately Macklin froze, leaning forward to lick Caine's nipples. "Let me know when it stops hurting."

It didn't actually hurt so much as it stung, but Caine appreciated the moment to catch his breath. Even more than that, he appreciated the obvious concern behind Macklin's offer. Caine didn't know how Macklin treated a casual fuck, but he was getting the hang of how to treat a lover.

The dual stimulation to his nipples and his prostate were enough to keep Caine from giving Macklin permission to move in words, but he tilted his hips so Macklin's cock slid deeper into him. The foreman took that as permission, surging even deeper until he was fully sheathed in Caine's body. "You feel too good," Macklin murmured in Caine's ear. "I'm going to come too fast."

Caine simply bucked his hips harder, urging Macklin to move. He'd proven the night before that even if he came first, he wouldn't leave Caine hanging, and that was good enough for Caine now.

Burying one hand in Macklin's shaggy hair, he pulled his lover down for a kiss. The other hand dug into Macklin's ass, for leverage and encouragement both.

That silent permission given, Macklin stopped holding back, driving into Caine with all the force and fury Caine had imagined. Caine planted his feet on the mattress and met Macklin thrust for thrust, reveling in the clash of bodies as they strove for mutual pleasure. Macklin worked a hand between them, closing his fist around Caine's cock and shunting along its length in time with their movements. Caine threw his head back, a choked cry escaping as his orgasm blindsided him. Macklin pounded into him a few more times, extending Caine's release, and then Macklin was shuddering against him, his hips stuttering as he collapsed on top of Caine.

Caine stroked Macklin's hair and back as their breathing returned to normal. Eventually he felt able to speak again. "You didn't learn to make love like that fucking in an alley."

Macklin shrugged. "No, but I've had a lot of years alone in this bed to dream of what it might be like to have a lover, of what I'd want someone to do to me and what I'd want to do in return. I tried a few of them, and you seemed to like them, so I tried a few more."

Caine leaned up and kissed Macklin tenderly. "Try as many as you like. I won't complain."

"You'll tell me if you don't like something, though, right?"

"Of course," Caine promised. "And you'll let me try a few things out on you too."

"I'll try," Macklin agreed.

Caine figured that was the best he was going to get at this point, so he wriggled out from under Macklin and snuggled against him. Macklin rolled away for a moment to toss the condom, but he kept one hand on Caine's hip as he did, making it clear he wasn't really pulling away. "I guess I should clean us up."

"Use your dirty boxers," Caine said. "I don't want you to move now. We can clean up in the morning."

"You'll have to get up early if you stay," Macklin warned. "You have to be back at your house before anyone else is up."

Caine suppressed a sigh. "I know," he said simply. "I'd rather wake up early than spend the night alone."

"I'll set the alarm."

Caine grimaced when he saw Macklin had set the alarm for four thirty. That was so early Caine almost got up and left, but while he would accept Macklin's need for discretion for a time, he wouldn't accept not sharing a bed with his lover. He'd keep trying to convince Macklin to relax his restrictions, and in the meantime, he'd abide by Macklin's desires. It really was better than sleeping alone.

CAINE grumbled to himself all the way home the next morning in the predawn chill. He had slept poorly, the comfort of Macklin's arms warring with the awareness he would have to wake up in a matter of hours, and so he had jarred himself awake every half an hour or so to check the clock so he wouldn't overstay his welcome. He'd make Macklin sleep in his house tonight so Macklin would have to be the one to get up and leave, not Caine.

Opening the door quietly, Caine slipped through the dark room toward the stairs.

"It's a little early for a walk."

Startled, Caine spun around, searching for the owner of the voice. "K-kami, you scared me."

"If you'd turned on a light instead of skulking around in the dark like a Galah, you would have seen me." Kami switched on the light as he spoke. Caine blinked a couple of times as his eyes adjusted.

"I c-c-couldn't sleep. I went for a w-walk."

Kami pursed his lips and crossed his arms over his broad chest, making Caine feel like a student called before the principal.

Caine looked away guiltily. "I fell asleep at Macklin's house. We were talking and I must have dozed off. I didn't want anyone to get the wrong idea, so I came home when I woke up."

"Seeing you sneaking in at four thirty is far more likely to give people ideas than you walking out of his house at a reasonable hour like you didn't have anything to hide," Kami pointed out, "but I don't believe that's the truth either."

"Why is this your business?" Caine asked.

"Because Macklin's my friend. If you're just messing around, you need to stop now," Kami ordered. "Having the men find out you were fucking around with him would ruin him."

"And if I'm not just f-fucking around?" Caine asked. "If I want history to repeat itself too?"

"Then you need to start acting like you're proud of him and your relationship," Kami advised. "The men respect strength. If you're strong enough to stand up for yourself and for him, they'll shrug and move on. If you act like you have something to be ashamed of, they'll never let you live it down and you'll both be laughingstocks."

"He's the one who's afraid to stand up for us," Caine said softly. "Not me."

"Because he knows what could happen," Kami insisted, "but you're different. You're the boss. They don't have to like you, but they can't drive you off. If you're strong enough to win their respect, Macklin's position won't ever be in doubt, but if they can't respect you, how can they respect him when he's with you?"

"How do I do that?" Caine asked.

"You be yourself," Kami said. "All of yourself. You've got your uncle's strength or you wouldn't have lasted more than a few weeks out here. The men have begun to see that. They don't call you blow-in anymore. Now it's time to let them see the rest of you. That doesn't mean you have to make any big scene. Macklin would skewer us both if you did, but you can't act like you're ashamed of him. No more hiding, Caine, because if they find out without it being on your terms, you'll have a much harder time winning them back over."

"I'll keep that in mind," Caine said. "I have to talk to Macklin first, though. I can't do anything without at least warning him what I intend to do."

"That's fine," Kami said, "but the longer you wait, the harder it will be. Now get upstairs and get cleaned up. I have breakfast to make."

"Thank you, Kami," Caine said, hugging the other man impulsively. "I won't let you or Macklin or Uncle Michael down."

"I don't think you will at that," Kami agreed, patting Caine's back before sending him toward the stairs with a gentle shove.

Caine climbed the stairs and walked into his bedroom, his thoughts racing as he pulled off yesterday's clothes and found something to put on after his shower. He'd known Kami was sympathetic, but he hadn't considered going to the man for advice. Now he wished he'd thought to ask sooner, not that it had really been an issue before now. He walked into the bathroom and turned the water on hot. He needed a plan because he had no real idea how to do what Kami suggested.

The first step, he supposed, would be to let people know he was gay. Coming out had been anticlimactic as a teenager. He had two older cousins, one on each side of his family, who were gay, married now in Massachusetts and Maine, but even before they got married, Caine had their example and his family's acceptance of them to assure him of his own. They had given him the sex talk his parents hadn't known how to give, they'd given him his first box of condoms, and they'd helped him download his first gay porn. In college, he'd joined the Gay Straight Alliance right away, and when he moved to Philadelphia, he'd spent most of his time in the Gayborhood even before he lived there. He wouldn't get the same reaction here.

It didn't matter. The men respected strength, both Kami and Macklin had said repeatedly. Fine. He would be strong and face down their reactions, whatever they were. Maybe he'd lose a few men in the process, but they'd deal with that if it happened. The important thing was not to falter where they could see him. He had to be the strong, confident man he'd never known how to be.

He thought about Macklin, lying in bed, too edgy to make love to him this morning because of the time. He didn't want his life to go that way. He wanted to wake up with his lover, his partner, and make love if they felt like it, or snuggle back beneath the covers and simply hold each other if they didn't feel like making love. He wanted a life with Macklin, and if having that life meant tapping reserves he hadn't known he had before coming to the outback, then that's what he'd do.

Now he just had to figure out how to come out without making it a bigger deal than it needed to be.

EIGHTEEN

MACKLIN wasn't in the canteen when Caine came in for breakfast, but some of the other jackaroos were already heading out, so Caine figured Macklin had come and gone and was already busy somewhere around the station. Caine would see him or not as the day went on. Caine hoped to catch a glimpse of him, maybe even time for a kiss or two, but if not, they would have their evening beer, not that they drank a beer very often these days.

Caine was grateful for his new long underwear when he headed out to the barn. He didn't see Macklin, but a glance in the stalls revealed a definite need for attention. "He told me I'd be shoveling shit," Caine said with a chuckle as he grabbed a pitchfork and the manure cart.

He'd finished three stalls and was starting the fourth when he heard the barn door open. He poked his head out to see who was there. "Hey, Neil."

"I heard a rumor when I was down at Taylor Peak yesterday picking up hay."

Caine sucked in a deep breath, but he remembered what Kami had said and refused to back down or let his nerves show. "Rumors are nasty things."

"Taylor says you're a poof."

"Not the word I'd choose to describe it," Caine said, surprised when the words came out without a stutter. "But if you're asking if I'm gay, then yes."

Neil's face twisted with disgust. "Fucking pillow biters," he spat. "Go back to Sydney or to America where you belong."

"What does me being gay have to do with me being here?" Caine demanded, leaning the pitchfork against the wall and coming out of the stall. He hoped it wouldn't get physical, but he wasn't going to let Neil's comments pass either. The men respected strength, Kami had said. Caine would show them strength. "I either do my job or I don't, no matter who I fantasize about when I'm alone."

"There's no place for sissy-arsed poofters in the outback," Neil insisted.

"Why not?" Caine demanded. "I might not know everything, but I'm pulling my weight around here now. You weren't complaining when I helped with the breeding or when I gave you a break from the cold."

"I didn't know what you were then," Neil retorted.

"I'm the same man now that I was before you knew," Caine pointed out. "The only thing that's changed is your perspective, not who I am or how I'm going to act."

"It better not change how you act," Neil said, advancing on Caine. "If you try anything, I'll put you flat on your arse."

Caine looked Neil over from head to foot. The man wasn't unattractive, other than his attitude, but he wasn't Macklin. "You don't have to worry about that," he said with forced nonchalance. "You're not my type."

"What is your type?" Neil demanded. "Prissy nancy boys? Some flaming shirt lifter?"

"What's going on here?"

Macklin's voice broke through Neil's tirade. Caine was tempted to tell Neil that was his type, a shaggy, sexy foreman who'd made love to Caine like no one else ever had, but he didn't think Macklin would appreciate being outed that way. "Neil and I were just talking."

"We weren't bloody talking," Neil said. "You say things like that, you'll have everyone thinking I'm a poof like you."

"If that isn't the most ignorant thing I've ever heard," Caine said with a shake of his head. "Get back to work, Neil. The sheep won't feed themselves."

"And remember who you're talking about before you go spouting off," Macklin said, his voice hard. "That's the boss you're talking about. If he decides to fire you because you're an ignorant bigot with not enough sense to keep your opinions about him to yourself, you'll have no one but yourself to blame."

"You knew about this?" Neil spat.

Macklin shrugged. "He's not exactly hiding it. He mentioned it the day we met."

"And you didn't think to tell the rest of us?" Neil demanded.

"What business is it of yours?" Caine interrupted, drawing their attention back to him. "I already said you aren't my type, so it's not like I came on to you when you didn't want me to, and even if you were my type, I'm certainly not going to come on to you now. If I make a bad decision, it's because I'm still learning my way around here, not because I'm gay, and if I make a good one, it's because Macklin's taught me well, not because I'm gay. The only person who has any reason to care is the person I'm interested in, and since that *isn't* you, I don't see where this is coming from."

"Bloody poofter," Neil said, storming out and leaving Caine and Macklin alone.

"He didn't hurt you, did he?"

"He said some n-nasty things," Caine said, cursing silently at the return of his stutter, but he didn't have to be strong with Macklin. "That's all."

"I told you it could be rough if the men found out."

"T-taylor told him," Caine said with a shrug. "I'm not going to deny who I am, Macklin. I chose to come out when I was fourteen, and I'm not going back in the closet for anyone. I'll be discreet, but I won't deny who I am."

"He's going to tell the others, and every time you turn around, someone will make a comment," Macklin warned. "They'll make your life hell."

"They can t-try," Caine said with a shrug. "I d-didn't stutter once the entire t-time I was talking with Neil. Not once. I couldn't have done that before I came here. I might have said all the same things, but it would've been broken up. They can say whatever they like. I'm stronger than that now."

"For how long?" Macklin asked seriously. "How long before you decide it's easier not to have to listen to them? How long before you leave?"

"Are we back to this?" Caine asked incredulously. "After last night you can ask me that question?"

"Keep your voice down," Macklin said, his voice a sharp hiss.

"I thought you were g-going to g-give us a chance," Caine said.

"You saw how Neil reacted," Macklin said. "Do you really want to live with that?"

"I'm going to live with it one way or another," Caine replied. "It would be worth living with if you were there with me."

"If we're lucky, most of the men will stay out of loyalty to me and Michael," Macklin said. "If we aren't lucky, they'll leave. We can't risk damaging that loyalty."

"Fuck that," Caine said. "You're scared. Macklin Armstrong, unshakable rock of a foreman, is scared that people will look at him differently if they know he's gay."

"I know they will," Macklin repeated. "You saw Neil's face. You heard what he said."

"He's one man," Caine said. "One prejudiced man. That doesn't mean everyone else will have the same reaction, and even if they do, that's their problem, not ours. Not unless we let it be."

"It's our problem if the station goes under because they leave."

"It all comes back to the station, doesn't it?" Caine said.

"It's all I have," Macklin protested.

"No, it's not all you have," Caine replied. "You have me. Or you could if you'd stop fighting me at every turn."

"You're asking me to risk everything I've spent twenty-five years building for a few nights of sex."

Caine recoiled as if Macklin had struck him, the words so sharp and painful he would have preferred a fist to his face. "Is that r-really all it w-w-was t-to you?"

"That's all it can be out here."

Caine nodded once, gritting his teeth to keep the emotions racking him off his face. "Then I guess there isn't anything else to say. I'll expect an update on the breeding at the end of the week. Good day, Mr. Armstrong."

Keeping his head high, Caine pulled the shreds of his dignity around him and left the barn. He'd come back later for the pitchfork, but he couldn't stay where Macklin was a second longer. He wouldn't beg. He wouldn't cry. He wouldn't let anyone, not even Macklin, see what those few words had done to him. They wanted strength? He'd give them strength.

He made it as far as Uncle Michael's office, shutting and locking the door, though he had to struggle to get the latch to fall into place, before he slumped into the chair and buried his head in his hands. He didn't cry, but he let the despair wash through him. He'd been so certain that Macklin's tenderness and attention to his pleasure had been signs that the other man was coming to care for him. He'd obviously been wrong.

"What do I do now, Uncle Michael?" he asked the empty room. "You lived with a stubborn Aussie foreman. You obviously convinced him it was worth the risk. How do I do the same when he won't even acknowledge we might have something worth taking a risk for?"

He ran his hands through his hair, noticing that it had gotten long since he'd arrived. If he'd thought about it last night, he'd have asked Macklin to cut it for him, but that wasn't an option anymore. Maybe Jason's mother would cut it for him if she was still talking to him after Neil spread the news around the station. He hoped she wouldn't forbid Jason from seeing him, but he'd live with it if she did. He'd live with it the same way he'd live with Macklin's choice: this was his life now, and he wouldn't let their prejudices run him off.

Firing up the computer, he went back to searching for sources of organic hay in their area so they could move forward on the organic certification while they were looking at producing their own feed for the sheep.

CAINE worked right through lunch, a fact he excused by reminding himself that a lot of the jackaroos choose not to come in from the fields for lunch. He couldn't ignore dinner, though, and not merely because his stomach wouldn't let him. He was sure Neil had told the entire station about his sexuality by now, and if Caine didn't show up for dinner, they would view that as a sign of weakness for sure. He might spend the entire meal at a table eating by himself, but he would be there. They would see he wasn't ashamed of who he was or cowed by their opinions of him.

Kami had a rare smile for him as he handed him a plate, making Caine wonder just how bad it really was if Kami was trying to be supportive. He took a seat and started eating, not really looking around. A moment later, Jason plopped down next to him.

"Hi, Caine. I didn't see you working outside today."

"I was working on the organic certification application," Caine explained. "I didn't get a chance to come out and see what you were up to."

"Schoolwork as usual," Jason said, "and pretending I couldn't hear my dad arguing with Neil."

"What were they arguing about?" Caine asked, sure he knew the answer.

"You," Jason said. "Dad told Neil to keep his mouth shut because if he was too mean to you, you might leave and sell the place and we could all end up working for someone like Devlin Taylor."

"And your dad thinks working for someone like Mr. Taylor would be worse than working for me?" Caine asked.

"Oh, for sure," Jason replied. "You care about Lang Downs. You might not know everything about sheep, but you're trying to learn and trying to make improvements. Mr. Taylor doesn't care about anything but the money in his pocket, and that's not good for any of us. Have you seen Taylor Peak?"

"Excuse me, boss."

Caine looked up to see Ian, another of the jackaroos, standing in front of his table, hat in hand. "Yes?"

"One of the rams busted out of the pen this afternoon. We rounded him up, but we're still missing a few of the ewes. We searched for them, but we haven't found them yet."

"Thanks for telling me," Caine said. "Have you told Macklin?"

"We haven't seen him all day," Ian replied. "What do you want us to do about the missing sheep?"

"It's getting dark," Caine said. "Searching for them now isn't going to do any good. We'll look again in the morning. If you see Macklin, make sure to tell him as well."

"Will do, boss," Ian said, walking away with a nod of his head.

"Ian thinks you're a better boss than Taylor would be too," Jason confided in a whisper. "Dad said Neil was a stupid Galah and I shouldn't listen to him."

"I hope he's not the only one who feels that way," Caine muttered.

"Being gay doesn't have anything to do with how you run the station," Jason said with a shrug. "You're a good boss. Even I can see that."

"Does that mean your dad's okay with me being gay?" Caine asked.

"I don't know about that," Jason said, "but he said it wasn't any of his business as long as you didn't go bothering him or me or anybody that didn't think the same as you. I told him you weren't like that."

"No, I'm not like that," Caine agreed. Since Jason was willing to talk, he took a deep breath and asked, "Are there others who feel like Neil?"

"I don't know," Jason said. "I don't get why it matters so much. I mean, sure, if you were trying to do stuff to me, I could understand people being upset, but you wouldn't do that. Who cares who you fall in love with?"

"I don't know why Neil cares," Caine replied honestly. "Some people say it's against their religion and that makes it wrong. Some people say it's unnatural and that makes it wrong. I say God doesn't make mistakes and it doesn't feel unnatural to me, so it obviously isn't wrong as long as I respect the preferences of the people around me. That includes other gay men who might not be attracted to me, not just straight men."

"Well, duh," Jason said. "That would be the same for me if I liked a girl. If she didn't like me back, I'd have to deal with it and move on."

"Exactly," Caine said. "The only difference is that I'm going to look for a cute guy to like instead of a cute girl."

"Dad's right. Neil's a Galah. Don't listen to him."

"I won't," Caine assured him. "I just hope nobody else listens to him either."

"I don't know about that, but nobody's making anyone stay here. I mean, if someone doesn't like you, they can just leave, and you can hire someone who won't care to take their places."

"I sure hope it'll work that way," Caine said.

"Boss? Did Ian tell you about the sheep getting loose?"

"He did," Caine said, looking up to see Kyle standing on the other side of the table. "I told him we'd look for the stragglers tomorrow."

"That's not the only problem. I was fixing the pen where they busted out. I think they might have had help."

"Did you get the pen fixed?" Caine asked. He hated to think someone had deliberately sabotaged their fences, but he had to think about the sheep first.

"No worries about that, boss," Kyle said. "We completely replaced the broken section. They won't get out through there again."

"Okay, then let's go look at what you found," Caine said, standing up and putting his plate with the other dishes to be washed. "Jason, are you coming with us?"

Jason stacked his plate with the others and ran after Caine and Kyle, his face so joyous that Caine ruffled his hair affectionately.

"Can't get a real man, boss?" Caine spun around at hearing Neil's accusation. The jackaroo stood on the veranda of the canteen with a couple of other men.

Before he could answer, Jason flew at Neil. "How dare you say something like that? Caine has been nothing but nice to me since he got here, and he hasn't ever done anything inappropriate."

"You're wasting your breath, Jason," Caine said, dismissing Neil completely. He could argue with someone like that until he was blue in the face, but nothing he said would register. It wasn't worth the effort. "He isn't going to hear what you say. Your parents know we're friends and they don't mind. Neil can think what he wants."

"That's really low, Neil," Kyle added. "Just because he's a poof, it doesn't make him a pedophile. Get over yourself."

At least one hand besides Jason's father didn't seem to care about his sexuality. He hoped there would be others, but he didn't have time to worry about that now. He needed to see about the potential sabotage.

"Show me the damage to the fence," Caine said to Kyle, leading Jason away from where Neil and his cronies stood.

Kyle led Caine to the outmost pen where the ewes had been separated for breeding. They grazed peacefully, oblivious to the excitement they had caused earlier in the day. Kyle pointed to the far side of the pen. "This is the section we repaired. You can see the slats are new. These are the slats that broke."

Caine examined the wood Kyle handed him. The boards showed all the ragged edges to be expected when wood cracked under force. "I obviously don't see what you're seeing."

"Look here," Kyle said. "The wood broke, but do you see that hole? It looks like something bored through it. That could have weakened it enough to break. And they all have marks like that in the same spot. On one slat, maybe it was a hungry insect, but the same spot on four boards is suspicious."

"I agree," Caine said. "I'm going to take this one with me. Any idea who would have done something like this?"

"Yesterday, I would have said Taylor," Kyle replied immediately. "After today, I could add a few names closer to home."

"He's a bigoted Galah, to borrow a phrase, but that doesn't mean he'd resort to sabotaging the station," Caine said, "and wouldn't someone have seen him if he'd done it in broad daylight?"

"Maybe," Kyle said, "but with just the year-rounders here, the station isn't exactly swarming with people. We trust the pens to keep the sheep safe since the dingoes don't come down into the valley unless the weather gets a lot worse in the highlands, which means no one was actually standing watch. If he timed it right, he could have done it today."

"Couldn't he have done it last night?" Jason asked. "Or a week ago for that matter."

"He didn't know I was gay until this morning," Caine said. "If that's his reason for doing this, that is. He said he heard a rumor yesterday at Taylor Peak, but he didn't confront me until this morning. If it wasn't him or that wasn't the reason, then yes, I suppose it could have been done at any time."

"And then when something spooked the sheep, they charged the fence and it gave way," Kyle concluded. "He, whoever he is, wouldn't have to be anywhere nearby and it would probably look like an accident and no one would be any the wiser."

"I need to talk to Macklin," Caine said, stomach churning at the thought of going to Macklin's cabin, where they had made love so tenderly the night before. "He needs to know what's going on. Jason, could you find him and ask him to come to the big house so I can talk to him?"

"Sure, Caine," Jason said, running off.

"In the meantime," Caine said to Kyle, "it's too late to check the other fences tonight. Is it worth setting a watch to make sure no other sheep get loose or that the person responsible doesn't try again?"

"You're the boss," Kyle said. "If you think it needs to be done, we'll do it."

Caine stifled a sigh that would surely be misunderstood. Macklin wouldn't hesitate. Macklin would order done whatever needed to be done. Taking a deep breath, Caine nodded. "Set a watch tonight," he said. "Two men at a time for an hour each. That way they can take breaks to get warm, and it won't be too long for anyone. We'll check the other fences first thing in the morning."

"Yes, boss," Kyle said.

Caine grinned. "Give Neil the 2 a.m. shift."

Kyle grinned back. "With pleasure, boss."

NINETEEN

CAINE paced the living room of the big house, waiting for Macklin to arrive. He didn't think the foreman would refuse a direct request to come talk to him, especially if Jason explained any of what he'd seen or heard in relation to the pen and the sheep, but he didn't expect Macklin to be happy about it.

When the door slammed open and then closed, he discovered how right he was. "You wanted to see me?"

No "pup", no "Caine", not even "boss", just that one terse sentence.

"We have one problem, we may have two," Caine said, struggling to keep his voice steady. If Macklin didn't want to be his lover, then Macklin didn't get to see his vulnerability anymore either.

"Besides Neil?"

"He might be part of it, but it's more than that," Caine said. "Ian said some sheep got out of their pen today, and they couldn't find all of them before it got dark, and then Kyle came to tell me he didn't think it was an accident that they got out. He showed me the boards they busted through, and it looks like someone drilled a hole in them to weaken them. Less obvious than using a saw on them but still enough to allow the sheep to break free."

"You think Neil's responsible? Until this morning, he's been a model employee."

"I didn't say he was responsible," Caine replied immediately. "I think Taylor is a much more likely suspect, although I don't know how we'd prove it unless we can catch him or one of his men in the act of sabotaging something, but I think we have to consider the fact that Neil is pretty disillusioned at the moment. He practically accused me of molesting Jason a few minutes ago. Jason jumped to my defense and Kyle told him to stuff it, but wherever his prejudice comes from, it's pretty strong."

"So what are you going to do about it?"

Caine's jaw clenched at the choice of words. Macklin hadn't even treated him this way when he first arrived at Lang Downs. "I asked Kyle to set a watch through the night in case whoever did it comes back and tries again. I told Ian we'd search for the missing sheep in the morning. That said, if you have suggestions, I'd like to hear them."

"That's pretty much what I would have done," Macklin said.

"Not all the men reacted the way Neil did," Caine said softly when Macklin didn't say anything else. "Ian and Kyle are still calling me boss like they always have, and they brought the problems to me when you weren't around. Kyle even told Neil to stuff it when he made the pedophile comment. And Jason said his dad didn't mind Jason and me being friends."

"Just drop it," Macklin said, his voice flat. "We said everything we needed to say this morning."

"Did we?" Caine asked. "I don't want to lose you."

"I'm not going anywhere."

"Really?" Caine asked. "Then come over here and prove it. Kiss me, or better yet, come upstairs with me and make love to me again. Spend the night in my bed and come down to breakfast at my side."

"You're asking for things I can't give you."

"Won't give me, you mean," Caine insisted. "You can do those things because you did them when we were in Boorowa. I won't hide, Macklin. The men are shocked right now, but in the long run, they'll respect me far more for being honest and not hiding who I am. If we skulk around and they find out about it, then it's a dirty secret. If we're proud of who we are and what we are to each other, they'll accept it because it simply is. Isn't that what you said happened with Uncle Michael and Donald?"

"I can't discuss this tonight," Macklin said, going to the door. "I'll make sure Kyle has the watch set for the night."

He was out the door before Caine could stop him.

"Well, fuck," Caine muttered.

"He's a stubborn one," Kami said from the door to the kitchen hall.

"How much did you hear?" Caine asked, embarrassed.

"Not much. Enough to hear him dismiss your logic," Kami replied.

"Your logic," Caine reminded him. "So what do I d-do now?"

"You give him a few days to see that the world hasn't come to an end because the jackaroos know about you," Kami said. "He'll come around."

"How do you know?"

"I've known that man for twenty-five years, and I've never seen him act like he has since you arrived. He may not be willing to say it, but he can't stop thinking about you."

"That's not the same as loving me," Caine said. "If he can't do that, if he *won't* do that, it doesn't matter how often he thinks about me."

"If he's thinking about you that much, he's fallen in love with you," Kami assured him. "He just doesn't know it yet."

"I hope you're right."

ALONE in bed later that night, Caine struggled to hold on to Kami's reassurances. The doubts that had always plagued him were stronger in the darkness, making him all the more aware of the empty space next to him, a space he had hoped Macklin would fill. Perhaps not every night, but most nights. If Macklin had been on watch or out with the sheep for some reason, Caine wouldn't be nearly as troubled by his absence. It would be a temporary one, related to work, not to Macklin's desire to be with him. His absence tonight had nothing to do with work and everything to do with Macklin's desire to be with him.

Unfortunately.

Caine forced himself to consider the possibility that Kami was wrong, that Macklin wouldn't come around if Caine gave him enough time. Caine didn't want to leave Lang Downs despite his promise to Macklin that he would leave rather than make the foreman go, which begged the question of whether they could coexist as colleagues at the station after having spent three nights together as lovers.

Caine wanted to believe they could. He wanted to think they could be adults and act courteously to each other even if they never regained the ease they'd had with each other in the first month Caine was at Lang Downs. Macklin hadn't refused to come speak to Caine today about the missing sheep, and he hadn't dismissed Caine's decisions. It wasn't the same camaraderie from their evenings drinking beer on Macklin's veranda or in his living room, but it was proof they could have a working relationship.

So he could stay, but he wouldn't have a lover and partner at his side to support him the way he'd started to dream of having with Macklin. He could follow Macklin's example of going to Sydney or Melbourne once or twice a year if the loneliness got to be too much, although he'd never been a fan of one-night stands. Still, the touch of any hand had to be better than his own. He could be open to the possibility that his orientation being public would bring others to the station who shared it. They wouldn't be Macklin—a thought that tore at his heart—but he might find someone else who would be willing to be his partner openly the way he desired.

The disloyalty of that thought left him feeling ill. They hadn't even been separated twenty-four hours, and he was already thinking about someone else. So maybe he wouldn't find a partner the way Uncle Michael had. Not everyone did. Some people filled their lives with work and close friends and a kind of extended, adopted family. He certainly had that with Jason. Given enough time, he might even have it with some of the other men at the station. If it was less than he'd begun to hope he might have, it was still more than he'd had in Philadelphia.

He ran his hand down his stomach. The softness that had plagued him all his life was gone. In a few short months, he'd gone from being a soft city boy to having muscles, not from the gym but from living his life in the outback. If a few months could do that, what would a few years do? Living in the outback had transformed more than his body.

He had argued with Neil that morning without stuttering once. He didn't believe for a moment that he'd never stutter again, but the confidence he'd felt as he faced down the jackaroo and his prejudices was new. He'd never had that kind of nerve before coming to Lang Downs.

He was making a life for himself, a good life, one that he could be proud of regardless of whether he had a lover to share it with him. The passage of years would only make that better as he grew even more confident with himself and his role at Lang Downs. If they could get the organic certification, he could proudly say he'd taken his uncle's legacy and built on it even more than simply maintaining it. He could make plans to set it up as a trust so that after he was gone, the station would become a joint venture of the families who had invested so much of themselves in it, or maybe he could look into adopting a child to take over the station after his death. The possibilities were limitless, even without Macklin at his side. His life would be richer with someone to share it—he had no doubt about that—but he could do this alone. He could have a life at Lang Downs as Caine Neiheisel, not as Michael Lang's nephew or Macklin Armstrong's lover, but simply as himself.

"I don't know what the future holds, Uncle Michael," Caine said into the darkness, "but I'm not going to let falling in love with Macklin when he doesn't feel the same way keep me from being happy. It might not be what you had with your Donald, but I'm going to make this work."

CAINE went down to breakfast early the next morning, determined to carry out his resolutions of the night before. Macklin wasn't in the canteen, but several of the men spoke to Caine as he came in, making him feel better about the reaction of the year-rounders as a whole.

Caine grabbed a cup of coffee and some breakfast. He would eat first and let the men finish their meals, and then he would check in with the ones who had stood watch during the night and give orders for the day.

If Macklin came in while he was eating, Caine would consult with him, but Caine refused to sit around dilly-dallying like he couldn't do anything without Macklin's approval. He'd just finished his breakfast when Kyle came in. "Morning, boss," he said. "We set the watch like you said."

"Good," Caine replied. "Get something to eat and then we'll talk about it."

Macklin walked in a moment later. Caine nodded politely in his direction, making no move to invite him over but not pretending he didn't see the foreman either. They were colleagues; Macklin was his foreman. That relationship had to abide.

Kyle came back with his plate, obviously torn between reporting to Caine and reporting to Macklin as he had always done. "Macklin," Caine called, "Kyle wants to give us his report from the night watch. Why don't you join us?"

Both men looked at him in surprise, but Caine simply waited until they had both joined him at the table before gesturing for Kyle to begin.

"It was pretty quiet," Kyle said. "The only person who reported seeing anything was Ian, but he was pretty sure it was just a pair of dingoes checking out the valley from the ridge."

"Is it normal for dingoes to come that close?" Caine asked, looking at Macklin.

"Not normal, but not unheard of," Macklin replied. "It means it's cold and snowy up at the higher elevations, and they've come down looking for food. They'll have to get pretty hungry before they'll come into the valley, even with the lure of the sheep. There are too many people around."

"But it means the sheep that got loose yesterday will be easy prey for them," Caine concluded. "Kyle, find Ian and have him come to my office. We need to know where he found the sheep that got loose and where he looked for the strays he couldn't find."

"Yes, boss," Kyle said, gulping the last of his coffee and hurrying off to do Caine's bidding.

"I'll need your help organizing the search," Caine said to Macklin. "I don't know the station as well as you do."

"I was beginning to wonder if you still needed me at all," Macklin said, his voice bitter. "You certainly took charge well enough this morning."

"Not here," Caine said, heading toward his office. Macklin followed more slowly. When they were alone, Caine faced Macklin and took a deep breath, trying to put his revelations of the night before in words that would explain without shutting any doors forever. "I would be happy to have you as my partner," he began slowly. "That hasn't changed and probably won't change, but that's not what you asked me. You're worried about your job and the life you've built here, the one that's so important you can't risk it. We're both adults. We can continue to work together as boss and foreman, but I *am* the boss and I need to act like it. Not for the men, not for us, but for me. I will always listen to your advice and probably always follow it because I don't have your experience, but I need to make decisions and be involved and be the leader this station deserves, and that means you have to accept me too."

A knock on the door interrupted them, but Caine ignored it for a moment. "Can you do that?"

"Answer the door, boss," Macklin said. "We have a search to organize."

Caine let out a sigh of relief. If Macklin had refused his offer, Caine would have found a way to keep going, but knowing he had the other man's support with the station relieved the one fear he had left. He called for Ian to come in.

They spent the next half an hour listening to Ian's report and dividing the nearest paddocks into quadrants so they could search for the missing sheep. Caine and Macklin divided the hands into groups of two and sent them out to search with orders to check in every hour and to find a drover's hut for a break at lunch. It was too cold to be out for longer than that without the opportunity to warm up again. A couple of times, he thought he caught an admiring expression on Macklin's face, and once he even thought he saw a hint of wistfulness, but the emotions were always quickly hidden the moment Macklin realized he was looking.

They found the sheep that afternoon, cold and straggly but seemingly unharmed. Caine stood across the pen from Macklin, overseeing their return, the gulf between them feeling insurmountable.

TWENTY

THREE weeks later, Kyle came in to Caine's office, his face grave. "You need to come see this, boss. I sent Ian to find Macklin. It happened again."

"What happened?" Caine asked.

"A broken fence, a drilled hole in the boards," Kyle said. "I sent everyone else out to round up as many sheep as we could as quickly as possible. This late in June, you never know when a storm will pop up."

They walked out to the pens where the sheep spent the winter. The one that had trouble previously was fine, but one of the pens on the south side of the valley had a fence down. Ian and Macklin arrived at almost the same time as Caine and Kyle.

"Look here," Kyle said, picking up the damaged wood and showing it to Caine and Macklin. "It's the same as the last time. Someone is damaging our fences deliberately."

"But who?" Caine said. "And why?"

"That isn't important right now," Macklin interrupted. "Yes, we need to figure it out, but first we have to get the fence repaired and the sheep back in their pen. I don't like the look of those clouds."

Sure enough, dark clouds hovered on the horizon to the west of the station. "Macklin's right," Caine said. "We'll worry about the whos and whys later. You said you'd already sent everyone else out after the sheep. That means we get to repair the fence."

"Get started," Macklin ordered. "I'm going to ride out and check on the others."

Caine felt the rejection keenly. He and Macklin had managed to avoid each other most of the time and remain cordial to each other when they couldn't, but it was obvious to everyone that the camaraderie of Caine's early days on the station was gone. None of the jackaroos had worked up the nerve to ask Caine about it, and he was sure they hadn't dared ask Macklin, but Caine could see the question on their faces each time Macklin made an excuse not to work with Caine.

Over the next few hours as Caine, Kyle, and Ian repaired the fence, jackaroos rode back in, driving a few sheep at a time before them. "Why are they so scattered?" Caine finally asked. "I thought they usually stayed pretty clumped together for warmth and protection."

"We saw dog prints," Ben replied. "If they got out of the valley and ran into a pack of feral dogs, they would have run in any and every direction they could. It could take days to find them all."

"Days we don't have if that storm keeps moving in," Kyle said.

"We'll do what we have to do," Caine insisted. "The fence is ready. Kyle, Ian, I think it's time for us to ride out too."

The rain held off until three that afternoon. The jackaroos put on their drizabones and kept right on searching for the missing sheep, but when it had not abated by the next day and got steadily worse, Caine had enough. He could barely feel his fingers on Titan's reins, and he couldn't imagine anyone else was faring better.

"We're not doing anything in this mess but risking out own lives," he declared. "Call everyone back in."

"Yes, boss," Kyle said, pulling out the radio and passing on Caine's orders. The radio crackled as replies came back, acknowledging Caine's decision.

The ground was muddy, even boggy in places, the horses' hooves squelching in the mud as they struggled to keep their footing on the steeper inclines. At one point, Caine jumped off Titan and let the horse find his own path to the bottom of a bad hill. He knew there was a risk the horse would bolt, but since he was sure they wouldn't make it down the hill together, it was a risk he decided to take. Fortunately, Titan waited for him at the bottom of the hill. Caine remounted, and they continued on toward home when Kyle's radio crackled to life again.

"It's Neil, boss. He says he can't get back. He's going to wait it out in the drover's hut near the western boundary fence."

"Tell him to radio in every fifteen minutes until he gets there," Caine ordered. "I can deal with losing sheep. I won't lose men."

Kyle relayed the order. Neil checked in once before he radioed back to say the hut was cut off as well.

"Bloody hell," Caine cursed, Macklin's favorite phrase slipping out of his mouth without conscious thought. "Kyle, do you know more or less where he is?"

"More or less," Kyle said.

"Okay, what's keeping him from getting home?"

"Floods," Kyle said. "There's a run-off gully he'd have to cross that can fill up fast in weather like this. Without a guide to get across, he's stuck on the other side."

"And how do we give him a guide?"

"Two strong ropes to create a passage so he doesn't get swept downstream if his horse loses his footing."

Caine looked down at the length of rope on his saddle. "I've got one. You've got one. Is anyone closer to him than us?"

"No."

"Then let's go. I meant it when I said I wasn't losing men, and it's too wet and cold for him to survive out here without shelter."

"Are you sure, boss? We could radio in to the station, have someone ride out."

"We're a good hour from the station, probably more at the rate we're riding, and Neil's farther out than we are," Caine pointed out. "That's time for the weather to get worse, the floods to get worse, and Neil to get hypothermia. Tell them what we're doing and where we're going. Have them send help if they can, but we can't afford to wait."

"Okay, boss," Kyle said. "Let's go." Kyle talked as he rode, leading Caine back into the outback. Caine could hear the shouts as Macklin protested their decision, but Caine refused to listen. Neil needed help, and Caine could give it.

"He's going to tear you a new one when we get back."

"If we all get back in one piece, he can yell all he wants," Caine replied.

It took longer than Caine expected to reach the flooded gully that had Neil trapped. Then they had to ride along it until they could find Neil and a place where they could secure the ropes to create a guide.

"You all right, Neil?" Caine called above the noise of the rushing water.

"A little cold, but nothing I can't handle."

"You're about to get wetter, if not colder," Caine warned, "but I don't see any other option."

"No worries. A little water isn't going to hurt me."

They all knew it was a lie as they watched the flood waters race down the mountain. "Any idea how deep it is?" Caine asked.

"A good meter would be my guess," Kyle said, "maybe even a meter and a half in places. Too deep for a man to cross on foot. The problem for the horses isn't the depth but the current."

"So how do we get the rope across?"

"If Macklin were here, he'd ride that bloody-minded beast of his across," Kyle said. "Nothing fazes that horse."

"Well, he's not here, and we don't know when or if he will be. Any other suggestions?"

"We can try tossing it across. It might be heavy enough to go the distance."

"It's worth a try," Caine said.

Kyle took the coil of thick rope from his saddle and tied one end to a tree along the bank. He threw the other end toward Neil, but it fell short, landing in the water. Kyle pulled it back in and tried again, but laden with water, it fell even closer to the near bank the second time.

"Give it to me," Caine said, "and tie the other one as well. I'm only doing this once."

"Boss, I'm not sure this is a good idea."

"Neither am I," Caine admitted, "but I won't ask someone else to do something I'm not willing to do myself. Tie one end to the tree and the other end to me. That way you can pull me out if you have to."

Kyle looked like he wanted to argue more, but he did as Caine requested, knotting the dry rope around Caine's waist and to the same tree as the first rope. "Okay, Titan," Caine said, patting the gelding's neck, "Macklin said you were a good, steady mount who knew what you were doing. He hasn't been wrong yet. Take good care of me, buddy."

Titan shook his mane and snorted, prancing a little when Caine directed him into the water, but with enough prodding, he started across the flooded gully. The water rose over Caine's boots, soaking his feet and calves as they crossed. Titan lost his footing once but regained it before he pitched Caine into the water. Then suddenly they were at the other side.

Caine handed Neil the other end of the wet rope. "Tie it around your waist. It's not what Kyle suggested, but if I have to choose between saving you and saving the horse, the choice is to save you."

"I'm sorry for all the names I called you, boss," Neil said. "You didn't have to come back out here to help me. You didn't have to risk your life to save mine. I won't give you any more trouble. From here on out, I'm your man."

Caine nodded. "Good to know. Now, we're both soaked and those waters are still rising while we sit here talking. Get across."

"What about you?"

"I'm right behind you," Caine promised. "I'm ready to be home and dry."

"On my way, boss."

Caine waited until Neil was halfway across the gully before he urged Titan back toward the water. The horse balked more firmly this time. "I know," Caine said, patting the animal's neck reassuringly. "I don't really want to get back in there either, but it's the only way to get home. The sooner you get across, the sooner we can both get dry."

By the time Titan moved into the water, Neil and his horse were climbing free on the other side. Caine turned his attention back to Titan, steadying him as best he could, doing everything he knew how to keep the horse calm. They had almost reached the far bank when a branch from upstream crashed into Titan's legs. The gelding reared, unseating Caine as he bolted for the bank.

Caine went under, struggling to find his footing in the rough water. A second later, the rope around his chest pulled tight. He held on with both hands, swimming as best he could in his soaked clothes and heavy coat. Within minutes, hands were pulling him to shore.

"Bloody hell, Caine Neiheisel! Of all the fucking stupid things...."

Then hot lips covered his, and Caine nearly sobbed in relief. Macklin was here, holding him, cursing at him, kissing him like he'd never let go. Somebody let out a wolf whistle, but Macklin ignored it, the kiss continuing, deepening even, as if Macklin had to prove to himself Caine was still there with him.

When Macklin finally lifted his head, Caine had to catch his breath.

"Um, boss?"

"Get Neil home," Macklin ordered, not waiting for Caine to speak. "Kyle, check Titan's legs and take him with you. I'll see to Caine."

"I bet you will," one of the men laughed.

"Shut it," Neil snapped. "Caine saved my life. I don't want to hear anybody saying anything about this."

"G-g-go home," Caine ordered, the cold seeping into his bones and making him shiver. "Everybody."

"You're soaked through," Macklin said. "You aren't going to make it home if we don't get you warm."

"How do you suggest we do that?" Caine asked. "It's raining. Everything is soaked."

"Ride with me," Macklin said. "You can wrap my drizabone around you too. It won't be perfect, but it will get us home."

"Neil might b-bully Kyle and the two who came with you into silence, but if we ride into the station with me wrapped in your coat, there won't be any hiding it anymore."

"I'm done hiding," Macklin said, urging Caine toward his horse. "I nearly lost you today. That puts things in perspective." He helped Caine up onto the back of his horse. Caine shivered as the wind picked up. Then Macklin mounted behind him, folding him in the warmth of his coat. "Let's go home."

Even with Macklin's body heat and the extra drizabone, Caine was so cold by the time they reached the station that every inch of his body hurt and he couldn't stop his teeth from chattering. Macklin swung down from the saddle, pulling Caine into his arms. "Jason, take care of Ned!" he snapped, striding toward the main house with Caine still in his arms.

"Yes, sir!" Jason called back as Macklin crossed the veranda and went into the living room.

"Kami! He needs coffee!"

Caine turned his head enough to see the cook's horrified expression as he raced to the kitchen.

"Bring it upstairs," Macklin shouted down the hallway as he carried Caine up the stairs to the big bathroom. "Can you stand?" he asked Caine tenderly.

Caine nodded, bracing himself on the wall as Macklin set him down and turned on the hot water in the tub. Caine flinched. As much as he wanted to be warm, he knew how much it would hurt at first.

"Come on, Cay," Macklin said. "Let's get you out of these wet clothes."

The new nickname surprised Caine. He'd gotten used to "pup," but he wasn't coherent enough to ask Macklin about it right now. He tried to help with his clothes, but his fingers had lost all coordination. They'd managed to peel off the drizabone and boots when Kami came rushing in with a thermos of coffee. "There's more downstairs, boss," he said. "Just yell down and I'll bring it up to you."

"Thanks, Kami," Macklin said, waiting until the cook had left to strip off the last of Caine's clothes. "Okay, Cay, into the water."

"It's g-g-going to hurt," Caine grumbled.

"Yes, but it's better than hypothermia," Macklin said, "and it's the fastest way to get you warm."

"You c-c-could take me t-t-to b-bed," Caine proposed.

"I will," Macklin promised. "As soon as I'm sure you're warm again. Go on. I'll even join you."

That was incentive enough for Caine to dip his toe in the water. It burned as he'd known it would, but even in the warm bathroom, he was shivering so hard he could barely stand. He forced himself to climb into the tub, hissing through the pain as he lowered himself into the water. Then Macklin was there with him, holding him, steadying him, encouraging him to relax and let the pain pass.

Caine leaned back against the strong chest, still shivering. Macklin soothed him, running his hands over as much of Caine's body as he could reach, rubbing his skin to help relax his muscles and increase his circulation. Caine's eyes drifted closed.

"Open your eyes, Cay," Macklin prompted. "You can't go to sleep until I know you're all warmed up."

Caine struggled to keep his eyes open, but lethargy had settled in, making him so sleepy.

"Caine!" Macklin said sharply. "Come on, don't do this to me. Open your eyes and drink some of the coffee Kami made for you."

Caine opened his mouth, even if he couldn't quite open his eyes. The coffee warmed his insides, and the caffeine helped stimulate him as well. He forced his eyes open to meet Macklin's worried stare. "I'm ok-k-kay."

"Not yet, you aren't, but you will be," Macklin promised, pulling Caine into his arms again. "I won't let you be anything else."

Caine burrowed deeper into the embrace, the shivers finally easing somewhat. "S-so what happens n-now?" he asked.

"I take you to bed and make love to you until neither of us can see straight," Macklin said. "And then when I'm done with that, I'll beat you black and blue for doing such a bloody stupid thing in the first place."

"What would you have done?" Caine demanded, not pulling away because it felt too good to be held, but tipping his head up so he could look Macklin in the eyes. "If you'd been in my shoes, with Neil trapped on the other side of that gully with no way to get to shelter, what would you have done?"

"Tossed him a rope," Macklin said.

"We tried. We couldn't get it across the gully to him. Would you really have left him there?"

"No," Macklin replied, "but I'm a better rider than you, and I'm used to Ned."

"Titan and I were doing fine until that branch hit us," Caine retorted. "And we put the rope around me precisely so we'd have a safety net if something did happen. Yes, it was dangerous, but it was also necessary, so don't yell at me about it."

"You aren't stuttering anymore," Macklin observed. "You must be warming up."

Caine wasn't sure if that was an admission on Macklin's part concerning the logic of his argument or simply a change of subject, but he was too relieved to have Macklin there with him to worry about it now. They could argue about it later if Macklin insisted. "Warm enough to exchange the tub for the bed?" he asked hopefully.

"I think that could be arranged," Macklin said, standing and pulling Caine to his feet as well. With the chill gone and the air cleared between them, Caine became suddenly aware of the hard cock pressing against his belly as Macklin held him close. Feeling bold, Caine slid a hand between them, circling both their cocks and stroking them together. "Bloody hell, that feels good."

"Then dry me off and take me to bed so I can do it some more," Caine proposed.

Macklin grabbed a towel, drying Caine thoroughly and lingering over his nipples, cock, and ass, much to Caine's delight. Even better, Macklin let him return the favor. Caine wanted to take his time and linger, but even in the steam-filled bathroom and with dry skin, he started feeling chilled again. "T-time for b-bed."

"Cold or horny?" Macklin asked.

"B-both," Caine replied, leading Macklin down the hall to the room he'd claimed as his own, although if Macklin agreed to move in with him, they'd have to use the master bedroom to have enough space.

"Horny is good," Macklin said, switching on the heater in Caine's room. "Cold is not. Get under the covers. I have to go back out. The lube and condoms are in my cabin."

"I have that little tube of lube," Caine said. "It's in my backpack."

"That doesn't take care of the condoms."

"When were you last tested?" Caine asked.

"A couple months before you got here," Macklin replied, every muscle in his body visibly tense. "You aren't suggesting…."

"Why not?" Caine asked. "Was your test negative?"

Macklin nodded.

"So was mine. I got tested when I had my physical before I came here, after John and I broke up. You just kissed me in front of a bunch of jackaroos and then carried me inside when we got back to the station," Caine pointed out. "You can't go back in the closet now. You're out, and if that wasn't a declaration of commitment, I don't know what would be. I don't see the problem here."

"One more thing I've never done," Macklin admitted.

Caine smiled slowly. "I'll enjoy showing you what you've been missing."

Caine could see the shiver of desire that went through Macklin at the words. "Where's the lube? Once I get in that bed, I'm not getting out any time soon."

"In my backpack," Caine said. "In the toiletries kit."

Macklin found what he was looking for and stalked toward the bed, everything in his expression and body language sending frissons of desire through Caine. He opened his arms and pulled Macklin down on top of him.

"Don't scare me like this again," Macklin ordered, bracketing Caine's head with his forearms as he hovered over Caine. "You won't like the results."

"Don't send me out with one of the other jackaroos when I should be out with you," Caine retorted, lifting his head to kiss Macklin lightly. Macklin's tongue surged into his mouth the moment their lips met, taking possession of Caine's senses with a masterful touch. Caine let his head fall back to the pillow, unable to support its weight with Macklin bearing down on him. Macklin followed, never letting up on the kiss as he explored every inch of Caine's mouth and then did it again.

When they finally broke the kiss, Caine was fully hard and completely warm again. "If I could stand to share, I'd patent that as a cure for hypothermia," he joked.

"I'm not kissing anyone but you," Macklin insisted. "I want to make love to you, but I don't know if I have the patience."

"So fuck me this time and make love to me next time," Caine said, rubbing his hands down Macklin's back in encouragement. "I'll love it either way."

Macklin reared back onto his knees. "Turn over," he ordered.

Caine scrambled onto his hands and knees, uncaring of the covers that fell to the side. Between the heater and Macklin touching him, he didn't need them.

Immediately Macklin's fingers worked their way inside him, stretching urgently. It burned, but Caine ignored it, rocking back against the probing digits, letting the pressure on his prostate ratchet his desire high enough that the burn didn't matter. Before long, the fingers withdrew and Macklin covered Caine with his body, his cock slipping into place, hot and hard and completely bare inside Caine. Caine shuddered with need, but he stayed where he was, ceding control of their lovemaking to Macklin. It might be hard and fast, with nothing but a few kisses in the way of foreplay, but Caine felt the way Macklin paused when he hit bottom, felt the brush of lips across his neck, and knew they were still making love.

Then the moment of respite ended and Macklin began to move, riding Caine hard and fast, harder than he'd ever been fucked before. He lowered his head to his forearms, braced his hands against the headboard, and held on for dear life. Even though Macklin's hands never left his hips, Caine felt every inch of his body grow sensitive as Macklin's cock plowed into him. He sobbed out his need, too far gone to put his request into words, but Macklin understood, moving one hand beneath him to stroke his cock. Caine cried out again, his climax blindsiding him. Macklin fucked him all the way through it, drawing it out until Caine felt like a ragdoll caught in a dog's teeth. He collapsed forward onto the bed, only Macklin's grip on his hips keeping them lifted to the right angle.

If Caine could have formed the words, he would have begged Macklin to hurry up and come already, but words were beyond him. Instead he clenched his muscles around his lover as best he could, trying to provide the stimulation Macklin needed to find release.

Whether that had been the signal Macklin was waiting for or whether it was something else entirely, it worked. Macklin's movements lost their rhythm, his body convulsing against Caine, shooting his load into Caine's body. Macklin slumped forward, his weight forcing Caine's hips down onto the bed and dislodging his cock from Caine's passage. Caine could feel the fluid seeping onto his thighs. He pressed them together, trying to hold as much of Macklin inside him as he could.

"Next time will be better, I promise," Macklin murmured against his ear.

Caine was pretty sure "better" would kill him completely.

TWENTY-ONE

THEY slept after that, the cold and the sex enough to leave both of them exhausted. Macklin nudged Caine awake several hours later. "It's almost dinner time, Cay. I can hear Kami shouting in the kitchen."

Caine rolled onto his back so he could look at Macklin. "What happened to calling me pup?"

Macklin shrugged. "It doesn't exactly fit anymore. You've outgrown that nickname."

"But I like it," Caine said. "I don't mind if you still call me that."

Macklin shook his head. "You're the boss now. The men don't need to hear me questioning that."

"I'm their boss. I'm your lover," Caine disagreed, "and chances are, they all know it by now. I don't think you calling me pup will be construed as questioning my authority. Fucking me into oblivion might be, but we won't tell them who tops."

"Do you think for a second they'd believe I'm a bottom?" Macklin scoffed.

Caine grinned and slid his hand over Macklin's ass, his fingers probing the crease. "Give me time. I'll convince you."

Macklin tensed but didn't pull away, so Caine worked his fingers a little deeper, finding Macklin's entrance and tracing it lightly. "I've wanted to rim you since you fucked my mouth in Boorowa. Think about it."

Macklin shivered, his hips rutting against Caine's side, his cock twitching in interest.

"I think you l-like the sound of that."

"I think you do, too, if you're stuttering just thinking about it," Macklin teased. "Be patient with me, pup. We're going to do this because the alternative isn't an alternative at all, but I'm not any better at relationships than I was last week or last month."

"We'll figure it out," Caine promised. "So do we have to go down for dinner or can we stay here and make love again?"

"Food first, then sex," Macklin declared. "After your adventure today, you need to eat. You expended a lot of energy just staying alive."

"How do you want me to act at dinner?" Caine asked. "I mean, I'm not going to hang all over you because that isn't who I am, but can I touch your hand or your arm or anything?"

"I told you I was done hiding and I meant it," Macklin said, "but I probably won't ever be comfortable with kissing or anything in public."

"It sure didn't seem that way this afternoon," Caine teased.

"That was extenuating circumstances," Macklin retorted. "Don't expect it to happen again."

"All teasing aside," Caine said, "what will you be comfortable with?"

"I don't know," Macklin replied. "I've never done this before. If you do something that makes me uncomfortable, I'll tell you."

"Sounds like a plan," Caine said. He shifted on the bed, feeling the stickiness between his legs. "I need a shower before we can go anywhere."

"I need dry clothes," Macklin said with a chuckle. "I came in here with you to dry off."

"I'd offer you some of mine, but they wouldn't fit," Caine replied. "I could get dressed and send Jason or someone to get some for you so you'll have something dry after your shower, or I could put your wet clothes in the dryer here and just bring dinner up to you."

"Send Jason to get some," Macklin decided. "You're not going anywhere without me for a day or two until I'm sure you don't have any lingering effects from your dunking today."

Caine pulled on dry pants and a sweatshirt, not bothering with underwear since he was coming back up to take a shower as soon as he found someone to either get Macklin's clothes or send Jason to do it. He padded downstairs in sock feet to find a pile of clothes sitting on the living room table. "Where did these come from?" he wondered as he carried them back upstairs.

"It would seem we have a fairy godmother," Caine said, setting the clothes on the bed. "Someone left these in the living room."

"Kami, probably," Macklin said. "The whole station saw me come inside carrying you, and Kami probably guessed I wasn't leaving."

"He knows about us," Caine agreed. "I think he knew about us before I did."

"He's a superstitious old aborigine," Macklin said, affection obvious in his voice despite the disdainful words. "He probably thinks Michael waited until Christmas to die so you could break up with the Galah and be free to come to Lang Downs."

Caine smiled. "I'm not opposed to thanking fate for my good fortune. We should clean up so we can go down to dinner. You can use Uncle Michael's shower if you want. I'll use the small one down the hall."

"And miss a chance to get my hands on you?" Macklin said. "You can join me in the bath, or I'll squeeze into the shower with you."

"That won't get us to dinner on time, and we'll get enough teasing as it is without being late."

"Fine," Macklin said, "but after dinner, your arse is mine."

Caine grinned and tweaked Macklin's buttocks as he walked by. "As long as your ass is mine as well."

Macklin didn't reply to that, and Caine didn't push any more than he already had. He was skirting the edge of Macklin's comfort zone, and while he intended to keep skirting that line until the line moved back a bit, he didn't have to accomplish that goal tonight. He could give Macklin time and space to get used to the idea of Caine's tongue, fingers, and maybe even his cock inside him.

They showered quickly and headed down to the canteen for dinner. Caine walked inside first, Macklin two steps behind him, not at all sure what kind of reaction they'd face from the rest of the crew. Caine had barely gotten over the threshold before he was mobbed, the men shaking his hand, patting his back, asking if he was all right, thanking him for helping Neil. The throng of people carried him forward deeper into the room. He looked for Macklin, but the crowd around him had separated them completely. Caine smiled at Macklin, surprised and touched by the reaction he was getting. He hadn't known what to expect, but it hadn't been this.

Macklin's sharp whistle cut through the hubbub in the room. "Let him get some tucker," Macklin ordered. "He's had a rough day."

"Here, boss," Neil said, pushing through the crowd. "I got a plate for you."

"Thank you," Caine replied, taking the plate and finding a seat at the nearest table.

Jason plopped down next to him almost immediately. "You're a hero, Caine! All the men are talking about it."

"I just did what had to be done," Caine said with a shrug. "Anyone else would have done the same."

"Maybe, maybe not," Neil interjected, taking a seat across from Caine, "but you're the one who did it. Whether anyone else would have doesn't matter."

Before Caine could think of a way to ask what kind of reaction Macklin's coming out and the revelation of their relationship had gotten, Macklin plunked his plate down next to Caine's and glared at the men who were hovering nearby. "Don't you have work to do?"

"No," Neil said. "Nobody's given us new orders now that the search for the sheep was called off."

"Do we need to be worried about flooding here in the valley?" Caine asked.

"No," Macklin said, "we may get more runoff than usual, but the valley is open at the far end so the water doesn't build up enough to be a danger to the buildings. Michael planned well when he decided where to build."

"Then our next concern is finding the person who's been damaging our fences," Caine said. "I hate to make people stand watch in this weather, but we can't keep losing sheep."

"We'll take short watches," Neil offered. "Like you said, it has to be done."

"Can you organize that?" Caine asked. "Macklin has already decreed I'm not allowed back outside tonight."

"Anything you need, boss," Neil said. "I meant what I said today. I'm your man."

"Have you recovered from the cold?" Caine asked. "You weren't as wet as I was, but you got pretty soaked crossing the gully too."

"I'm fine. I might take an early morning shift, though, so I have the night to stay warm."

"You'll stay inside just like Caine will," Macklin snapped. "Tomorrow night you can stand watch with everyone else. Neither of you is going outside tonight."

Neil looked like he wanted to argue, but Caine smiled and shook his head. "You heard the man, Neil. We're under house arrest tonight."

"UNDER house arrest?" Macklin said when they were alone in Caine's room again.

Caine smiled. "You didn't really want me to tell them I couldn't stand watch tonight because you had to make love to me since you fucked me earlier, did you?"

"Um, well, no, not really," Macklin said. "They'll think it, but we don't have to tell them they're right."

"You don't mind that they're thinking it?"

Macklin shrugged. "I'd rather they not think about it at all, but because it's private, not because I'm ashamed of you."

"That's fair," Caine said, pulling his sweatshirt over his head. "Come to bed. The nap this afternoon helped, but I'm still exhausted."

"Too exhausted to make love?" Macklin teased, stripping down with an ease he'd never before had in Caine's presence.

"I'll never be too tired for that," Caine said, climbing into bed and pulling the cover up to his waist. Macklin climbed in on the other side, drawing Caine toward him. Caine moved willingly enough, latching onto one of Macklin's nipples and sucking lightly.

"So you want to be in charge tonight?" Macklin asked.

"Will you let me?" Caine replied seriously.

"For now," Macklin said.

It was more of a concession than Caine had expected. Mulling over his options and which would be most likely to give him a shot at what he really wanted, he rolled over to his back and urged Macklin to straddle his chest.

"You can face me and watch as I suck you or you can turn around and suck me too."

Caine hoped Macklin would turn around, but he didn't want to be too obvious about it. If Macklin knew what Caine had planned, he'd never give Caine the chance to get started.

"As tempting as it is to watch, it's even more tempting to reciprocate," Macklin said, shifting around and giving Caine a prime view of his backside as he bent over to lick Caine's erection.

Caine took his time, fondling Macklin's cock and licking his balls. Macklin trembled above him, giving Caine the courage he needed to slip back enough to bury his face between Macklin's buttocks and lick the tight entrance.

Macklin froze, Caine's cock in his mouth, every muscle in his body tense.

Caine licked him again.

Macklin shivered, starting to pull away, but Caine wasn't done yet. He grabbed Macklin's hips, holding him steady as he pressed his tongue against the tight iris, barely penetrating.

"Caine!"

Let me love you, Caine begged silently, his actions conveying the request his words could not.

Macklin stayed where he was, his body tense as Caine continued to rim him, focusing on the outer ring more than on pushing inside.

When he pressed a finger against Macklin's entrance in place of his tongue, the foreman's control broke. He pulled away, flipping Caine onto his stomach and pulling his hips into the air.

Caine squirmed around, trying to get comfortable, expecting to feel fingers and Macklin's cock in short order. Instead, Macklin's hands gripped his buttocks, spreading them and exposing his entrance. Caine held his breath, not daring to hope Macklin would reciprocate.

"P-p-please," Caine begged when Macklin didn't move. "D-d-do something."

Macklin's teeth nipping his ass was the only answer he got. Caine pushed up onto his elbows, looking back over his shoulder. Macklin's hands still held him open, his eyes fixed on Caine's entrance. "You d-don't h-have to."

"No, I don't," Macklin agreed, his voice rough, "but now that you've done it to me, I can't stop thinking about it."

"So t-try it. If you d-don't l-like it, d-do something else."

"I can't imagine not liking something that will make you feel like you made me feel," Macklin said.

Caine trembled, the anticipation adding to the desire for the man behind him. Then Macklin bent his head, his whiskers rubbing Caine's skin as he leaned in, licking his way up Caine's crease from his balls to the base of his spine, the flat of his tongue passing over Caine's entrance but not lingering. It wasn't enough, and yet it was already so much more than Caine had expected to get so soon. Then Macklin's tongue was back, circling Caine's entrance and pushing inside.

Caine dropped his shoulders and pushed his ass back against Macklin's mouth, breath catching in his throat as he absorbed the sensation of Macklin rimming him. He smiled at the stray thought that next time, he'd get to rim Macklin longer. If his lover liked it well enough to do it to him, the next time he'd be less hesitant to let Caine do it.

One of Macklin's hands slipped between Caine's widespread thighs, reaching for his cock and stroking it in time with his teasing tongue. The stimulation was too much for Caine's control. His release slammed through him, leaving him panting and oversensitive.

Macklin's tongue kept teasing him, but the sensation became almost unbearable. "S-s-stop," Caine gasped, pulling away. "T-t-too much."

"I'm not done with you yet," Macklin teased.

"D-do something else," Caine said, rolling onto his back again. "Or l-let me d-do something to you."

"You just want another shot at my arse," Macklin said.

Caine batted his eyelashes jokingly. "C-can I?"

To Caine's surprise, Macklin turned back around after grabbing the lube from where he'd left it earlier. "Only until you're ready for a second round," Macklin warned. "I'm not coming anywhere but in your arse tonight."

"I c-can't w-wait," Caine said, pulling Macklin back so he could reach his prize.

The taste of sweat and musk was stronger this time, Macklin's arousal clear in every judder that went through his body as Caine licked him. Caine didn't repeat his mistake from the first time, keeping his hands firmly on Macklin's hips rather than trying to finger his lover as well. That could wait for another time, when Macklin had grown accustomed to the idea of switching roles. Caine didn't need to top every time, but he refused to give it up entirely. Macklin was already far too smug and controlling. He didn't need to always control their lovemaking too.

It was hard to concentrate with Macklin's tongue coaxing Caine's cock back to life and his fingers pressing on Caine's prostate, but Caine refused to be distracted. He would make Macklin feel so good that the next time Caine suggested it, Macklin wouldn't hesitate at all.

Macklin pulled away sooner than Caine would have liked, but given that Macklin turned and kissed him deeply, mingling the tastes in their mouths, Caine let it go. Then Macklin covered him completely, pressing him down into the mattress as he fit their bodies together as intimately as possible, burying himself deeply and rocking against Caine like he never intended to move again.

Caine wrapped his arms and legs around the foreman and gave complete control to his lover. He was hard again, but he didn't really expect to find a second release. Macklin was determined, though, the tip of his cock nudging Caine's prostate relentlessly as Macklin's treasure trail rubbed against Caine's erection with every movement.

"Come on, pup," Macklin urged, breaking their kiss. "Let me see you."

The expression in Macklin's eyes as he stared down at Caine stole Caine's breath. In that moment, he had no doubt that Macklin loved him. The foreman might not ever say the words, but as long as he kept looking at Caine that way, Caine didn't need them. He stroked Macklin's cheek gently.

Macklin returned the tender gesture, the emotion on his face and the matching emotion in Caine's heart enough to trigger a second, unexpected climax. Caine cried out, his body squeezing around Macklin, and that was all Macklin needed, his body tensing, every muscle taut as he groaned and found his release, filling Caine's body as he filled Caine's heart.

Caine pulled Macklin down on top of him, refusing to let the foreman roll to the side. He didn't want the moment to end. *I love you*, he mouthed silently against Macklin's cheek.

Macklin lifted his head, staring down into Caine's eyes again before kissing him slowly, tenderly, deeply. Caine returned the embrace, closing his eyes and slumping against the pillows. "Sleep now?" he murmured through a yawn.

"Sleep," Macklin said.

"Stay?"

"Brumbies couldn't drag me away," Macklin promised.

EPILOGUE

AFTER a month of standing watch at night, the men were frazzled, frozen, and worn to the bone. "We can't keep doing this," Caine told Macklin as they walked to dinner. "Half the men are sick, and if we aren't careful, the other half are going to fall sick. I know we can't afford to lose sheep, but we're going to lose men."

"I know, pup," Macklin said. Even his usually implacable face showed signs of strain. Caine doubted the others could see it, but he'd learned to read every nuance of Macklin's expression over the past month. "I don't know what else to do."

"If we had a shelter, something like a drover's hut, so they could stay dry and warm during the night, we could put two men on a night shift together and then let them sleep through the next day. If we did the schedule right, they wouldn't have to do it but once every couple of weeks instead of half the men having interrupted sleep one night and the other half the next," Caine said.

"We can build anything you want," Macklin said slowly.

"What else would you suggest?" Caine asked. "I'm out of ideas otherwise."

"I want to catch the bloody bastard who did this," Macklin said. "I don't want this dragging on all summer. Even with the summer jackaroos coming back before long, this will still be a strain. We need every pair of hands for the shearing."

"I want to catch him too," Caine agreed, "but I don't know how else we can do it."

"Don't listen to me, pup," Macklin said, squeezing Caine's shoulder. "We'll build your hut and we'll get the men well and on a better schedule. We'll catch the person responsible or at least have the peace of mind of knowing he can't come back and do more damage. We'll hire a few extra jackaroos if we can find them to ease the load enough to keep the night watch going."

That little squeeze was all Caine ever got when they were where anyone could see them. Caine hadn't given Macklin cause to repeat his public kiss, and he intended to keep it that way. Flaunting their relationship wasn't in either of their natures. The year-rounders knew, and they'd all found subtle—or not so subtle in Kami's case—ways to show their acceptance and even their approval of the situation, and that was good enough for Caine.

"Hey, boss," Neil said as Caine and Macklin walked in. "Hey, boss."

"Hi, Neil," Caine said. Macklin tipped his head in Neil's direction. Caine still couldn't decide if Macklin's cool reaction was simply the way he was or if Macklin hadn't forgiven Neil yet for his ugly comments when he'd first found out about Caine being gay. Caine had stopped worrying about it. Neil had stayed true to his word, not uttering another negative statement about Caine and not tolerating it from anyone else either.

They were halfway through dinner when the canteen door opened and Devlin Taylor came in.

"Taylor," Caine said coolly. "What are you doing here?"

"I need to talk to you," Taylor said.

"I'm listening," Caine replied.

"Alone," Taylor insisted.

Caine could feel the tension in the room growing. With a brief nod to the men, he rose and walked outside. Macklin followed right behind him.

"I'm listening," Caine repeated.

"I fired a man today," Taylor said. "I overheard him bragging about how he'd damaged your fences. I don't like you. You're a blow-in and a pillow biter, and there's no place for either in the outback, but I won't keep a man at Taylor Peak who would do something like that. I thought you should know so you don't start thinking I had anything to do with it. I don't want a station war."

Even if Caine had found proof Taylor was responsible, he wouldn't have retaliated that way, but he suspected Taylor would have, were their situations reversed.

"It's good of you to come tell us," Caine said. "You could have simply left us in the dark."

"I thought about it," Taylor admitted, "but I didn't want the blame to land on me."

"Everything okay, boss?" Neil asked, sticking his head out onto the veranda.

"I'm surprised to see you still here, Johnson," Taylor said. "What happened to all that noise about not working for a poofter?"

Neil had crossed the veranda before Caine and Macklin could react. "He might be a poofter, but he's *our* poofter," Neil said, hands fisted in Taylor's coat, "and he's more of a man than you'll ever be." Neil turned back to Caine. "Can I throw him out?"

"No," Caine said, "but you may escort him back to his ute and make sure he makes it home safely."

Neil's face brightened.

"Safely," Caine repeated. "Taylor came to apologize for the damage one of his former employees did, not to cause trouble."

"Yes, boss," Neil said.

"He's going to get himself in trouble if he goes after every man who makes a comment about you," Macklin warned as Neil escorted Taylor back to his truck.

"He'll learn or they will," Caine said with a shrug. "Let's go back inside. I'm hungry."

Macklin caught Caine's shoulder before he could turn away. "Taylor's wrong, you know. You aren't a blow-in who has no business out here. You're a grazier at heart. You've learned so much in five short months. Taylor could learn a thing or two from you if he'd look past his idea of you to see who you really are."

"He'll never see me as anything more than a 'poofter'," Caine said.

"That only proves what a fool he is," Macklin replied. "What a fool I nearly was."

"You weren't a fool," Caine insisted. "Just scared, and that's all in the past. Neil may say I'm their poofter, but I'm really all yours."

Macklin smiled, if a tad uncomfortably. "Don't tell Taylor that. He won't survive the news."

Caine laughed and squeezed Macklin's hand before going back inside. He'd have to apologize for his choice of words later, but since that would inevitably lead to makeup sex, he'd wait to do that until they were alone in their bedroom—the big bedroom—to mention it.

Macklin shook his head and followed Caine inside.

ARIEL TACHNA lives outside of Houston with her husband, her daughter and son, and their cat. Before moving there, she traveled all over the world, having fallen in love with both France, where she found her husband, and India, where she dreams of retiring some day. She's bilingual with snippets of four other languages to her credit and is as in love with languages as she is with writing.

Visit Ariel's website at http://www.arieltachna.com/ and her blog at http://arieltachna.livejournal.com/.

Contemporary Romance by ARIEL TACHNA

http://www.dreamspinnerpress.com

Also by ARIEL TACHNA

http://www.dreamspinnerpress.com

www.ingramcontent.com/pod-product-compliance
Lightning Source LLC
Chambersburg PA
CBHW070009260626
47159CB00005B/1735